25p

QUEEN OF THE STREET

D1634917

QUEEN OF THE STREET

The Amazing Life of
Julie Goodyear

SALLY BECK

BLAKE

Published by Blake Publishing Ltd,
3 Bramber Court, 2 Bramber Road, London W14 9PB, England

First published in the UK in hardback 1995
Published in paperback 1996

ISBN 1 85782 1688

British Library Cataloguing-in-Publication Data:
A catalogue record for this book is available from
the British Library.

Typeset by CentraCet Limited, Cambridge
Printed in Finland by WSOY

© Sally Beck 1995

To Brian Roberts and John Kelly

'When I go and watch Shakespeare plays I always find myself thinking: "When's the interval?" ... My favourite television programme is *Coronation Street*.'

Sir Anthony Hopkins

'The standard of acting is mind-boggling. I'd jump at the chance if they offered me a part in the show.'

Derek Jacobi

Contents

Foreword and Acknowledgements

Julie Goodyear claims to be mystified at the fact so many stories are told about her and her colourful love-life. The rest of us are not. Millions of fans who admire her as the undisputed Queen of *Coronation Street* also, understandably, relish every detail of her fascinating personal life.

Bet Lynch is the raunchy, voluptuous landlady of the Rovers Return. She can flirt, she can manipulate, she can give as good as she gets. But she is only human. Unlucky in love, she can cry. Rejected by those nearest, she can hurt. That's why, as a nation, we are hooked on her. Every performance is a lesson in life, and with Bet as the teacher it's fun to learn.

Scriptwriters don't struggle over her words. They have actress Julie to inspire every sentence. They create the storylines, which brilliantly capture the day-to-day reality of life in a suburb of Greater Manchester. And they write the basic outline for her to work to. But it is Julie and no one else who makes it all real. This is self-evident to even a casual viewer. So it is no surprise at all that everyone who has ever met Julie Goodyear is proud to boast about it.

Many people have come forward to contribute to this book – a definitive look at the phenomenon that is Julie Goodyear and, at the same time, Bet Lynch.

There was sadness in her childhood – a sadness she does not care to reflect upon. Through the eyes of those who shared part of that childhood, a picture emerges of an extrovert little girl – 'show off' is the description some have used – who desperately sought attention and affection as a means of escaping inner loneliness.

Young Julie had the striking looks to match her big personality. She won all the attention she craved, outside of her home life, and it was such a successful substitute for the real thing that a stage career was always going to be the answer to her emotional needs.

There was a long way to go, though, before she could sublimate all true feeling into her showbiz persona.

There were the early years of pain as her parents' marriage deteriorated. The young Julie, an only child, was to overhear repeated rows between her mother and her father. Bitter accusations of infidelity, incomprehensible and frightening to the small girl lying in her bedroom upstairs, unable to sleep.

She developed an outer toughness that would stand her in good stead many times in later life. By the age of seven, Julie had a new 'Dad'. The upsetting domestic battles had stopped, but now there was something difficult and new to deal with: her mother's total dedication to this stranger, her stepfather. Friends and neighbours have described over and over the loneliness caused by Julie's exclusion from this relationship. How she was left at home on her own while the newly-weds partied until late at night; how her stepfather criticized and belittled her in front of friends; how the two adults closest to her were too wrapped up in one another to notice her needs.

Many children have lived through the trauma of their mother's divorce and remarriage. Many have retreated into themselves and borne the emotional scars for life. Not Julie Goodyear. She fought back from the word go. Her naturally sunny personality combined with a crying need for attention, and her striking appearance saw to the rest. She began to 'show off', to perform, to sing and dance and act. Aged six, she was beginning her brilliant career.

Today, she is still described as someone who wants and needs others to like her. Some say it is easy to like Julie Goodyear, but hard really to know her. They do not always speak of her with respect.

Julie has said: 'My fans would commit murder for me if I asked them to. They all love me, you know. They would die for me. I know what ordinary people feel about me. They're protective of me. That's why when anything bad is written about me, I don't have to fight back in print. The public does it for me. You don't think they believe half the rubbish that's written about me, do you? They're not fooled for a minute. Because they know me. They know I'm one of them.'

Secure in the certainty of a bulging mailbag and the loyalty of her army of fans, Julie seems to have decided to bring her screen persona – Bet Lynch, her alter ego – into her real life. She does not want to cast Bet aside when she takes off her professional make-up. She does not want to be vulnerable Julie Goodyear, off the *Coronation Street* set. She can bring the whole thing – the ready wit, the clever put-down, the brittle manner — with her. Today, they are part of Bet and they are also part of Julie.

So does anyone really know the woman inside? The woman who looks back on a childhood thoroughly documented as difficult and upsetting, and states carefully: 'My mother died four years ago and I loved her dearly. I also loved the man who brought me up from the age of five. He was my Dad to me and always will be...'

Anyone who tells a different tale, she says, is simply willing to make a quick buck out of a passing acquaintance with her.

Not one contributor quoted in this book — and there are many — was paid a single penny for an interview. All memories, views and opinions were offered unprompted, for no reward. The result is a truly fascinating insight...

Many, many people have helped with the research for this book but I would like to say a special thanks to journalist Nikki Murfitt, who encouraged me to 'go for it' in the first place, Lawrie Masterson and Jacki Harvie. Sue Sumner, Audrey Brogden and Kenneth Alan Taylor were particularly helpful. I would also like to thank Ada Kemp, Rod Simpson, Ida Boardman, Sandra Thornley, Elsie Bowden, Edna Barlow, Alan and Elsie Chadwick, Edith Collinge, Alice Wellings, Joan and Rodney Deardon, Dot Stand, Janet Leech, David Liddle, Pam and Peter Hughes, Tony Whitehead, Annie Maskew, Sylvia McNally, Anne Eatough, Brenda Wilkinson, Kath Jepson, Peter Wild, Connie Parker, Jack and Frieda Little, Bob Pauls, Peter Birchall, Sydney Yates, Jack Sumner, Malcolm Wright, Rod Lockley, John Bradley, Glyn Griffiths, Jack Diamond, Dolores Visco, Jean Morris, Jenny Morton, Peter Rushworth, Gorden Allen, Teresa Wilkes, Judith Barker, Pam Holt, Jimmy Rowbotham, Annie

Coates, Carolyn Preston, Geoff and Barbara Nuttall, David Hamilton, Adele Rose, Fred Feast, Graham Watson, Richard Shaw, Vicky Ogden, Sue Jenkins, Madge Hindle, Fanny Carby, Jim Bywater, Nick Stringer, Brian Peck, Bobby Howarth, Cyril Smith MP, Dr Robert Yule, Jane Beck and those few who wished to remain anonymous.

Many thanks to MSI, the Press Association, News International, the Blackpool Evening Gazette, All Action and all those people who contributed pictures for this book.

'Being in the *Street* has given me somewhere to belong as a person.'

Julie Goodyear

'The Rovers is more than a pub to Bet – it is her whole life.'

Alec Gilroy

Prologue

She is haughty, but at the same time undeniably earthy. She has an acid tongue, but a kind smile. In a life crowded with love and laughter there has also been heartbreak. She is the brassy landlady of *Coronation Street*'s Rovers Return, the indomitable Bet Lynch. But she is also the actress Julie Goodyear, whose loyal fans have cheered her on through the good times and the bad; in her colourful life there have been plenty of both.

Curiously, the ups and downs that have marked Bet's long career in the famous *Street* have been mirrored in the personal life of her creator. Or is it the other way round? Is it possible that Julie Goodyear *is* Bet Lynch? Did the woman who spent her childhood years in a state of lonely confusion, and who as a result pursued love and affection so relentlessly that it backfired on her many times, turn to the acting trade and hit on the one character she could play to perfection?

Many millions believe that the two women are one and

the same. Interestingly, Julie Goodyear disagrees: 'There is a lot of me in Bet, but there is very little of Bet in me. I never get the two confused. It's other people who do that.'

Hardly anyone from her past agrees with her. All those who helped with this book offered their views on the extraordinary parallel and volunteered, without prompting and without exception, the unshakable opinion that Julie and Bet are remarkably similar. This may not please her, but the evidence I unearthed is overwhelming. Former neighbour Elsie Bowden, who knew Julie as a lively ten-year-old, said: 'That is her on television.' Fellow pupil Peter Birchall, who acted with Julie in a school play, added: 'Julie is absolutely superb as Bet Lynch; she's just like Bet in real life.' Her best friend at school, Sue Skelton, confided: 'Julie is like Bet, you know.' Audrey Brogden, former landlady of Julie's local pub, the White Hart, knew her in her twenties. She said: 'She doesn't have to do any acting, she's like that in real life.' Former neighbour Edna Barlow, who has known Julie for years – having looked after her as a child – said: 'Julie's no different in real life.'

A brief potted biography of Bet, and one of Julie, make interesting comparisons:

Full name: Elizabeth (Bet) Theresa Lynch

Date of birth: 4 May 1940, Weatherfield

Background: Bet's father disappeared when she was six months old. Brought up by a domineering Catholic mother, she rebelled and became pregnant at sixteen. She had baby Martin adopted but had already gained a reputation as something of a good-time girl. There was disapproval – and probably envy – from neighbours and family friends. She entered

beauty contests and in 1955 became Miss Weatherfield.

In November 1970, Billy Walker took Bet on as the new
Rovers' barmaid one day when his mother was out
shopping. Annie Walker took one look at Bet, in her
body-hugging black dress and false eyelashes, and
instructed Billy to give Miss Lynch notice straight away:
'Am I biased or does her name sound as if it should be
over a porn shop?' said Annie. Billy refused, claiming she
would be a hit with the customers and that profits would
soar. He was right. Annie swallowed her pride and
allowed her to stay.

Annie was amazed when grown men fought to get Bet's
attention. Headscarf and curler-wearing cleaner Hilda
Ogden announced to the pub, 'The day I have to look like
that to attract the fellas is the day I give up the struggle as
a *femme fatale*.' Bet fell in love easily with rogues who
misused her and made her feel cheap. She had a run of
disastrous affairs with various men, including builder Len
Fairclough, factory boss Mike Baldwin and taxi driver
Jack Duckworth. Later, she married Alec Gilroy because
he offered security and was the only man to court her
without pretending to love her. A year later, she was
devastated when she miscarried his baby. In 1975 her son
Martin was killed in a car crash in Northern Ireland. He
had once turned up at the Rovers but had left without
speaking to his mother, upset by her behaviour towards
the male customers. Devastated, Bet attempted suicide.

For fifteen years Bet worked for the Walkers, some of
the finest times being when she manned the pumps with
Fred Gee and Betty Turpin, between 1976 and 1984. After
Annie retired, Billy Walker sold the pub to the brewery

and Bet stunned regulars when she applied for the licence. Backed by a petition from customers, she was taken on as the brewery's first single manageress and, in 1984, became the first barmaid to run her own pub.

She married Alec Gilroy in 1987. They ran the pub together for five years, but when Alec was offered a job in Southampton, Bet refused to leave and the marriage broke down. Later, she started dating handsome trucker Charlie Whelan, who stuck around for a year then disappeared with bitchy barmaid Tanya.

Name: Julie Goodyear (formerly Julie Kemp)

Date of Birth: 29 March 1942

Background: Julie's father George and her mother Alice divorced when she was six years old. Alice remarried when Julie was seven. Her stepfather Bill Goodyear was something of a bully by all accounts, but Julie found ways to escape the unhappiness she faced at home.

As a teenager, Julie lived above The Bay Horse Hotel, a small pub in Heywood. There she often volunteered to help out behind the bar, and soon became an expert in the art of pulling pints. The pub was a popular meeting place and Julie met a number of young men keen to take her out. Many of them were lucky – but Julie was gaining a reputation. By the time she was seventeen the rumour mongers were gleeful: Julie was pregnant.

Soon afterwards she married Ray Sutcliffe, the father of the baby she was expecting. Their son Gary was born on 28 April 1960, one month after Julie's eighteenth birthday. But the marriage, shaky from the start, had already begun to disintegrate. Ray claimed that Julie was cheating on him, and that he was regularly left babysitting their child while she went out to enjoy herself. She, on the other hand, longed for an acting career and had no intention of spending her days as a housebound wife and mother.

The way Ray tells it today, there were rows when he tried to put his foot down, telling her she couldn't use the car for her evenings out. Soon, she moved out and a legal separation followed. In an attempt at a new beginning, Ray suggested a move to Australia, where his parents had settled. He would set up a new life for his family, and then send for her. Instead, within a few months of his emigration he received divorce papers in the post. He didn't contest Julie's claims of mental cruelty, and the decree nisi came through within a year. It was 1963 and baby Gary was just three years old.

Julie now set out in earnest to capture the beauty-contest titles she longed for. In 1965 she became Miss Britvic. That success was closely followed by others: she was Miss Astral Cream, Miss Aeronautical Society and Miss Langley Football Club. Her ambition blossomed, and she took up modelling. Talent-spotted as a stunning blonde with a personality to match, she was chosen for a bit part in *Coronation Street*. For six weeks she played Bet Lynch, the typical Lancashire lass who worked in Elliston's raincoat factory.

It was that other formidable *grande dame* of the *Street*, Pat Phoenix, who spotted Julie's raw talent. After the six-week stint was finished, she advised Julie to learn her craft thoroughly at Oldham Repertory Company. Julie made the tea for the acting troupe, served out her own apprenticeship in each and every part she was offered on stage, and landed several minor television roles before she secured her permanent place in *Coronation Street* in 1970.

After her divorce, she had become involved in a number of relationships, most of them short-lived. She lived with three different men and had been engaged twice before marrying businessman Tony Rudman, in 1973. He was the friend of an old flame of Julie's, and both claimed afterwards the marriage didn't even survive the wedding reception. Later there was an annulment.

As her career stabilized, and Bet Lynch grew into one of the nation's favourite soap characters, Julie's love-life became even more chaotic. She was engaged at one point to *Street* director Bill Gilmour, but the wedding was cancelled two weeks before the register-office service. She had been dallying with an American airline executive, Richard Skrob, and married him in 1985.

It was around this time that details of a bizarre love-life began to emerge. The marriage faltered, and as divorce loomed two men claimed she was a lesbian.

By 1987 the marriage was well and truly over. A succession of female personal assistants have since lived with Julie at her home in Heywood, and she recently also took a fancy to married actor John St Ryan, who played her screen lover Charlie Whelan.

Julie has played Bet Lynch for twenty-five years.

1

Fractured Childhood

George Kemp's eyes smarted as he groped his way through a shroud of choking soot. The Royal Engineers sapper could do battle with a tangible enemy, but this thick smog, caused by belching cotton-mill chimneys and roaring coal fires, had him beaten. Black smoke coated the rows of red-brick houses, making them look as though they had been tarred. Carefully hand-scrubbed linen sheets, pegged limply on lines, all told the same story as sooty pollution turned them grey. This cobble-streeted scene of northern hardship could have come straight from an L. S. Lowry painting.

Returning after the Second World War, the handsome twenty-seven-year-old soldier was minutes from his home, but in a suffocating pea souper like this it could take an hour to walk half a mile. George struggled to get his bearings. He knew the mucky Lancashire mill town of Heywood as well as the trenches he had dug in the desert, but because of the smog he barely recognized the cobbled streets. Desperate to see his vivacious twenty-two-year-old wife Alice and pretty three-year-old daughter Julie, sapper number 2011168 perservered.

Alice was in a panic. She smoked cigarette after cigarette as she hared around checking for shreds of evidence which could alert George to her infidelities. Chucking out crates of empty beer bottles, she scrubbed their tiny terraced house at 8 Pickup Street, then gave the sheets a good wash. While her husband had been at war, Alice had become lonely and bored. To relieve the tedium, she and her best friend Florrie had been entertaining American GIs from the massive base at nearby Burtonwood, near Warrington. But it was an Englishman who had captured her heart. Alice had become rather too friendly with a tall, quiet and handsome master builder, Bill Goodyear.

Now she was anxious there should be no slip-ups when George arrived. To make sure the reunion went smoothly she gave her bright daughter an acting lesson. She tutored young Julie not to blurt out anything about the 'uncle' figures who had come into her life.

'Now remember, when Daddy comes home run and give him a big kiss,' she coached.

'Yes, Mum,' Julie said, concentrating so hard that a small frown appeared under her blonde curls.

After Alice finished Julie was ready to give her first performance.

Shop assistant Alice Duckworth was seventeen when she married twenty-two-year-old electrician George Kemp. They made their vows at the Baptist Chapel in Heywood on 13 April 1940. Alice's father, George Duckworth, a moulder at the local ironworks, proudly walked his daughter down the aisle while retired butcher Emmanuel Kemp, George's father, watched as his son slipped a gold band on the third finger of Alice's left hand.

To start their married life the young couple rented a small terraced house in Pickup Street, Heywood. The town, six miles north of the city of Manchester, snakes between the larger towns of Rochdale and Bury like an unruly funeral procession. Today, it is still much the same as it was in the 1940s, with its rows of cobbled streets and sprawling mish-mash of jerry-built back-to-back terraces, thrown up to house thousands of industrial workers migrating to the town in search of work.

During the war years the community was close. Neighbours could often be spotted washing their front steps, whitening them with donkey stone while they caught up with the gossip. In fact, the place could have been a model for Coronation Street.

Two years into the Second World War, on 29 March 1942, Alice gave birth to her only child, Julie Kemp, at Bury Infirmary. Alice was nineteen when she had Julie, too young to be saddled with a baby. She wanted to be out dancing and enjoying herself, not indoors with a bucket full of dirty nappies for company.

So, while her husband defended his country, Alice did her bit for the war effort and set about 'entertaining' the troops. 'After Julie was born, Alice was determined to enjoy herself,' said George. 'I didn't see much of it because I was away. But I heard plenty when I got back.'

Whenever she could, party girl Alice palmed Julie off on her mother Lizzie Duckworth. Consequently, Julie grew very attached to her 'Nan', who always had time for her. While Lizzie minded Julie, Alice continued to see different men, including Bill Goodyear. However, it was

3

not until her husband finally came home in 1945 that she admitted to herself that the marriage was over. When George knocked on his own front door that smoggy night, Alice took one look at him and felt nothing.

It was an awkward reunion. Julie gave a flawless performance, but even her superb acting could not save her parents' marriage. Alice made no attempt to hide the fact that she was being unfaithful. In fact, she positively flaunted her affair with the dapper Bill. 'I think George once threw Bill Goodyear out of the house when he found them in bed together,' said Ada Kemp, George's second wife of forty years. 'But then they were cruel enough to send him a hotel bill giving details of where they had stayed. 'They didn't make any secret about what was going on. They just carried on right under George's nose.'

Alice wanted out of the marriage and goaded George until he broke down and agreed to a divorce. He left 8 Pickup Street in 1947 and Lizzie moved in to help with Julie.

Julie soon grew to regard Lizzie as a mother. She loved the days when Lizzie allowed her to pull out the drawer in her bedroom and root through its contents. It was full of interesting bits and pieces she could play with, and she spent hours creating a rich and colourful kingdom, full of imaginary friends.

Now aged five, Julie was already learning about life alone. Her mother, often out on dates with Bill, left her to live in a fantasy world. Julie's favourite daydream centred on a pile of coloured buttons she kept crammed in a jar. Picking up each one, she pretended they were diamonds, pearls and emeralds, and she would lie on the floor making up stories about princes and princesses wearing the jewels. Or she would practise her favourite song, 'Away in a

Manger', which she sang all the time.

It was two years after George left before Alice finally married Bill, who was fourteen years older than George and had once been his boss. Before they set a date for the wedding, Alice decided that Julie should be formally introduced to her new father. On the bus ride to Bill's house in Rochdale, she told Julie to say 'Hello, Daddy' when they met. Alice knocked on the door, Bill opened it, and a terrified Julie shrieked hysterically at the sight of this tall, intimidating older man. All she wanted to do was hide. Eventually she calmed down, but she was still viewing him with suspicion by the end of the visit.

Julie's adverse reaction did not prevent the wedding going ahead on 23 July 1949 at Rochdale Register Office. Alice was ecstatic, but Bill's former neighbours from the Rochdale area were surprised when he decided to marry at all. At forty years old, still a snappy dresser, and a hard drinker, they had always known him as a man with an eye for the ladies. Former neighbour Ida Boardman said: 'He liked his women and he fancied himself.'

After the wedding the couple set up a new home, but Julie never came to terms with the arrangement. She saw Bill as a surly man who drank too many pints of Carlsberg and had no patience with her. She looked forward to visits with her 'real Dad', and a family friend often came to collect her to take her to George's house. For a special treat George would take her to a seaside boarding house in Blackpool – twelve shillings and sixpence for bed and breakfast. Julie loved their trips to promenade cafés, and at the top of her voice would sing her party piece – a passable rendering of 'Away in a Manger', whatever time of year it was!

'I remember what a beautiful child she was,' said

George sadly. 'And how happy we were together.'

Julie attracted a great deal of attention when she performed, which of course encouraged her. Once, aged six, she gatecrashed a talent contest, staged by the well-known talent spotter and radio personality Carroll Levis in a Rochdale public hall. In between acts, Julie leapt on stage and started singing and dancing for all she was worth. She was furious when the judge turned round and gave her a pat on the head. 'How dare they treat a performer like that,' she thought. 'I was furious. I was really ambitious,' she said later. Julie might not have been appreciated by the professionals, but George loved to watch his precocious daughter perform. It was not long though before Julie's visits stopped. Flitting between mother and father had worked well during her parents' two-year separation, but after Alice married Bill and George started dating Ada, whom he met in 1950 on a bus going to work, the outings were suddenly cancelled. Julie was almost eight years old.

No one told George why the visits stopped, and he was hurt and annoyed. He thought about kidnapping her or fighting for custody, but, 'I didn't think it was right for a child to be in the middle of two people trying to tear her apart,' he said.

Julie would probably have had a more settled, stable home life with George and Ada. The couple were happy together but Ada, unfortunately, could not have children. Instead Julie was stuck with Bill, a bully who had no time for her.

Julie was at Harwood Primary School in Heywood when the visits to her father stopped. For comfort she stuck close to her best friend Joan Ogden. Fellow pupil Joan Deardon thought the pair were twins: 'They always wore similar clothes,' she said. 'They both had red coats and bonnets with little ears, and pompoms hanging off the strings. And they always used to skip in the playground.

'I remember Julie being a bit bossy and always wanting her own way. And I also remember her Mum would come and pick her up. We used to be jealous because she always had little treats for her like sweets and biscuits, which the rest of us didn't have.'

At home Alice was not an attentive mother, but she spent ages dressing Julie before they went out. 'Julie always looked immaculate,' said neighbour Edna Barlow, a close friend of Alice and occasional childminder to Julie. 'She always made sure she looked pretty no matter where she was going.' To the outside world young Julie looked fine, so no one could possibly accuse Alice of neglect.

Julie was soon uprooted from school and Heywood, and on 1 May 1950 she began at Spotland County Primary School in Rochdale, three miles from her old home. The move meant she would see less and less of her Nan, a prospect which disturbed her.

Alice and Bill took up residence above a grocer's shop in Molyneaux Street, Rochdale, which they ran, and a new life began. Overnight, Julie's surname was changed to Goodyear. There is no record of a formal adoption. One day Julie was Kemp, the next she was told she was Goodyear. Then a whispering campaign to discredit George began. 'Alice started poisoning her mind against me,' said George. 'Julie told me her mother said I left them destitute. But it wasn't true.'

Divorce rips families apart today, but in the 1940s, when most couples tried to stick together no matter what, it must have been devastating. George had failed with

Alice, but could have no idea – until thirty-five years later – how badly the split would affect his tearaway daughter, although distress signals soon became apparent.

Julie hated living in Rochdale and yearned to be back with her Nan in Heywood. 'It was cosy and secure,' Julie said years later. She often ran away. 'Sometimes my parents would wake up in the morning and discover I had sneaked out in the middle of the night and walked from Rochdale back to Heywood. 'It's only a ten-minute car ride now, but then it was a long trek for a little girl in her flannelette nightie and thin coat.'

When she finally arrived, her Nan would always send her smartly back home.

2

Puppy Love

For three years Bill shifted his new family from house to house, then decided to move back to Slattocks – a Middleton village four miles east of Heywood – where he had lived in his bachelor days.

By now Bill was a fledgling property tycoon who owned several houses, together with his partner Jack, in a pre-war cul-de-sac called Clifton Road. They had built the terrace of semis in 1938 and had either let them or sold them off.

One of the houses would be perfect for his new family, thought Bill, though there was one major problem: none of his houses was vacant. Drastic action was clearly called for, so he evicted a woman whose elderly mother had recently died.

Gladys Tonge and her mother Florence had lived at 9 Clifton Road for years. It was filled with their things, and, modest though it was, they considered it home. Florence had just died, and Gladys was at a stage when she desperately needed the security of the familiar surround-ings Bill was taking from her. She wasn't rich, but she bid £375 to buy the three-bedroom property. Bill simply refused her offer and moved in with his new family.

'He forced her out,' remembers Gladys's sister Ida Boardman, who still lives in a house backing on to Clifton Road. 'He didn't give her long to move. Then as soon as she'd gone the Goodyears moved in.'

A sturdy Lancashire woman, Ida was philosophical about the eviction and bore no grudge against Bill. 'It was just one of those things,' she said with a shrug. Ida's daughter Sandra, a lively, inquisitive girl, became best friends with Julie, and the pair frequently skipped between the back-to-backs to play in each other's houses. Ida, in her turn, became a mother figure to Julie. She looked after her while Alice and Bill, with eyes only for each other, enjoyed frequent nights out together.

Ida remembers: 'Bill and Alice used to go out and leave her. They didn't bother about her, so she was here a lot. They would never ask me to look after her; she just trotted over and parked herself here. I thought she was very lonely, really.'

Over the years, several of Julie's friends observed her parents' apparent indifference towards her. Sandra was the first close pal to notice things were not all they might have been. 'I don't think her parents were very loving towards her,' said Sandra. 'She was very much left to her own devices. When her parents went out I used to go over and keep her company.'

The girls were bosom buddies but Julie never confessed that Bill Goodyear was not her real father. 'I don't think I found out Bill was her stepfather until years afterwards,' she recalls. 'It was something she didn't talk about.'

It seems Bill hankered for nights out with his mates, and he wanted his new wife along with him. But Julie, the daughter who wasn't his, never seemed to be included. She would be left at home while the adults enjoyed themselves at the pub.

During the day Julie's young life was just as solitary, as Alice and Bill would often take long afternoon 'naps'. At ten years old, Julie started to notice that her family life was different from that of her best friend Sandra, and it wasn't long before she became curious about her parents' odd habits. One afternoon she popped an off-the-cuff question to Ida which made Ida's jaw drop. 'Totally straight-faced, Julie asked me: "Do you never go to bed?" I said: "What do you mean? I go to bed every night." She looked puzzled for a minute then she said: "Don't you ever go to bed in the afternoon?" When I told her of course I didn't, she said: "Ooh, me mum and dad do all the time."'

With Alice and Bill spending long afternoons wrapped up in bed together, Julie needed an antidote to loneliness. Physically forward for her age, she found a temporary cure in the local boys.

One lad with whom Julie became friends was twelve-year-old choirboy Rod Simpson. 'Our relationship was hotter than best buddies,' recalls Rod, who was already at senior school when they met. 'Julie was my first serious girlfriend.'

Rod's parents, also called Bill and Alice, were leading lights in the village. His father ran the youth club and staged two important annual events, the summer play which was the focus of the annual summer fair, and the winter pantomime. The whole village joined in to help out with these dramatic occasions, with Rod's mother round-

11

ing up all the village mothers to help make the costumes.

Julie adored these events and longed for her family to take part, but although they encouraged her, Alice and Bill were too busy to get involved. 'Most mothers would bring their sewing machines to make up costumes as the kids rehearsed, and the fathers would help with the scenery. Alice Goodyear never brought her sewing machine and Bill never helped with the props,' said Alice Simpson.

The entire village looked forward to Slattocks's summer fair, a weekend event which centred on Smalley Memorial Hall, a pivotal meeting place next to the church. Inside, the hall overflowed with cake stalls, flower stalls, bric-a-brac and white-elephant stalls. Outside, on a playing field, sporty villagers took part in an athletics meeting. As the sun slowly disappeared from the sky, everyone prepared for the staged event, a 'Go as You Please', a sort of *Opportunity Knocks* for locals with stars in their eyes.

Everyone took part, children, parents and grandparents. Julie adored this event, as it gave her the opportunity to showcase her blossoming acting talent.

One year, about 1952, Rod's best friend Neil Ramshaw formed a jazz band called the Slattocks Swingsters. He and a group of scouts got up on stage and mimed to jazz records. There were six of them in the band, with Neil playing trumpet and the rest of the scouts impersonating musicians karaoke style, on trombone, clarinet, banjo, piano and drums. The band went down a storm.

It was also the year Julie teamed up with Rod to sing a duet.

Rod first met Julie at Sunday school and youth club, but nothing romantic happened between them until they started rehearsing an old music-hall number which called for them to act as a shy courting couple just falling in love.

'Julie and I ended up on stage together singing "You Made Me Love You". Either I was singing and she was being coy behind or I was being coy and she was singing, I can't quite remember. I met Julie off stage, held her hand and our relationship developed from there.'

Rod was capitvated by Julie, with her natural blonde hair and bubbly personality. 'I thought she was one of the most attractive girls in the village,' he said. 'It came as quite a shock to realize girls weren't that bad after all.'

After the hand-holding session Rod sought ways to get Julie alone, although he was not quite sure what to do once he succeeded. Neil Ramshaw's sister Helen came to his rescue. 'She encouraged me to put my arm round Julie one night,' said Rod. 'It was after rehearsals and we were sitting in the hall. Smalley was a typical church hall, with a stage at one end and a balcony at the far end which was really dark. When we weren't on stage we cleared off to the balcony. Once Julie and I were alone I put my arm round her. We sat there for ages holding each other. Then we started kissing. There was a fair amount of kissing – not proper French kissing; don't forget we weren't even teenagers – we would just have our lips stuck together for about ten minutes.

'From then on we spent hours and hours together. It was a big romance. Wherever I went Julie was there and vice versa.'

It sounds very innocent, but in the 1950s sex was rarely discussed and children of ten and twelve, Rod and Julie's age, were far more naive than young people today.

Even aged ten, however, Julie was considered quite a trophy, already bewitching friends with her lively personality and 'Pears soap' looks. Rod thought he was quite a prize too and was not surprised when she chose him over his rivals. He said: 'I played football for the school and I played cricket. I was in the youth club and the scouts. I think I would have been a bit of a catch.'

The whole village was aware that Julie and Rod were courting, although their first steps to adulthood caused some sniggering among Rod's friends. Rod remembers one morning in the local parish church when an in-joke about Julie earned him a serious ticking off from the vicar. He said: 'I was head choirboy at Thornham St John's Church. One of the hymns had a line which went: "I hope to follow duly." I looked up and saw my mate Neil Ramshaw in the main congregation waving and mouthing Julie instead of duly. I started laughing my head off. It was very irreverent and I got into serious trouble.' But in spite of the behind-the-hand giggling and teasing from his mates Rod was obsessed with his little girlfriend.

The pre-pubescent couple had lots of opportunities to indulge their passion. After the summer fair, rehearsals began for the Christmas pantomime. In the 1950s, there was a show called *Where the Rainbow Ends*, rivalled only by *Peter Pan*. Staged every Christmas, it was carefully guarded by producers, who kept it under licence for theatre professionals. As soon as it came off licence Rod's parents snapped it up.

'We were the first to put it on,' said Alice proudly. 'It was about two children looking for their parents.'

Rod and Julie both had parts, but Julie did not have the starring role. 'I think I was the family's cat and Julie was some other minor character,' remembered Rod. But neither cared; the panto meant they had plenty of excuses to meet.

Apart from these rehearsals, the other event on which they were hooked was Sunday night at the Boardman house. Sandra remembers: 'My Mum and Dad used to go out for a drink and everybody would come over to my house and play cards. There would be Rod, his sister Anita, a chap called Eric Cheetham, me, Julie, a girl called Doreen Kenworthy and Rod's best mate Neil Ramshaw – who Anita had a crush on. We'd play pontoon, betting with matches.'

The youngsters retreated to the Boardmans' house when they could and, like all kids, occasionally lost track of time, which once landed Rod in serious trouble. It was Christmas, and Julie was nearly sick with excitement, not at the thought of Father Christmas filling the stocking hung at the end of her bed, but because she had a date with Rod at the Slattocks Christmas dance. She arrived in a full-length black gown, a little too sophisticated for a ten-year-old, perhaps, but she looked lovely.

Rod and Julie had a row at the dance and Julie refused to speak to him, even though he apologized. Later, both went back to the Boardman house together and Rod remembers: 'We were sitting on opposite sides of the room until eventually we kissed and made up. I didn't arrive home until a lot later than I should have, probably about midnight, and got into terrible trouble with my Dad.'

Rod can't remember if Julie's absence was noticed. Perhaps her parents thought she was tucked up in bed with a cup of Ovaltine and an Enid Blyton book, or maybe Bill and Alice were unable to check as they were still out themselves.

Apart from her dates with Rod, Julie cultivated a busy social life. She spent Monday evenings from 7 p.m. to 8.30 p.m. at Guides, and 7 p.m. to 10 p.m. on Tuesdays and Thursdays with the 'gang' at the youth club. The club was a godsend for the children who had little or no money to spend on entertainment.

'We used to really enjoy the youth club,' said Sandra. 'It cost money to go to the cinema and we hadn't got any. I didn't go to the pictures until I was about fourteen or fifteen.'

The club, run by Rod's Dad, was held at Smalley Memorial Hall, like most village events. The kids played badminton, table tennis and snooker or listened to the *Goon Show*, which they loved.

Although Julie would join in with most of the games, when it came to anything requiring physical exertion, she preferred to bow out. 'She wasn't really into sport,' said Sandra.

At Guides, neither Julie nor Sandra earned many of the badges for sewing, cooking or knitting, for which the girls were encouraged to compete. But whenever there was a staged affair, Julie came into her own. The Guides formed a concert party and elected Julie their star performer. 'It was at the Co-op Hall in Middleton,' said Sandra, recalling Julie's debut. 'That was the first time it dawned on me that Julie had something we didn't; she had a real talent.'

Julie starred in a production with a Middle Eastern flavour, written and produced by the girls. By all accounts she stole the show – she was spectacular.

'We were all dressed Eastern style in huge pyjama pants. We sang and belly danced and Julie was very, very good. Everybody loved her.'

Always the centre of attention, Julie's sense of fun and natural good looks made her immensely popular, especially with boys. Sandra said: 'The lads were always round her like bees round a honey pot. She was always quite pretty. She always had nice hair – quite fair – and she was always well developed for her age.'

It was the era of the eleven-plus, the exam taken by pupils in their final year of primary school as a passport to grammar school. If you passed and were sent to grammar school, you were guaranteed a first-class education and, you hoped, a better job in a white-collar career like accountancy, teaching or the legal profession. If you failed, you went to a secondary-modern and would probably enter one of the solid working-class trades such as building or plumbing.

Julie passed the eleven-plus and Sandra failed, which meant they were allocated to different schools. Julie went to Queen Elizabeth's Grammar, in Middleton, a prestigious forward-thinking school with excellent teachers and top-rate facilities. Sandra got a place at the more downmarket Durnford Street secondary-modern school, which was actually next door to Queen Elizabeth's. Every day, Sandra and Julie travelled together on the bus, but separated at the school gates; inevitably they drifted apart.

After a year, Julie ended her relationship with Rod and started dating an older boy who was also at Queen Elizabeth's. 'I can't remember exactly what happened, but I think Julie went off with a bloke called Paul Carney,' said Rod. 'He was higher up the school than me, older still. I was distraught when we finished.'

The split happened just before Julie started senior school. Rod had already been at Queen Elizabeth's for two years and was just beginning his third year when Julie arrived.

On his first day back at school after the long summer

holidays, Rod dreaded bumping into Julie. Like the male lead in the hit teen movie *Grease*, Rod decided it was not cool to have an old flame around who knew your intimate secrets. Rod said: 'I got a feeling of dread because this ex-girlfriend was arriving. I was highly regarded in the school and it wouldn't do my credibility any good to have had a serious girlfriend. The thing was to have several.

'Personally, I was never short of girlfriends. I was far more sought after than Julie,' he boasted. 'I played soccer for the school in the second year. In the sixth form I was first XI captain, house captain, prefect and cross-country champion.'

Unlike Sandra Dee, the innocent girlfriend in *Grease*, Julie could not have cared less about Rod and preferred the company of older boys. She actually avoided her ex and made it clear she had set her sights somewhat higher.

Rod now says defensively: 'I never dealt with her at school. She was out of my league. Firstly, she was two years below me and I had no interest in girls younger than me. Secondly she was busy with other boys and getting a bit of a reputation. I felt I didn't want to be with a girl like that anyway.'

Julie's kissing and cuddling behind the bike sheds seems innocent now, but in a school where boys and girls had separate playgrounds and even the teachers had single-sex common rooms, this sort of behaviour was pretty racy.

Julie was enjoying her popularity at school, but away from the playground she was facing another upheaval. Her mother and stepfather were on the move.

First they took a little terraced house in Gregge Street, Heywood, then because they spent so much time in the pub they started to think about managing one. Eventually, when Julie was twelve, they found a tenancy at a small local round the corner from Gregge Street called the Bay Horse Hotel.

As the removal van packed up their things neither Julie nor her mother showed any signs of regret at leaving Slattocks. Sandra remembers: 'Once they moved they shut the door and that was it. There was no big lead up. One day Julie was there the next day she wasn't.'

That final slam of the door closed the chapter on their two-year friendship.

Years later, Sandra, aged seventeen, bumped into Julie at a local club, but says there was no warmth between them. 'She said hello,' remembers Sandra. 'Julie looked utterly grown up, quite sophisticated with a cigarette in a holder and flashy clothes. She was more like the person on television than the person I knew. 'The friendship was gone though. I thought it was pretty clear that she wasn't that interested in me just by the look she gave me.'

And Rod, who, despite being cool at school, secretly adored Julie for years, bumped into her one day when he was out shopping. He said: 'It was in Tesco, and she didn't recognize me.'

3

Loneliness

Julie is the first to admit she was no genius at school and could not whip up much excitement for the three 'R's'. But she was never a quitter, and to make the whole learning experience more exciting she looked for ways to cheer up lessons. Julie liked nothing better than to push her books aside, take centre stage and sing a song or two. Not caring whether she was in music, history or maths, if Julie got the urge, she performed.

'Once, Julie got up in front of the whole class and sang "Black-eyed Susie",' said Anne Thomas, a close friend of Julie's who shared her first-year class. Julie serenaded her history master with all the confidence of a girl much older. 'I never saw anything like it in my whole school career,' Anne continued. 'I was very impressed. I thought she sang it very well; she was incredibly good. She had a very deep, full, voice. Most children would get up to sing and it would be childish, but Julie sounded authentic and quite sophisticated.'

The performance set her apart from the shy first-year pupils. Sylvia Henderson, who later became head girl, was overawed by Julie's nerve. 'I remember when she volunteered to go to the front and sing,' she said. 'We all thought she was incredibly pushy. We wouldn't have dared sing in front of complete strangers and to volunteer to a strange teacher, well!'

The teacher appeared to love the attention and thought the episode cute. 'He wasn't at all embarrassed,' said Anne.

Pretty Dot Huggins, also in Julie's form, remembers being in music teacher Alfred Hull's lesson when Julie treated a visiting maths teacher to her Hollywood song-and-dance routine. 'She was more Marilyn Monroe than Marilyn,' said Dot. 'Julie was all over the maths teacher. She sang "I Can't Give You Anything but Love" and "You Made Me Love You".' It was Christmas 1954 and Julie was fourteen. When she finished the song, she grabbed Mr Hull and kissed him under the mistletoe.

'He was very embarrassed, but secretly loved it,' grinned Dot. Julie was delighted that she had the power to make a teacher blush.

'Julie was a great flirt,' remembers Anne, who travelled to school on the bus with Julie. 'She flirted with all the teachers, especially with Mr Hull. She had a lot of confidence with them.'

In the playground Julie was just as confident, and her impromptu performances made her a legend. She loved the attention and performed encore after encore. As well as her song-and-dance routines, Julie could tell a riveting story. Every Monday a crowd gathered underneath the classrooms in the out-of-bounds boiler room or coal hole to listen as Julie span her yarns.

Sue Skelton, a smaller, quieter girl who became close

pals with Julie in the second year, remembers how she held court and told fantastic tales of their weekends together. 'They would be very theatrical, film-star type of stories. Things like we'd met two guys and they'd taken us to the Ritz, or somewhere fantastic, and then they'd flown us to Paris. They were incredible tales, but everybody loved them.'

Anne Thomas also remembers Julie making up stories about imaginary brothers and sisters, or describing in gruesome detail how her real father, George Kemp, beat her mother so badly she had had to leave home.

'Nobody disliked her for telling fibs or challenged her,' said Sue, 'they just enjoyed listening.'

What none of her fellow pupils realized was that Julie's fantasies about a glamorous life were prompted by unhappiness. Julie felt trapped at home, where she became increasingly miserable with her stepfather, Bill. 'She was very unhappy when I first met her,' said Sue.

By her second year at school, Julie had moved from Gregge Street to the flat above The Bay Horse Hotel in Torrington Street, a small, back-street pub, filled with regulars who enjoyed a pint and a game of darts or dominoes. Sue regularly visited the flat and was distressed to witness Bill, red-faced from drinking, shouting at Julie. 'I wasn't very fond of Bill; he used to be a bit peevish,' said Sue. 'In all the years I was going there I never saw him speak to Julie nicely, I never heard him say a loving word or make a loving gesture. He just made her do jobs and things that I didn't have to do at home, and if she didn't do her chores she would get into trouble. Then he would criticize her work, always finding something to pick on.

'I felt so sorry for Julie because our lives were so

different. I used to go home and my mother would have the tea made. Julie would have to go into a cold house with nobody there, light the fire and get the tea started.

'I saw her in tears quite a lot, especially if Bill had been giving her a hard time, and although her mum loved her in her own way, Bill seemed to regard her as a bit of a nuisance.'

Sue says Julie refused to cry in front of Bill. When he was rough, crude and coarse towards her there would be no temper tantrums or hysterics. She would just stand behind Sue and giggle.

Julie's mother seemed to be a bag of nerves. She smoked constantly as she made ineffectual attempts to mediate between her husband and daughter.

In her early teens, Julie suffered a terrible torment. She regularly escaped the unhappiness at home by popping round to see her Nan, Lizzie Duckworth. Then one morning, thirteen-year-old Julie caught sight of a newspaper headline which rocked her to her knees. 'WOMAN FOUND DEAD IN CANAL,' it said. The woman turned out to be her Nan and Julie lost an important ally.

No one knew whether, depressed by her husband's death, and facing years of loneliness, Julie's Nan had decided to end it all, or whether she simply slipped and drowned. The coroner's verdict was accidental death.

The old lady had been a spiritualist, and Julie liked to think she used her powers to stay in touch from beyond the grave. If Julie ever got depressed she only had to think of her Nan and her face would light up. Then she would notice the smell of mothballs and lavender. These were her grandmother's smells and Julie knew her ghost was present.

Schoolfriend Kath Jepson remembers that she and Julie played with a Ouija board around that time. 'We'd made it ourselves,' she says. 'We used to turn the lights down in the lounge at my parents' council house. We played by the light of the coal fire.'

Julie's own home life remained short on warmth during the years living over the pub. Most nights her hard-working parents rarely sat down to eat dinner before midnight, by which time Julie would be fast asleep. During the day they had admin and books to worry about, so Julie would walk over the road to see friendly neighbour Edna Barlow.

Pub life seemed to be taking its toll on the marriage of Julie's parents, and her mother began seeing a married man, a regular customer at The Bay Horse, who lived nearby. Far from objecting to the friendship, Bill appeared to encourage it.

Edith Collinge, one of the best friends of Julie's mother remembers how the man waited in the bar one night while Mrs Goodyear was busy getting ready upstairs. Bill sat having a good-natured chat with the fellow, then shouted up to her, 'Hurry up, you're keeping the lad waiting.'

Her home life in turmoil, Julie looked forward to going to school. She travelled on the bus with her pal Anne Thomas, who was nicknamed Tommy. She remembers how Julie would often jump on the bus chewing a pickled onion sandwich, having missed breakfast.

In and out of class Julie found it a simple matter to get the attention she was missing at home. Apart from the pranks and her dramatic performances, Julie flouted strict school regulations and tinkered with her school clothes. Even her conformist friend Sylvia Henderson admits, 'The uniform was pretty abysmal. In summer we had red or green gingham or plain green dresses. They were just like a sack, with elbow-length sleeves. They tied in the middle and had a gathered skirt, which did nothing for your figure.'

Julie adapted hers so it enhanced her figure. With the help of Edna, who was a part-time seamstress, she made subtle alterations. 'Julie managed to make her uniform look stunning. She looked sexy and glamorous while everyone else looked like shapeless bags.' Sylvia laughed. 'Her summer dress had cap sleeves, which weren't regulation. The fashion was waspie belts, so she had her dress pulled in with a waspie belt. Those were also the days of paper nylon petticoats. So she had one to make her dress stick out. Her hair was in a ponytail with a little kiss curl dangling over her forehead. And she always looked stunning in her sports shorts.'

Senior mistress Annie Maskew, who was in charge of the girls, spotted the first signs of Julie's uniform baiting. She said: 'They were supposed to wear their hats all the time. Julie would always keep her hat off until she turned the corner and came into view of the school. I'm sure she never knew that we knew.'

The school colours were green, red and grey. Boys wore white shirts with short grey trousers until they were fifteen then graduated to long. Ties had green and red stripes while blazers were green with red piping. In winter, the girls wore white blouses, green gym slips or skirts, and green berets with red trim and a red pompom sewn to the crown.

During the five years Julie was at Queen Elizabeth's co-educational Grammar School she was known less as a rebel and more for being simply mischievous.

The school – nicknamed Quegs – had an ambitious motto: Tout Bien ou Rien, which means All Good or

Nothing. And pupils were encouraged to live up to it. Their standards was those set by the school founder, Cardinal Langley, in 1412. Girls and boys educated there were expected to take up careers in the professions.

Several pupils exceeded expectations. Old boy Frank Tyson, the Northamptonshire fast bowler, helped win the Ashes for England against Australia in 1954 during one of their biggest Test defeats at Lord's. Ex-Quegian Francis Williams became editor of the now-defunct newspaper the *Daily Herald*, before joining the Labour government as Prime Minister Clement Attlee's press secretary. He also controlled press censorship in 1945.

Opera singer Ann Hood, who sings with the D'Oyly Carte international opera company based in Birmingham, was at the school around the same time as Julie. So was Norma Charlton, wife of former England footballer Bobby Charlton. Julie soon joined the ranks of famous old pupils, but teacher Annie Maskew, nicknamed 'Fanny' by the kids, said wryly: 'Julie was notorious rather than famous.'

When Julie arrived at her senior school on 9 September 1953, around 400 pupils were crammed into the impressive red-brick art deco building. Queen Elizabeth's expanded fast and soon ugly prefabs appeared on the playing fields opposite. Girls and boys had separate entrances and separate playgrounds. Sports were encouraged and the girls played hockey, tennis and netball while the boys played tennis, cricket and football. Boys were called by their surnames, girls by their first.

Julie was popular with classmates – especially the boys – and her good looks were universally acknowledged. Tommy, who like some of the other girls at school confessed she was a bit in awe of Julie, said: 'She was a golden girl. Golden hair, golden skin. Her nose was a bit too straight in a way. But she was lovely, absolutely lovely.'

In the playground, Julie was the school clown. One party trick was to put a whole crisp in her mouth without breaking it. Others remember her eating the middle out of a muffin and stuffing it with crisps, and it was noticed that her blazer smelled of beer from the pub.

Julie loved her schooldays and her old schoolfriends remember her with affection. Dot Huggins, Julie's best friend in the first year, says: 'Julie was always the centre of attention, she was very funny. She always had an answer for everything, and always got the last word.'

She mixed with everyone, not caring if they were more academic or older than her; Julie was a hit with them all.

Sylvia Henderson, who was far more studious than Julie, said: 'Julie was never unpleasant, catty or condescending, she was very warm-hearted.' Her friend Sue Skelton agrees. 'There was absolutely no malice in her.'

Teachers liked her too. Brenda Worrall, her art mistress, thought she was a hoot: 'There is no doubt Julie was fun to teach. Very bubbly and very chatty. She was quite popular with the teachers, she was not one of the notorious baddies who you screamed about in the staff room. She was quite mature, she had a knowing air about her. At the time she was quite sophisticated, and we all thought she was destined to do something special.'

Julie flouted the rules, but she was never in any serious trouble. Her English teacher Connie Parker remembers how she covered her tracks. 'She was too clever to be naughty in the wrong place at the wrong time.'

And her friend Dot recalls: 'Julie didn't disrupt classes, she liked to entertain us. In our mock biology 'O' level we were asked the question: "What regulates the body temperature?" Julie didn't have a clue and drew a picture of a horse sitting in a deckchair under an umbrella holding an iced drink. In the winter the horse was sat there with a scarf on and a hot drink. The drinks and the clothes were supposed to regulate the body temperature. The teacher gave her two out of ten for artistic impression.'

Teacher Annie Maskew remembers chiding Julie a few times for mischievous behaviour: 'Julie was in a religious education class, taken in one of the prefab classes. Heating pipes ran through one classroom to the next. She thought it was very funny shaking the pipes with her foot in one room so they rattled in the other room, but unfortunately she got her foot stuck. I told her: "We'll have to send for the caretaker, either to cut the pipe or to cut your foot off and I think it will be cheaper to cut your foot off!"' Julie thought that was hilarious.

Another time Mrs Maskew found a crowd of squiffy girls who had guzzled a whole bottle of rum, destined to flavour a Christmas cake. 'They were fourteen at the time,' she said. 'One girl, Wynsome Reynalles, who came from the Bahamas, had bought a whole bottle of Jamaican rum and they'd been swigging it. One of the teachers found them lolling around and sent someone to the staff room to fetch me. This teacher was really worried. She said she'd sent a lot of the girls to the sickroom because she thought they'd been overcome by fumes. I went to the sickroom, where the smell of drink was overpowering.

'I didn't have to punish them, because they were all so ill. I told them to tell their parents what they'd done and bring letters from home confirming they had confessed.'

Another time, Julie sent art teacher Brenda Worrell into a panic. Brenda said: 'I was teaching Julie's class one day and I remember I had just become engaged. My ring was a large square sapphire surrounded with diamonds, and I was very proud of it. We were doing something in class and my hands were plastered with printing inks, so I took my ring off and put it on the side of the sink. When I turned round it had disappeared. I was frantically looking around for it, and I remember panicking because I'd only been engaged for a week and I thought I'd already lost my engagement ring. Then I saw Julie sitting there with it on her finger, holding it up to the light. She just grinned and said: "It suits me, doesn't it?" '

Genteel, tweed-suited English teacher Connie Parker took her subject – English literature – very seriously. Unfortunately, not all the children shared her passion and Connie often had problems controlling her classes. Dot Huggins was in class when Julie actually made Mrs Parker cry. 'Julie used to like winding her up. She said to her: "Would you like a sweet, Mrs Parker?" and dropped it down her front.' The teacher went to the headmaster in tears.

Mrs Parker taught Julie throughout her school career and, despite being teased, had a soft spot for her. 'Julie was a bright girl,' she said. 'I think English was her strongest subject. She wrote quite imaginative essays. Sometimes they were very humorous. I remember one she wrote with some of the other girls which was so amusing I thought I'd send it to the satirical magazine *Punch*. It was about working at the seaside, burying people in the sand as an occupation. It was very amusing because it was so detached.'

Mrs Parker was right: Julie did love English, especially the performing side. Sylvia still remembers Julie surprising everybody by beating her in a Bible-reading contest. 'In the second year we had an arts festival organized by some

Welsh teachers, called an Eisteddfod,' said Sylvia. 'One of the events was a public-speaking competition. We had to read a passage from the Bible. I think Julie read a passage from Isaiah 35 – "The Road of Holiness." Julie won and I came second. I was a bit miffed, particularly because the Bible didn't seem to be the sort of book Julie would normally have chosen.'

The school was enjoying golden days. History teacher Bob Pauls remembers: 'The atmosphere was good and the pupils were mainly middle class. It was a happy school. The head Mr Wren, a very able man was very well respected. We did pretty well and had reasonably good exams results, with a few pupils getting to Oxford or Cambridge.

'The social work side of teaching didn't exist in those days. We didn't have to cope with truancy, vandalism and petty crime. The main problem we had was persuading the boys to wear their caps. The girls generally were very good, well behaved, middle class children. Julie fitted in very well.

'The children were very keen on charities. One famous occasion some of the girls wrote to Jimmy Saville, an upcoming DJ in those days, and persuaded him to come to school to support an African charity. To our surprise he came, turning up in a red sports-car, and giving a talk to the kids. He presented the headmaster with a bottle of whiskey, which went down very well, and gave us about £100 towards the charity.'

Although she kept her nose clean in front of the teachers, behind the scenes Julie was a bit of a villain. Each morning pupils who arrived on two wheels would leave their bikes in the shed at the back of the school. The bike sheds were out of bounds during the day because they were isolated and hard to patrol, which made them more alluring.

Children who dared, would sneak behind them for a quick puff on a Senior Service cigarette. Others would just stand and gossip, telling secrets not suitable for the playground. Couples a bit more advanced would risk a quick grope.

Tommy remembers: 'Once I was there with Julie, listening to her talking of her latest exploits, and we were caught by Miss Pauls the gym mistress who gave us lines.'

More typical was the trouble when Julie was spotted with a boy in the school fields – out of bounds of course. The teacher mistook her for classmate Janet Howard, who was then threatened with expulsion.

Julie was not above getting into the odd scrap, either. Classmate David Liddle was not quite sure what the fights were about – Sue reckons they were mostly about the pub – but remembers being on the receiving end of a few swift kicks. 'She certainly kicked me occasionally,' he claims. 'I remember her as this straw-haired thing who was very precocious, very flirty and who had the odd fight.'

Despite the scuffles, her schoolfriends bear no grudges and remember the things about Julie which made them laugh, not the ones which gave them bruises. Julie got involved in school life and joined the trendy Junior Poetry Reading Society (JPRS), quite an advanced class for a conservative grammar school. She also joined the literary and debating societies, although as Connie Parker quipped, Julie talked so much she could have debated with herself. She became a member of the Inter-Schools Christian Fellowship (ISCF), which met at lunchtimes. She also joined the music circle and the choir. Julie had a good voice and liked being in the choir because she got a special seat in front of the whole school.

Julie was not an outstanding academic. She took five mock O-levels: English language, English literature, history, geography and art, and obtained low grades in all of them. The lowest was 15, equivalent to an E pass, for geography, the highest 30, equivalent to a D pass, for English language and art. For English literature and history she scored 25. Not surprisingly, on 29 July 1958 at the age of sixteen, Julie left school. But we are jumping ahead of the story.

In the first year, pupils were separated into three forms and streamed according to their date of birth. Children born between September and December were in class X, December to April joined Y class and April to September birthdays were in Z class. At the end of the first year they were streamed according to their academic ability. The ten brightest from each form went into class X, average children went into Y, and those with least academic ability were relegated to Z.

Julie joined class IIZ with her pals Sue Skelton, Dot Huggins and Janet Howard and became part of a crowd known as 'The Fast Set'.

The traits which made Julie popular with classmates made her slightly unpopular with parents. Sue Skelton's Mum, Marion, disapproved of Julie although her Dad Harold didn't object. 'They thought she would lead me astray,' said Sue. 'Instead of doing homework we were always out enjoying ourselves. Mum used to worry about where we went and what we did when we got there. She thought that Julie would get us in to trouble, she worried about our reputations. Her favourite saying was: "Birds of a feather flock together."'

'When Julie got pregnant at seventeen, Mum thought

that was absolutely dreadful; she didn't want me to be tarnished by my best friend. Julie knew Mum disapproved, but it didn't bother her and Mum never banned her, she just worried.'

Occasionally, Julie would use the Skeltons as an excuse when she was staying out late with a boyfriend.

Mrs Skelton never really came to terms with Julie. Sue says: 'Years later when I phoned Mum and told her I was going to be on television as a guest when they had Julie on *This is Your Life*, she said: "Ooh, that's lovely. I just wish it was going to be somebody else's life."'

Despite their misgivings about Julie as Sue's closest friend, the Skeltons couldn't help liking her for her irreverent sense of humour. Sue's sister Pam remembers Julie's spontaneous one-woman vaudeville floorshow. 'She used to entertain us by telling rude jokes. Mother would be quite shocked but dad would say: "She doesn't know what she's saying." Mum would disagree and say: "She knows exactly what she's saying."

'She was a great mimic too and took off all the teachers. Her imitation of domestic science teacher Frieda Little was hilarious. Frieda had this very enthusiastic way of speaking, quite a presenters voice and Julie got her off to a tee.'

Julie often stayed at Sue's house and even joined the family for holidays. Away from home the two schoolgirls behaved like typical teenagers – always up to mischief. 'Our first holiday together was at a boarding house in Torquay with my parents,' recalls Sue. 'It was 1956 and we were fourteen. We got locked out one evening. It was only 10.30 p.m. but we had to hammer on the door. Mum popped her head out of the window and shouted that I was in trouble. She threatened to send us home. We burst out laughing, then the landlady came down and let us in.

We'd been looking for some dance place to rock'n'roll in.

'Two years later, we went to Newquay with my older sister Pam and her fiancé, Peter Hughes. I think we must have been an absolute nuisance. Julie was always in trouble for coming down to breakfast in her hair rollers. It wasn't the done thing.'

The Newquay holiday was in wakes week, the annual break for northern mill and factory workers. During wakes week the mills would close for repairs and maintenance and the whole town closed down with them.

'Peter and I probably wanted to go to Newquay on our own but had to chaperone Sue and Julie,' laments Pam. 'The journey took about 12 hours overnight. The train stopped at Exeter and Julie and Sue were so excited they wanted to get off and find a quicker way to get there. We stayed in a typical guest house. It had beautiful gardens and a lake.'

Julie made up for the intrusion by entertaining the troops. At breakfast, looking like a sexy version of Hilda Ogden in her rollers and saucy shorts, she launched into a comedy routine that had them all in stitches.

'There was a big black sambo money box in the corner of the dining-room,' recalls Peter. 'Julie would go over and do a ventriloquist act with it.'

Typically for England, it rained all week, but even torrential downpours were not enough to keep the girls away from the seafront. 'They would come running back from the beach in their swimming costumes with newspapers over their heads,' laughed Pam, remembering the pair looking like a couple of damp little characters from a picture postcard.

*

The late 1950s was the era of a new breed of youngster: a phenomenon of the post war years called the teenager. They were rebellious, had their own ideas and fashions, and were intent on having fun. Firing them up were pop stars like Elvis Presley and Buddy Holly, who rocked into view around the same time. British heart-throb Anthony Newley was also beginning to make a name for himself. The more staid groups like Bill Haley and the Comets were on their way out, and so was one-time heart-throb Dickie Valentine.

The dance craze Elvis and co fuelled was jiving. Couples would expertly flip each other over shoulders, through legs and round backs. Julie and Sue picked up on the craze and spent every spare minute practising the intricate moves. Julie – being the taller of the two – would flip, while Sue leapt, swung and spun.

The in venue for rock 'n' rolling near Heywood was a Mecca dancehall called the Carlton. On Saturday afternoon the local teenagers would flock to Rochdale to dance under the hall's spinning mirrored ball. Manager Ernie Mills hired huge dance bands, like those of Joe Loss and Geoff Love, to entertain the hoards of dancers who flocked in their hundreds for a slow waltz or hectic jive. At some stage each evening the band would launch into the Carlton capers, the hall's version of the hokey-cokey. Dot's mother banned her because she called the place 'a trapping spot'. Julie and Sue were regulars, though, and would always arrive together. Sue often made her own way home, leaving Julie smooching on the dancefloor. Her sister Pam remembers: 'My parents worried sick about Sue making her own way home.'

Julie and Sue were mad about jiving and spent every spare minute practising. 'That's all we used to do at playtime, practise all the moves,' Sue said. 'We spent hours jiving in the school yard and fields and people gathered to watch us.' The practice paid off. 'We won quite a few competitions at the Carlton. We didn't get trophies, there was a tray and a vase plus clothes and things like that.'

To their parents they pretended to be at each other's houses, heads down doing homework. Carrying off the charade took expert planning. 'We used to sneak off in ordinary gear, then change when we got to the dancehall,' said Sue.

Julie, aged fifteen, would step out of the front door dressed demurely in a blouse and knee-length skirt. But the second she was out of sight she would whip off the skirt to reveal a perfect pair of legs clad in figure-hugging shorts. She would then stride down the road to wolf-whistles galore as the lads ogled her slender figure.

Her quick changes are remembered with affection by former neighbour Edna Barlow. 'Young Julie could turn any man's head when she was dressed like that,' said Edna. 'Her stepfather would have gone mad if he knew because he never liked her in clothes that showed her off too much.

'Julie found a way round it by putting on a modest skirt and then whipping it off when she was out of sight. Often she would throw the skirt into my lobby and pick it up on her way back home. All of us had a laugh over it because it was typical of Julie.'

The girls loved to borrow each other's clothes. 'We'd wear sleeveless polo-neck-type tops, or sleeveless blouses with stand-up collars, and we both had felt skirts, flat shoes and socks,' said Sue. 'One skirt was royal blue with gold and silver thread round it, the other was like a wigwam with orange and yellow zig-zaggy things on it. We bought them from C&A with our pocket money.'

Bill did not approve of Julie's outings, and would have been furious if he'd known what she was up to. But then that was Bill, about as understanding as a drill sergeant. It was small wonder Julie looked for affection in the boys she met, and luckily found plenty willing to offer it.

Julie had turned into a stunning young woman, with her blonde hair and slender figure, and even at fourteen she was the talk of the school.

Friends Sylvia and Tommy remember tales of her dates, whispered in confidence behind the bike sheds. Tommy said: 'Julie would talk to me about boyfriends, and what she got up to with them. I didn't know much about sex or anything, but from the anecdotes she told me I got the impression she did.'

Tommy experienced Julie's powers of attraction first hand when her French teacher father invited an exchange pupil called André to stay. 'André had bright red hair,' said Tommy. 'He was about four years older than us, we would have been about sixteen, and he came from Marseilles. I was wondering what on earth to do with this André. I didn't actually think he was very nice.

'Somebody said there was a dance on at the Young Conservative club in Middleton. You went there simply to dance it had nothing to do with politics. I invited Julie who turned up dressed girlishly in white. When I saw her I just thought: "Oh Julie". She managed to make an innocent colour like white look very, very sexy.

'André took one look at her and was smitten, so was Julie. They paired up and spent the rest of the night dancing together. Afterwards I had to endure a whole week with him going on and on about what an innocent, fragile, wonderful girl Julie was. She had him round her little finger.'

Julie had a personal allure far beyond her years, and soon she was dating local lads she met at The Bay Horse, which she began to refer to as The Bay Horse-A-Go-Go. 'Julie was popular with the boys,' Sue said. 'There was a gang in Hopwood who we used to pal around with. We used to go on Hopwood Rec and gather round and chat until about 8 p.m. We occasionally had a snog in the corner. Not with anyone special. We'd try them all out!'

Malcom Wright was a Hopwood lad who first met sixteen-year-old Julie in The Bay Horse. 'The lads used to go berserk over her,' he enthused. 'She had a fantastic figure. She was fairly well endowed, with lovely legs. She dressed provocatively in revealing clothes. We used to have bags of fun with her; she was always bubbly and game for a laugh.'

One 'lad' besotted with Julie was Trevor Saxon, who lived in Bing Street, a couple of roads away from the pub. 'She went out with him for quite a long time,' remembers Sue. 'He really worshipped her, he would have laid down his life for her. But she was always leaving him for someone else. Then they'd get together again and it would be back on.'

Trevor was intelligent, with hair the colour of Hovis and a wicked glint in his eyes. He was about 5ft 8ins tall and rode a motorbike. He was also a tolerant lad, the sort who would watch somone make a fool of themselves at a talent show and say: 'Well at least they had a go.'

When she and Trevor were not dating, Julie joined a crowd of others and would go off dancing. She was considered pretty knowledgeable in the sexual arena, having grown up in a pub where she had listened in to adult conversation, while hiding on the stairs with Sue.

One boy who dated her occasionally, when Julie was fourteen, says: 'I was a couple of years older than her and she was pretty advanced for a fourteen-year-old. It wasn't serious between us; we went out to youth clubs and things, but nothing more. Julie liked to go out with different lads, she liked to play the field a bit.

'Some people seem to attract more attention than others and she was one of those. It was partly a personality thing, not just looks. She talked to shock. She was a live wire with the looks to go with it, which all added up to magnetism.'

It was a great disappointment to her male classmates that Julie was not interested in them, but her lack of availability did not stop them dreaming that one day they might be honoured with a date.

Peter Birchall who later starred with Julie in the school play, was in the year above her and one of the lads who hoped Julie would be forward with him. Instead he watched from the sidelines. 'Unfortunately, she was never interested in me. She was attractive to the opposite sex. When skirts shouldn't have been short she wore them short.'

While boys' tongues hung out of their mouths gathering gravel from the playground Julie side-stepped them and concentrated on her acting career. She was a member of the school dramatics society and she loved drama.

It wasn't until the fifth form, though, that Julie's showbiz talents were noticed. Domestic-science teacher Frieda Little, who also taught comedienne Victoria Wood, remembers that she could see Victoria's potential from the start, but she didn't spot Julie's emerging talent.

'Vicky composed words and music for a sixth form review. It was superb. She had a flair for English and music but didn't fit in with tradition. She was a bit of a rebel, untidy and chaotic.

'Julie didn't make the same impact. She wasn't what I would call outstanding.' Nevertheless, Julie surprised the school with a performance which would not have shamed a professional actress when she landed the lead in the school play in 1958. It was a comedy thriller called *We Must Kill Toni*, set in a country mansion.

Julie, as Toni Opera, stood to inherit the family fortune. Her half-brothers, played by Sydney Yates and Albert Darby, were left out of the will. Incensed, they plotted to kill her, but not before one brother – Sydney – tries to seduce her. Anita Simpson, as investigative journalist Miss Richards, got in the way.

As in all riveting thrillers the butler played a major role. In this part, Peter Birchall was to discover the brothers' iniquitous plot and tip off a shocked Miss Opera. In the end, thanks to her scheming, the brothers killed each other instead.

The young cast gave four performances of the play, the final being on 29 March 1958, Julie's sixteenth birthday. To play innocent Toni Opera Julie had to iron out her broad Lancashire accent, and behave like a naïve young woman. She had been picked for the role from four hopefuls because classics teacher and deputy head Tony Whitehead said she oozed sophistication beyond her years. 'I chose her because of her brightness, poise and assurance, which was rather unusual for a fifth-year girl. She was very outgoing and extrovert and had a good voice and a good sense of movement.

'She was younger than the others in the cast, but came

out the boss of the play. She was a natural for acting, she needed very little direction. Although there was one scene where she had to walk up stairs and I made a note that she was wiggling her bottom a bit too much.'

It was Julie's first serious performance. Of course, the boys watching the production were more interested in her looks than in her talent. 'She had some natural assets, if you know what I mean,' says schoolfriend Peter Birchall. 'When blokes talked about her they would say: "You know, that blonde bit with the big tits."'

What they could not see was the help Julie gave her 'assets'. To make them look bigger and more uplifted she padded her bra with tissues and cotton wool. 'Or anything at all,' said Sue. As she got older, however, Julie's 36b bosom no longer needed artificial help.

Julie had been delighted to land the role of Toni, but had some trouble finding time to learn her lines. Her busy social life created an appealing diversion. But on the night, like a true professional, Julie was word-perfect and the school magazine gave her a rave review: 'This light comedy of crime in the grand manner had for its brave and innocent heroine Julie Goodyear, of VZ, who played her part most vivaciously . . .'

On school speechday Julie was awarded the head-master's prize for dramatics, a silver trophy, at a ceremony at Middleton baths. Bursting with pride Julie – who had already left school and come back specially – walked across the boards covering the swimming pool towards the makeshift stage. The applause was deafening: 'She thoroughly deserved it,' said Tony, who knew he was watching a star in the making. 'I was sure at the time that she would go on to act. I wouldn't necessarily have thought she would take the role of Bet Lynch in *Corona-*

tion Street, I thought she would probably so something more dramatic, but I knew she would do something.'

Julie became addicted to drama. She loved being the centre of attention and glowed as teachers responsible for hair, make-up and wardrobe fussed over her. She loved the rehearsals, first-night nerves and applause as the curtain dropped. It gave her the feeling of being in a supportive family unit, of pulling together working for a common goal.

The rapturous applause gave Julie's spirits a much needed lift. After years of turning in very average school-work, it proved she was outstanding at something. It also gave her a warm glow, a feeling of being loved, a feeling friends claimed she was used to living without. It gave her the glimpse of an exciting future. She made up her mind to become an actress and looked for allies within the school to help her.

Despite Julie's success, teacher Annie Maskew who advised the girls on careers, scoffed when Julie said she wanted to train as an actress. 'I said: "You can forget that Julie, it needs far more intelligence and far more staying power than you have. You've been in school plays but that's not acting." She was very, very average, perhaps a bit below average. I thought she would make a good secretary or clerk, so I sent her to the aviation firm Avro's for an interview.'

Avro's liked Julie and gave her a job as a trainee shorthand typist, which she started in September 1958. It wasn't acting, but Julie still took centre stage. Mrs Maskew was staggered when Avro's distributed a recruitment leaflet to schools. On the cover was a picture of Julie sitting on a desk.

Julie also started her first serious relationship at Avro's, with a draughtsman called Ray Sutcliffe.

When they started work, Julie and Sue saw less of each other. Sue had a job at ICI as an administration clerk. Both were keen not to drift apart, though, and the following September they decided on a holiday in the Isle of Man.

The Isle of Man was the in venue for teenagers lucky enough to be let off the leash, and Julie and Sue spent weeks persuading their parents that they were grown up enough to be trusted.

Julie checked in to a boarding house with Sue, but was soon off doing her own thing. Sue claims she hardly saw her in the evenings. With Ray Sutcliffe temporarily forgotten, Julie was intent on enjoying herself. 'We probably went out during the daytime, but I have no idea where Julie spent her nights,' said Sue.

Dot Huggins remembers Julie writing to say what a great time she was having with all the boys she met on holiday. What Julie did not say was that she had at last discovered the joys of steamy nights spent making love . . .

4

Teenage Mum

Once Julie discovered her sexual allure, she turned the heat full up. By now, aged sixteen, she was gorgeous. It was no exaggeration to say that she looked like a young film star. Men fell for her left, right and centre, bewitched by her mix of raw sex, humour and charisma. The good part was that she was just as fascinated by them as they were by her; the bad that her fascination would end in tears. By the time she reached seventeen she was unmarried and pregnant.

She met the young lad who supposedly got her into trouble at Avro's, the aforementioned aviation firm. Avro (which has since been taken over by British Aerospace) was located in Chadderton four miles to the south east of Heywood, and was a big employer in the area. Built in 1939, the factory was, and still is, massive. When Julie joined in the late 1950s nearly 6,000 staff were involved in churning out Lancasters, 748s and other aircraft.

It was September 1958 when, fresh from school, Julie

joined thirty raw recruits employed on the Avro training scheme on a weekly salary of £2 17s 6d. Half of the newcomers would train to be shorthand typists and the other half would be trained to work in the accounts department. The company took the instruction of new staff seriously and built a separate training school. Miss Earnshaw, a quiet ex-teacher in her mid-fifties, was responsible for training the secretaries. For the first three months of their induction course, the thirty school-leavers would study company law, maths and English. Then the group split in two and the accountancy recruits went off to be trained in accounting, while the secretaries studied shorthand and typing. Julie graduated six months later as a shorthand typist and became a secretary in the accounts department.

The training school was at the back of the firm's huge aircraft hangar, which covered two-thirds of a mile end to end. To get to the school meant walking a quarter of a mile past hoards of engineers and factory workers studiously riveting aeroplanes together. From the minute she walked through the door she caused a furore. Julie had the impact of a forces sweetheart visiting troops who have been exiled in the desert for a couple of years. As she sashayed past the lads they whooped and hollered and banged their hammers on the massive plane fuselages on which they worked. They behaved as though Brigitte Bardot herself had dropped in to see them.

At the time, the fashion was for huge, swirling skirts held out by layers of net petticoats, topped with demure twinsets and pearls or shirts buttoned way above the cleavage. On their feet girls would wear flat pumps. Julie bucked the trend and would turn up in skin-tight skirts, tiny jumpers, high heels and lots of jewellery. Her provocative clothes, stunning figure and catwalk poise caused a sensation.

Jenny Morton, who joined the firm at the same time as Julie and was in the same group, remembers the impact she had as the girls made their way to 'school'. Every morning a crowd of trainee secretaries walked in Julie's wake like little ducklings following their mother. And they bathed in reflected glory as Julie's appearance threatened to cause more damage than Hitler's bombs. Jenny said: 'Julie was a very, very good-looking girl. She had a perfect figure and terrific legs. Every day her hair would be different, one day in a chignon, the next loose or piled on top. She used to wear tight skirts and sweaters and very high heels. When I think about the rest of us she was very advanced. I was still in a ponytail and had virtually only just cast off school uniform. She was far superior, she seemed far older, although she was the same age as me.

'The training school was at the back of the building and, unfortunately, we had to negotiate the shopfloor to get to it. The factory then was absolutely bulging at the seams, it was like a small town. If you can visualize this massive, massive building which was very, very lofty with glass ceilings to let in as much natural daylight as possible, stepladders leading up to jigs, and scaffolding towers about fifteen feet high. The aircraft bellies and parts of the aircraft were suspended in these jigs with men crawling all over them. There was a constant rattle of pneumatic riveting drills, so there was a tremendous racket.

'Julie used to swing across that shopfloor and really set the place alight. As soon as she came into view, things would come to a sudden halt and the place would go quiet. There was an abundance of young men who would be hanging out of the fuselages, off the stepladders and scaffolding, whistling and cat-calling.

'She used to wave at them and give them a big flashing smile. The phrase "If you've got it flaunt it" could have been invented for her. She loved every minute of it – anybody would – and we were in absolute awe of her.'

Avro's was an old-fashioned, tightly-run company. Juniors were taught to respect their bosses and when senior staff were around you watched your Ps and Qs. The female head of personnel, Miss Jane Fraser, was ex-army, a spinster known as the 'iron lady' of Avro's. A real sergeant major, she terrified the girls.

The company had all sorts of rules which, by today's standards, seem petty. For example staff were not allowed to hang around in groups talking. Jenny remembers: 'If Miss Fraser walked past a group chatting in the corridor you were expected to disperse. If you weren't wise enough to skedaddle and she passed the same group as she was coming back down the corridor, you were fired.'

Julie was used to this type of authority and knew just how far to push it. In class she was the model student, never disruptive. She worked hard and was a good shorthand typist. When the bosses were around, Julie was never deliberately provocative but she did allow herself a daily devilish indulgence when crossing the factory floor.

When news of Julie's knock 'em dead appearances reached the bosses, it was decided that someone should have a word with her. She was becoming the talk of the factory, Avro's own celebrity, and it was not considered healthy. They reasoned that it would not be long before one of the men, too intent on ogling Julie, had an accident. Visions of missing fingers, broken limbs or worse, a fatality, fired the hierarchy into action. Julie had to be brought into line and the knuckle-rapping task was given to Miss Earnshaw.

Jenny remembers: 'It came to a head at one stage. Obviously, the foreman and different bosses got to hear of it. It was a very strait-laced place in the 1950s. Questions were asked and news was eventually given to Miss Earnshaw. She called Julie in for a chat. When Julie came back, she told us Miss Earnshaw had calmly pointed out to her that it wasn't really on to come dressed like this and she should be a bit more demure and not set out to call attention to herself. She was asked not to wear jewellery – earrings were fairly unusual for a girl of her age – she was asked not to wear high heels and tight skirts.'

Secretly, Julie thought 'silly old cow', but took the knuckle-rapping to heart – sort of. Jenny continues: 'The following day she'd done exactly as she was told. She came dressed like something out of the film *Seven Brides for Seven Brothers*. She wore a broderie anglaise top with a gathered scoop neck and little puff sleeves, a huge gingham skirt with masses of petticoats underneath, with little flat ballet pumps and her hair up in bunches. She looked just as provocative, just like Brigitte Bardot, very kittenish. She came across the shopfloor and had exactly the same effect.

'Of course, she couldn't be called into question because she'd done as instructed, she'd removed her jewellery, she'd removed her high heels and straight skirt. That sums her up, really. She was a devil with a small d.'

Gradually, Julie's attempt at being demure disappeared and she went back to wearing alluring clothes. She became the factory pin-up after appearing in the company's monthly magazine, the *Avro News*, wearing nothing but a leopard-skin bikini (model's own). Half-naked, Julie froze while the shot was being taken by editor Gordon Allen. She posed one lunchtime on the draughty stairs leading from Avro's reception area to the offices, for a regular feature Gordon called 'Beauty off Duty'.

In today's world of full-frontal nudity it is impossible to imagine the sensation the picture of Julie in her bikini caused. Peter Rushworth, who was then in his twenties and worked in the drawing office, explains: 'It was very risqué. Jane Fraser's eyes would have been out like chapel hat pegs. Good God, the only thing round that area were sheep, and they all had smiles on their faces. You never saw women like that. That picture was an absolute stunner. All the lads had the photograph stuck up on the top of their drawing board. And the factory was covered with that picture. When it appeared, everyone was aghast but pleasantly surprised and thinking, "Yes, this is the age of the youth; if you've got it, flaunt it."'

It seemed the whole factory fancied her. A click of her fingers and Julie could have had any man in the place. It was inevitable that she would end up dating one of her workmates, but her final choice staggered everyone.

The lad who caught her eye was twenty-two-year-old loner Ray Sutcliffe, a quiet but slightly rebellious, artistic chap with a passion for calligraphy. He looked like the American rocker Buddy Holly, with curly black hair teased into a slight quiff and tortoiseshell glasses like Buddy's. His speech was littered with Americanisms. He worked out at the gym and consequently was well built and muscular, and he stood around 5ft 10in. His clothes reflected his rock 'n' roll passion. At work he wore a white shirt, bootlace tie, drainpipe trousers and winklepicker shoes. In the evenings he liked to pose quietly in a powder-blue suit, which at the time – when men wore tweed or worsted – was almost as daring as Julie's leopard-skin bikini.

Ray was a trainee draughtsman and part of a 350-strong design team. He earned about £3 a week and worked in a side office in planning. His section was known as the routine drawing office. Ray would make minor alterations to aircraft drawings and schedules handed to him by the highly-paid chief draughtsman. He sat next to colleague Peter Rushworth and, in quiet moments, indulged his artistic talent by decorating Peter's set square with drawings of a voluptuous, semi-clad woman, who looked rather like Julie.

Julie decided she fancied Ray, there was something about Ray's genuine, gentle manner that appealed to her, and he was mesmerized by this extrovert wildcat with the dazzling smile and Mae West banter.

Once she decided she wanted something, it seemed nothing could get in her way. Peter remembers: 'Julie, being Julie, was every male's ideal young girl. She had the attributes (no silicone, if you know what I mean) to get a man and when she set out to do so, by God she made sure she won.'

Ray's first impressions of Julie were purely physical. 'She was beautiful,' he said. 'First I was attracted to her fantastic figure, then I got to know her.'

Before he had time to say set square, Ray was eating out of her hand. Julie expertly sent out the appropriate radar 'come-on' signals to her target. Ray picked them up and plucked up courage to ask her out and was very surprised when Julie agreed. 'It was a great boost to my ego,' he said.

Later, Julie told her version of how Ray had gone after

her. She said: 'He was tall, dark and handsome. All the girls in the typing pool fancied him like mad. Me, I wasn't bothered, but for some reason he picked me out and we went out a couple of times to the local cinema. Then one night he invited me on my first date.'

That first date came about six months after Julie joined Avro's. Ray borrowed his father's car for the occasion and took Julie, now seventeen, to the movies. A gentleman, and not the sort to boast about his conquests, Ray kept his coup quiet, but when word got out that he was dating the most sought-after woman at the Avro empire, workmates were stunned. 'I was absolutely gobsmacked that Ray was the one she chose,' said Peter. 'He wasn't the sort you would expect Julie to have chosen. He was quite quiet and arty and she was a flighty young girl. Ray was very secretive about it and even though I sat next to him I found out from someone else. I was flabbergasted when I knew. I said, "It can't be big quiet Ray." I confronted him and he sheepishly said, "Yes, it's me." He was absolutely over the moon that he'd captured Julie. The fact that he'd won the race was as much a surprise to him as it was to everybody else.'

An ex-grammar-school boy, Ray came from an ordinary, hard-working, working-class family. Ray, his older brother Joe, and younger sister Sandra lived with their parents Joe Snr and Betty, a dinner lady at Moss House School, on a faceless housing estate in Blackley, about twenty minutes' drive from Heywood. Joe Jnr also worked at Avro's, while Joe Snr was a drill setter at a local engineering company called Metropolitan Vickers.

Betty and Joe were well liked by the local community. Their former next-door neighbour, Dolores Visco, has nothing but praise for them: 'They were a lovely family. I don't think anybody had a bad word for them. Betty was a good lady, always happy to do you a good turn.'

Betty and her sister Mary shared the responsibility of looking after their elderly father. For six months of the year Granddad Pickering would live with Betty, then he would go to London and live with Mary. When old Mr Pickering stayed in Blackley, he would often hang over the front gate and chat to the local kids and neighbours.

All the Sutcliffe kids were well behaved. Ray was intelligent, hard-working and certainly no Jack-the-lad. Handsome and popular, he played cricket and football, liked to keep fit with trips to the gym and had a cracking physique. He was quiet, with a dry sense of humour, but once you got to know him he opened up.

Neighbour Jean Morris, who lived opposite Ray in Northland Road, remembers him as 'a bit of a clown, a bit of a dare devil. He had a cheeky face and curly hair. One curl came down over his forehead. He loved swapping comics like the *Beano*, *Dandy* and the *Eagle*.'

Ray had never had a serious girlfriend before Julie, but he apparently liked the experience. 'I think he was really potty about her in the beginning,' said Jean.

Julie was not often seen in Blackley and seemed to turn her nose up when she did put in an appearance. She appeared to make no effort to ingratiate herself with Ray's friends and neighbours. 'I was never friendly with her,' said Jean. 'We used to say hello when she came to Raymond's Mum's when they were courting. I felt she wasn't someone you could take to, always seemed a bit aloof and didn't appear to mix with any of Ray's crowd.'

Despite her apparent lack of interest in his friends, Julie persevered and, according to Ray, although she was younger she was more experienced than him in the sexual arena and even made the first pass. 'She made a play for me,' he said. 'She was my first serious girlfriend and it was the first time I had any sort of sexual encounter.'

After that first encounter Ray felt his life was being churned up in a giant concrete mixer. It was August 1959 when Julie dropped the first breezeblock and told Ray she was pregnant and that he was the father. At the time, Julie was seventeen, Ray was twenty-three.

Julie claimed the accident had happened after their first dinner date and portrayed herself as an innocent working-class lass from t'mill town, with cotton for brains, who got drunk and let a man take advantage of her. 'In those days I neither drank nor smoked,' she said, 'but on that night, nervous and excited at being in a big smart restaurant, I drank glass after glass of the cheap, sickly white wine Ray ordered. By the time we arrived back at his parents' home and found it empty I was feeling so giddy and light-headed I was not even sure who I was – never mind where I was.'

Ray's only comment was, 'It wasn't anything like that.'

However, in an interview with *The Sun* Julie created the impression that losing her virginity to Ray was a bit of a letdown. 'Girls are always led to believe that losing their virginity is a precious magical moment, something they will look back on and treasure for the rest of their lives,' she said. 'What's so marvellous about it? All I can remember through a blurred haze is wondering what could possibly be enjoyable about the fumbling and groping on the sofa in Ray's mother's front parlour. Certainly it could not be classed as the most memorable moment in my life.'

It was certainly not the most memorable moment in Ray's life, and in fact, he remembers a whole different version of events. 'I was certainly not her first boyfriend,' he insisted. Then he added, 'I know for a fact that she was going out with somebody in the army when she was dating me. I said, "Well, if we're going to go out together then you can't go out with other guys, you either go out with somebody else or with me, it's as simple as that." She said, "That's all right, I'd rather go out with you."

'We didn't have sex, although at the time, I was too naïve to realize we hadn't actually had intercourse, but Julie made a play for me,' said Ray. 'And I would certainly never have done anything like that at my parents' house or even a friend's house. It would have been out of the question!' he insists. 'I can't remember exactly where we were when we had our first intimate experience, we could have been in the front or the back of the car, but we definitely were not at anybody's house.'

Julie's best pal Sue Skelton says at the time Julie took the blame for her predicament. 'It's my fault,' Julie told Sue, after she confessed to her friend she was pregnant. 'Julie meant that Ray hadn't forced himself on her,' said Sue.

Julie said her mother was the first to notice she was pregnant and that she actually had no idea. She said: 'Naïve? I was so naïve that I did not even know I was pregnant until my mother sat me down and told me. She realized nature's monthly event had not taken place, questioned me about what had happened and then she broke the news that I must be pregnant. Working-class girls in Lancashire mill towns only learnt the facts of life by trial and error in those days. And boy, did I make an error! God, it was awful. It was as if my whole small world had come crashing down on me. I felt terribly hurt and ashamed that I had let my parents down.'

When Julie broke the news to Ray, they had been apart for about a month. He'd been on holiday to Spain, then she left for a holiday with Sue. When she came back and told him he was about to become a Dad, he was stunned. 'We'd only been going out a short time. It seemed like just a few weeks. When she told me I was amazed. My parents were shocked and disappointed in me. They were shocked to think that I could get somebody pregnant, but they didn't say too much to me about it.'

Former neighbour Dolores remembers Ray's Mum's reaction: 'Betty was a bit cut up about it. She didn't like the fact that Raymond had to get married. I think she was very surprised, I don't think she knew the relationship between Ray and Julie was that serious.'

It was a terrible scandal. Nice girls just did not have sex before marriage, and if they did they deserved everything they got. At work, the whole firm started whispering and gossiping about Julie's predicament. Julie could have been outcast and branded as 'loose' but, instead, the girls at work felt sorry for her. Jenny said: 'We thought, "Oh God, what a shame." I don't remember people thinking: "It serves her right."'

Illegimate babies were, however, frowned on and the reluctant fathers were expected to 'do the right thing' and marry the girl in trouble. Ray was not given the choice. He said: 'It was just taken for granted that we were going to get married and that was the end of it. I didn't have any say in anything. Julie's mother told me if I tried to make trouble there would be no wedding.

'I was told what to wear, when it was going to be and to turn up on the day.'

When he confided to friends that he was marrying Julie, one couple warned him: 'Do you realize you're going to have a job hanging on to her?'

Full of confidence, Ray replied, 'I don't find that a problem.'

At this stage Ray was actually thrilled at the prospect of becoming a father and delighted to be getting married, but Julie was not at all happy. Sue recalls: 'Julie was sad about being pregnant; she was too young to be married. I knew Ray and he was just a very nice ordinary guy, but she just didn't love him.'

Once the decision had been made, Julie asked Sue to be bridesmaid and the wedding preparations began. Family friend Edna Barlow was commissioned to make Julie's wedding dress and Sue's bridesmaid dress. But a white wedding was off. Ray said that, for obvious reasons, Julie's mother refused to let her wear a traditional white dress.

'Julie's dress was blue and mine was pink,' said Sue. 'They were 1950s style with a sticky-out, knee-length skirt. The head-dresses were crowns of little petals made of tulle.'

Julie's big day arrived and she and Sue spent the morning getting ready. Julie was only two months pregnant, so her bump did not show and she was still bubbling with energy. Before they left for the church, Julie in typical Julie Goodyear fashion decided she wanted one last fling – not with another bloke – but a quick rock 'n' roll with Sue to say goodbye to her old life. Sue remembers: 'There we were with our headgear and our posh frocks. We put some music on and had a quick fifteen-minute jive before we went to the church.'

On 26 September 1959, Julie walked down the aisle at the Saint Church, St Luke in Heywood, clutching a bouquet with an interesting mix of flowers – red roses, a symbol of love and passion, and white lilies of the valley, the flower of innocence. When Julie arrived at St Luke's, as the church was referred to locally, Jimmy Rowbotham, photographer for local paper the *Heywood Advertiser*, was waiting to snap her as she climbed out of the car. Over thirty-five years later, he still remembers Julie's radiance. 'She was the bonniest bride I've ever taken a picture of. I haven't snapped anyone who looked as good as her before or since, she looked so pretty,' said Jimmy, who already had nearly thirty years' experience as a photographer.

The caption which later appeared in the local paper read:

The bride wore a ballerina-length dress of blue nylon flocked with white roses and a coronet of white pearls. She carried a bouquet of red roses and lilies of the valley. The bridesmaid wore a pink nylon ballerina-length dress with a pink coronet and carried pink carnations.

Mr Joseph Sutcliffe (brother of the groom) was the best man and the groomsman was Mr James Henry Hefferan (friend of the groom). The bride, a shorthand typist, and the groom, a draughtsman, are spending their honeymoon in Wales and on return will live at 37 Torrington Street, Heywood.

Sue Skelton and Bill Goodyear were witnesses. Later, Ray took Mrs Julie Sutcliffe back to his parents' home in Blackley. Jean Barlow was peering through the curtains as the couple's car drew up, and watched Ray whisk Julie – still wearing her blue nylon wedding dress – off her feet. 'He carried her across the green in front of the house,' she said.

After the honeymoon in Rhyl in Wales, Ray and Julie rented a terraced house, 37 Torrington Street, two doors away from the Bay Horse.

Julie's wedding-day radiance faded almost as soon as the honeymoon was over. Being a young mother was not how she envisaged becoming a sexy screen siren. The writing was on the wall; her relationship with Ray was not going to last. She said later: 'Our marriage was destined for failure. There was nothing glamorous or exciting about life then. Two youngsters who hardly knew each other had been thrown together because they had made a mistake. They didn't even particularly like one another.' Ray said: 'I was still in love with her in those days, or so I thought; as soon as I got married I realized it was probably more infatuation.'

Gary Sutcliffe was born one month after Julie's eighteenth birthday, on 28 April 1960, at Fairfield General Hospital in Bury, seven months after the wedding. Julie gave a graphic description of her labour, which she said lasted forty-eight hours, and the sniffy disapproval heaped on her by the nurses. 'I lay on the delivery-room table screaming in pain, a frightened, bewildered animal,' she said in an interview with *The Sun*. 'No one had prepared me for this. I was about to have a baby and I didn't even know how it would be born. For two days I had lain there in labour suffering the snide looks of the other "proper" mothers and the stabbing bitchiness of the nurses who believed "my sort" deserved every second of suffering.

'Not until I had been lying in the delivery room for four hours after the birth, staring blankly at the bare walls, did I receive my first words of kindness. An elderly doctor came in, took one look at me and sized up the situation immediately. While he stitched and bathed me he talked in a gentle, reassuring voice and finally placed a sleeping 9lb 2oz baby in my arms. It was the first moment I realized I had given birth to a son. Straight away my boy became the most important man in my life.'

Ten days later, Julie was discharged from hospital and took Gary back to their rented two-up, two-down. The two-week-old baby was about to get a shock as Julie struggled with the concept of motherhood. As Gary's godmother-to-be, Sue would often pop round to help, and is amazed that Gary grew up so healthy. 'Julie had little idea of what to do and neither did I,' said Sue. 'When I think of when he was little what we did to him, I don't know how that child survived. I remember once we gave him boiling milk, we probably bathed him in red-hot water as well.'

For a while the youngsters seemed to enjoy their new family and, being a couple of doors away from The Bay Horse, would often pop in and lend Julie's parents a hand running the pub. Ray said: 'We both worked in the pub. I enjoyed helping out and a few times I actually ran it by myself. Those were great times. I enjoyed that part of it.'

Ray also joined the Bay Horse darts team and would drive the team to matches in Bill's Austin Cambridge, leaving Bill free to enjoy a good drink.

However, Julie found motherhood frustrating and missed her old lifestyle. As little Gary started to grow, Julie started to grow restless. Ray said: 'The marriage lasted for as long as it took for her to get her figure back. It was about three to six months maximum after Gary was born.'

Julie wanted to be back in the limelight and started

entering beauty contests. She indulged her hobby at every opportunity, even on holiday with her son and husband. 'When we used to go on our holidays I'd spend the week looking after Gary and she'd spend the week in beauty contests,' remembers Ray. 'There was really nothing I could do about it as such. I could have thrown a tantrum and put my foot down, but that wouldn't have got anything other than an unhappy holiday. Gary and I enjoyed ourselves though, we had the holiday, we had a ball.'

As soon as she could Julie went back to work and got a job in a solicitor's office. Ray was still at Avro's. Alice looked after Gary during the day and Ray took over in the evenings and at weekends.

Ray realized Julie was never going to be a typical housewife and in fact he did not mind if she went out to see her old mates. Sue remembers they made a pact: 'Julie and Ray decided they would go out on alternate nights.' In fact, Ray was happy at home babysitting and often forfeited his night out. 'In the evenings I babysat 95 per cent of the time,' Ray said.

Back at the Carlton, the role Julie played was not one of the contented wife on a girls' night out who was dying to get home to her husband. Julie relished the attention lavished on her by the men. When Ray got to hear the stories, he was livid and deeply hurt, but tried to ignore them. However, when these stories came too thick and fast to ignore, he decided to find the truth out for himself.

He said: 'Friends would tell me that they'd seen Julie around, then she would tell me stories and things that I'd find out weren't true. I used to see her getting out of other men's cars.

'We used to own a Hillman Minx and when I started to

get suspicious I found the car parked about half a mile away from home. Julie came back the next morning and said she'd been to Blackpool and stayed the night with a friend, which obviously wasn't true.

'Once I happened to walk round the corner from our house and found Julie and another man parked in an Austin Healey sports car. Because it was a sports car, I thought of turning the thing upside down, but my quietness got the better of me. Instead, I banged on the window a few times and walked away. I think that was the time I showed most emotion. Other times I thought it was going on, but couldn't do anything to prove it one way or the other.'

Away from his domestic nightmare the strain caught up with Ray. He had always been quiet at work but he now became postively brooding. Never one to advertise his deep emotions, he kept his problems to himself. When he did finally open up about the desperate state of his marriage he was clearly distraught.

His colleague Peter watched as Ray deteriorated. Peter said: 'Ray was absolutely devastated by what Julie turned out to be. He believed he'd captured something that he could tame. He was determined he was going to satisfy her every need. He didn't want any of his friends to know that that wasn't really the case, so he didn't talk about it very much.'

Ray decided to take control of the situation and thought he would lay down a few rules and regulations. He told Julie, 'You can't use the car, you should stay in more to look after Gary.' Her response was to move out. 'She only moved next door to the pub,' said Ray. 'She took Gary, but I still babysat in the evenings, apart from going out to the odd darts game every two or three weeks.'

A year after Julie had married Ray, their relationship was on the rocks. She had moved back to the pub, where she shared a room with Gary while Ray stayed in their terraced house at 37 Torrington Street, just two doors away. Ray hoped Julie would come home, but Julie had other ideas and started proceedings for legal separation.

Ray remembers the shock he felt when he received the solicitor's papers and an even bigger surprise when he got to court and saw the normally glamorous Julie. 'I nearly walked past her,' claims Ray. 'I didn't recognize her. She had no make-up on, her clothes weren't the showy things she would normally wear. I don't know if she was born to be an actress but she certainly put on an act that day.'

When the proceedings started he got an even bigger shock. 'I got hit with her barrister who made a lot of accusations against me; I was dumbstruck. He said that I didn't give her any money, then he said I wasn't bringing the child up right, horrible things. I didn't know what to say. Julie's mother was in the court and I didn't know what she'd told her mother, I didn't want to put my foot in it so I just kept quiet and listened to what he said.'

Later, he thought about fighting back. 'I spoke to a solicitor. He said, "It's just your word against hers."

'I gave him a brief run down on what was happening and he said, "Well, I can get somebody on her and follow her around and gather information together." But, (a) I couldn't afford it and (b) I didn't see what difference it would make because I really didn't want a divorce.'

Once Julie had moved out she picked up with Trevor Saxon again, but did not take their relationship seriously. To Julie, Trevor was therapy, claims Sue. 'She was always giving him the flick,' she said, meaning Julie was always picking him up and dropping him.

After the separation Julie left the solicitor's and took a job as a receptionist/typist in a small family business in Heywood called Bradley's Engineering. There, twenty-year-old Julie met John Bradley, who was on the first rung of the ladder in the family firm and is now company chairman.

He was smitten the moment he set eyes on her. 'She was a great girl, a very exciting woman,' he said, giving a saucy chuckle. 'She was very, very attractive. She had confidence and a great figure.'

Sparks flew between them. It was as though they had borrowed a couple of oxyacetylene torches from the Bradley workshop and were pointing them at one another. John said Julie wrapped him round her little finger. He knew Julie was separated from her husband, but not divorced, and the situation made any physical relationship between them taboo – going out with a woman who was still married was just not done – but even so, John found Julie irresistible.

John had already been engaged three times and, as he put it: 'Julie had had a few relationships.' They seemed perfectly suited and carried on seeing each other. At times their relationship sounded like a scene from a Brian Rix farce. Ray would be coming in the front door, hoping for a reconciliation, while John ran out the back. 'I never met Ray face to face although he saw the back of me a few times,' John laughed. The sense of danger gave the whole affair an extra edge of excitement. Ray occasionally caught a glimpse of John as he ran out the door. Perhaps that was exactly what Julie wanted. Perhaps that was the only way she could get the message across that their relationship was over.

John had a slightly uneasy conscience about the situation, but managed to override it. He said: 'In those days it wasn't really the done thing to mess about with someone who was still in the throes of marriage. It wasn't really right in the sense that she was still married and he was still keen. He was trying to patch things up. And why not, with a woman like that!'

Their turbulent relationship lasted for a year. John still has vivid memories of Julie and remembers one particular event where she totally stole the show. He said: 'I was a member of Tweedales and Smalley Football Club. [Tweedales and Smalley were a big textile machine makers in the nearby town of Castleton.] Every Friday they had a dance at the Carlton, and one cold night in November or December I took Julie. When I picked her up she was wearing a coat. When we got to the Carlton she went upstairs to the ladies to get rid of it. Underneath, she was wearing a tiny black mini dress about two foot long. I was the envy of every man in that dancehall.'

Julie stood at the top of the stairs and, when she had everyone's attention, swept down the staircase. 'She certainly made a big entrance,' he said. 'Mind you, she'd make a big entrance with a boiler suit on.'

Julie only stayed at John's firm for a month, but the pair continued to meet. They would constantly row, with the result that one or the other would storm off. Eventually, Julie stormed off for good. 'We were just two volatile people who wouldn't have lasted two minutes,' lamented John. 'One night, standing on the Carlton balcony, we had a row, and we didn't get back together.'

John, who is now happily married, is convinced their relationship could never have worked full-time. He felt Julie was always searching for unattainable happiness. 'You have to work hard at marriage to make it successful.

Julie was such a bubbly person I think the ordinary mundane life of being married would have seen her off. I met one other girl like Julie; these women are a certain type. I don't think they'll settle down when they're ninety. They always seem to be looking for something.'

Julie would agree. In an early interview, Julie said that the men in her life had not come up to her expectations. 'I've got very high standards,' she stated. 'I just think there's a very poor selection of men around.' Later, she told how her ideal man should have the qualities of seven famous performers. 'I call them the magnificent seven. My fantasy man would need the sex appeal of actor Lord Olivier, the looks of blond actor David Soul from the 1970s cop series *Starsky and Hutch*, the humour of comic Eric Morecambe, the voice of singer Jack Jones, the wit of comedian Woody Allen, the musical talents of French composer, conductor and pianist Michel Legrand, and the courage of a wonderful man, unknown to most of you, wheelchair-bound Granada TV historian, Eric Rosser, disabled during World War Two.'

Poor Ray had no chance; he was still trying to come up to scratch and failing. It became clear there was going to be no reconciliation and while Julie carried on enjoying every second of her life, Ray began to brood. He said: 'I felt she married me because of the baby and that was it. From the early days I felt it was a marriage that was doomed. The sex side soon died off and she began to go out on her own more and more.

'It sounds as though I was some sort of wimp sitting at home while she went out. But I always believed Julie would get this thing out of her system and we'd be a happy couple again.

'When we finally split I felt wretched. I'm from the old-

"Queen of the Street". Julie strikes the pose.

Above: The Coronation Street cast gather to celebrate the show's 25th birthday.

Opposite: On their first anniversary, husband number three Richard Skrob and Julie take a romantic trip to Puerto Vallerta Mexico.

The Street wedding of the year: Bet marries Alec (Roy Barraclough) in 1987.

Topless by the pool, Julie is snapped by paparazzi photographers in 1993, whilst holidaying with a lady friend.

Above left: Chat show host Des O'Connor invites Julie onto his show. Dressed top to toe in black spandex and leather, she sings "These Boots Are Made For Walking".

Above right: A touch of glamour: Julie is never seen without her trademark cigarette holder, or her Wonderbra.

Above: Cowboy Charlie Whelan and Julie are snapped together off set.

Below: Happily married actor John St Ryan, who played Charlie, claimed Julie got on well with him, but said nothing happened between them.

fashioned school, it's "till death do us part", or I thought it was. I don't think Julie ever cared for me the way I cared for her.'

On reflection, it seems Ray would have been perfect for Julie as he was willing to live in her shadow while she made a name for herself. 'One thing Julie was never going to be was a housewife, which was fine by me,' he said. 'If people have vocations that's fine, I'd have been quite happy if she'd been where she is now. They could have called me Mr Goodyear if that's what she'd wanted.' But Julie had other plans.

The couple were separated but not divorced and Julie was no doubt wondering how this could be achieved. Funnily enough, Ray was the one who opened the window of opportunity.

Ray's eighteen-year-old sister Sandra had fallen in love with Ray's best friend Jimmy Hefferan, who had been groomsman at Ray and Julie's wedding. The Hefferan family were seduced by the Australian government's 1960s offer of heavily subsidized fares for Britons wanting to emigrate. The deal offered a £10 passage to sail there providing you stayed for two years. Families who did not last the course had to refund the deferred payment to the government in full.

Engaged to Jimmy, Sandra decided to go too, and if Sandra was going, her parents wanted to be with her. Former neighbour Dolores said: 'Sandra was Betty's only daughter and she wanted to make sure she settled all right. The Hefferans went first, then the Sutcliffes followed.'

Sandra, Betty and Joe moved to Australia, leaving Joe Jr and Ray in England. They had been in Australia for about a year when Ray's marriage problems came to a head. Ray claims Julie persuaded him to join them and set up a new life for them. They were constantly arguing and she said she felt they needed some space.

Ray said: 'Originally the plan was for me to go to Australia and make a new life for Gary and Julie, and that's what I did. While I was getting established, I didn't go out, because I was a married man, and I sent money, virtually everything I earned, to Julie and presents to Gary. My mother bought him a huge koala bear, which cost a fortune to post. I know he got it because it was mentioned in letters. Then I wrote to Julie telling her that I was settled and she and Gary could come and join me. Later I received the divorce papers. She divorced me on the grounds of mental cruelty. As I wasn't in the country to defend myself, the divorce went through.'

In *The Sun*, Julie told a different story, a story of desertion, not separation. She said: 'Being left holding the baby was just one of the many occasions life has turned round and slapped me in the face. One night Ray knocked on the back door and told me he was leaving. "Do you want to come upstairs and say goodbye to your son before you go?" I asked. "What's the point?" he replied. "See you kid", he said, turning round on his heels and walking away. It was the last I ever saw or heard of my first husband. He disappeared out of both our lives without a backward glance. Gary has never even received a letter, birthday card or Christmas gift from his father.'

When Ray hears that word, 'desertion', he bristles, he cannot bear it, especially as his version of events is much more emotional and he claims he was expecting to see Gary and Julie again. He remembers his last day. It was 1963 and Ray was twenty-seven: 'I went to see Gary to say goodbye. I told him I was going away and he could come and join me. He started crying; the last time I saw

Gary he was crying his eyes out at the window of the pub. I'd brought him up for three years and I was walking out of his life. I felt terrible. That's the last memory I've got of him and I was very upset. It certainly isn't a happy memory.'

5

Bachelor Girl Again

A classy blonde, just back from a modelling assignment and dressed in an expensive fur coat, strode through the door of the White Hart in Birch. The jet-setters' pub, about half a mile from Heywood, was packed with regulars sipping pints of bitter or gin and tonics. The chat quietened as the sexy young woman in her early twenties lifted the bar hatch and slid behind the erect rows of beer pumps. Using the optics as a backdrop, she threw open the fur and, as it fell to the floor, revealed a stunning figure clad in a flattering white swimsuit. The sound of men's jaws dropping was deafening as Julie Goodyear practised the art of the show-stopping entrance.

Audrey Brogden, landlady of the whitewashed, oak-beamed local, remembers the impact Julie had on the men. 'They were agog,' she said. 'They couldn't believe their eyes. That was part of Julie's charm: she always enjoyed a laugh.'

With her marriage over and her ex-husband Ray on the

other side of the world, Julie's social life was in full swing. It was the early 1960s and Julie made the Hart her base, dropping in for a drink most nights. Audrey remembers how she loved to flirt. 'She was outrageous, a real tease. Of course the blokes loved it and egged her on, though some were terrified of her.'

Audrey, who worked in the pub for twenty-six years, remembers how Julie made one regular very nervous. 'It was one lunchtime in the pub car park and Julie was messing about, being playful,' she said. 'She put the fear of God into this poor chap. She had him spreadeagled over the bonnet of his car and said to him: "Shall we have it here, now?" She was kissing him and he was terrified in case his wife walked past. She didn't really fancy him. She just did it for a laugh.'

Another Julie teased was Heywood's answer to medallion man – open-necked shirt, hairy chest and a gold chain with a heavy gold medal hanging from it – whom the regulars nicknamed Mr Harry. One night, leaning casually on the bar, Mr Harry took a deep breath and threw his opening chat-up line to Julie. She caught it, juggled with it, then threw it back.

Geoff Nuttall, a White Hart regular who knew Julie well, said: 'It was hilarious to watch. You knew just by looking at her face she didn't fancy him, but she played him along. He went too far with his banter, though, so Julie told him: "Piss off, you're in the wrong league."'

Julie knew she was running the show, not the men, and while she didn't mind a laugh and a joke with them, she wasn't going to be seriously chatted up by someone she didn't fancy.

There was fierce competition to take Julie on a date. Audrey remembers: 'Nearly all the men tried to chat her up. She brought a lot of gaiety into people's lives. She could laugh at them and she didn't mind being laughed at. The men loved her; they always like someone outrageous in a pub. It was a battle of wits between them, but Julie could always hold her own.'

There was the odd bloke not bowled over by her over-the-top looks or wicked chat. Geoff Nuttall was one: 'I could never understand the attraction.'

Some of the women were cautious, while others thought she was great. Geoff Nuttall's wife Barbara said: 'Most women didn't like her. I think they felt threatened. They thought she might take their man from them. She was a man's woman, not a woman's woman. To my mind, Julie was straightforward and down to earth. I enjoyed her company. Some others tried to put her down, calling her common and that sort of thing, but you couldn't help admiring the wit and humour she had.'

Audrey added: 'Half the women would have loved to have done the things she was doing, but didn't have the guts. I think they were jealous and wished they could be more daring themselves.'

Geoff saw in her the makings of a brilliant actress: 'When she had her eye on a man she could act demure if that's what she thought they would like. Or she could be cheeky if she thought that would fit.'

It was the Swinging Sixties, a great time for women to be single, and they had plenty of opportunities to take advantage of their new-found freedom.

Julie and Ray were divorced in 1963, and within a couple of years Julie felt comfortable about getting involved in a new relationship. She fell for Geoff Cassidy, a man twelve years her senior, a respectable local solicitor and pillar of society. Geoff belonged to the Rotary Club, a charity organization called the Heywood Lions, the Conservative Club, the Royal Naval Association and Heywood Cricket Club. Then in 1958 he was appointed Deputy Rochdale County Coroner. When Julie met him he was a solicitor with local firm, A. S. Coupe.

Like Julie, Geoff was divorced and had a son Nicky, seven years older than Julie's son Gary. Nicky lived with Geoff's ex-wife Val and Geoff shared a house with his father. Geoff was quiet and slightly shorter than Julie's 5ft 4ins. He wore glasses, smart but sober clothes and drove an expensive Jaguar. His hobby was collecting old 78 records and he could often be found drinking alone at the White Hart or The Bay Horse.

Audrey liked him and thought he was perfect for Julie. She says today that she looks at Roy Barraclough, Julie's screen husband Alec Gilroy from 1987 to 1992, and can see Geoff in him.

Geoff's parents were working-class and his father worked his way up the ranks at the *Manchester Evening News* to become circulation manager. He also owned a newsagent's shop in the centre of Heywood.

Geoff was educated at Bury Grammar School then later at Manchester University and was articled to A. S. Coupe, a local firm in Heywood, in 1948. Julie met the wealthy thirty-four-year-old solicitor when she took a secretarial job there, and he fell for her immediately. At twenty-two, she had the sexy looks of a young Diana Dors and would not have looked out of place in Hollywood. The combination of her beauty, extrovert personality and young attitude took Geoff's breath away.

She gave him a taste of the youth he'd missed out on. Audrey explains: 'Geoff had been educated, and stepped up the ladder from the working class to the middle class, which was quite a feat. He'd worked hard to get where he was, and as a young man missed out on the good times. When Julie came into his life it was as though he was recapturing his youth. He could do things with Julie that he'd never had the chance to do before. For Julie it was all new – the money, the respectability – and I thought she was very much in love. Julie and Geoff became the talk of the town.'

The White Hart was *the* bar of the moment and everyone wanted to be seen there. *Coronation Street* stars Bill Roache (amorous schoolteacher Ken Barlow) and the late Bernard Youens (lazy window cleaner Stan Ogden) could often be spotted supping pints with the locals.

Julie was considered one of the Hart's most glamorous customers. Barbara Nuttall has vivid memories of her many different outfits. She said: 'Once she walked in wearing this pink gingham dress; her hair was in pigtails with pink ribbons on the end. My husband Geoff asked: "Is this the ingénue look?" and she told him, "I'm just a country girl at heart". The following night she changed and walked in wearing long dangly earrings and a sleek black dress.'

The Hart was the first pub in Lancashire to open a restaurant and people travelled for miles to eat there. Julie and Geoff were regulars and ate in the upstairs restaurant twice a week. They always sat in the far corner of the dining room.

Looking at Julie in character as brassy Bet Lynch, with her loud jewellery, leopard-skin-clad cleavage and short skirts, it's impossible to imagine her having a style of her own but in the early 1960s Julie's clothes were incredibly glamorous. She chose fashionable outfits which she searched hard to find or asked neighbour Edna Barlow to make, and is remembered as the Grace Kelly of Heywood. 'She had some beautiful clothes, and she was gorgeous. She looked like a young film star,' said Audrey.

Geoff spent thousands of pounds on presents for Julie. He bought her a white mink jacket and a white two-seater Triumph Spitfire with a white leather interior. The convertible sports car alone cost just over £1,000. Audrey remembers Julie turning up at the pub in the car. 'Everybody in the Hart had to come out and see it. Some people might have thought it was over the top but Julie looked absolutely right in it. She had the right glamour to go with the car. She drove it at top speed everywhere, revving the engine so that people would notice.' Later, she was spotted, with the roof down, driving into a petrol station, dressed in a skimpy bikini. Julie was enjoying golden days; her love-life was perfect and her career on the up and up.

To get noticed, Julie started modelling and continued to enter and win beauty contests. 'A week's royal treatment in one of Blackpool's leading hotels began last Friday for model Miss Julie Goodyear,' announced local weekly paper the *Heywood Advertiser*. 'Besides VIP wining and dining, she will be guest of honour at a late-night ball – all part of her prize for winning the "Miss Britvic" contest.

Julie preened. She was being treated like a royal, a real VIP. 'This is better than scrubbing clothes and washing pots!' she reckoned. Her dream, slowly materializing, was also being acknowledged in print.

The story continued: 'Julie won the title in the face of competition from fifty other models from all over the country, all trying for the glittering first prize which, in addition to the week in Blackpool, includes a substantial amount of money and an evening dress. During her week in Blackpool, Julie paraded through the streets on a float wearing her sash and crown, and wore the evening dress, Grecian-style in white tricel, at the ball.'

The six-paragraph story, pronouncing Julie the winner of a beauty contest sponsored by pub fruit-juice manufacturers Britvic, was illustrated with a picture of Julie, elbows resting on her knees, wearing a white swimsuit, white three-inch stilettos, her hair cropped short, bleached and back-combed, and – etiquette of fame forgotten briefly – a smile which said, 'This is the fiftieth time I've posed for a photo today. Hurry up and get it took!'

It was July 1965 and Julie, still only twenty-three but aware that she had left it a little late to begin a modelling career, lied about her age. She told the *Heywood Advertiser* and Britvic that she was twenty-one. As Miss Britvic she was asked to judge other beauty contests. One was Miss Piccadilly. To liven it up she called her friend Annie Coates, a sultry model with huge brown eyes. Annie said: 'Julie asked: "Do you want to enter a beauty contest?" I was never a beauty-queen image and I said: "I'm not the type." She said: "Well you are if I'm judging." In the end I fell off a catwalk and hurt my ankle, so I couldn't go, but I would have done it for a laugh.'

Miss Britvic was not the first beauty title Julie had won. Photographer Jimmy Rowbotham remembers taking pictures of her as she accepted the crown and sceptre for Miss Astral, Miss Langley Football Club and Miss Aeronautical Society.

Jimmy would take pictures of Julie performing her beauty-queen duties. 'On one occasion we were at the annual show at Woodford Aerodrome which we drove to in my motor home. Julie was presenting prizes,' said Jimmy. 'Later I took a picture of her with a huge model plane, posing on top of the bar at The Bay Horse pub, her legs stuck straight up in the air in the classic 1940s pose.'

Julie did not take the competitions too seriously, claimed Annie; she figured they were a good way to get noticed. If Julie wiped away any tears as she was handed her sash, they would be tears of laughter, not the release of pent-up emotion for which sobbing beauty queens are famous. She realized that winning a title was good publicity. If you won, you got your picture in the paper, embarked on a round of fête and supermarket openings, and picked up a fat cheque as a bonus.

To boost her career, Julie paid £25 to the Manchester branch of modelling agency and deportment school Lucy Clayton. The northern branch was different to the London establishment, a finishing school which taught shorthand and typing, cooking, deportment and grooming to daughters of the middle-class. 'It was a find-yourself-a-husband school,' said ex-pupil Carolyn Preston. The Knightsbridge establishment turned out the occasional actress, including Joanna Lumley.

Lucy Clayton's in Manchester concentrated on training girls with ambitions to model. Julie arrived for her interview plastered in make-up, with a beehive hairdo and wearing a tight short skirt and red stilettos. 'I wanted some of the rough edges knocked off me,' she said. She joined in the early 1960s and proved a fast learner.

Pam Holt, who ran the northern branch, remembers Julie clearly: 'She wasn't your elegant mannequin model, she was a girl who had a good figure. She wasn't tall for a model, she was only about 5 ft 4 ins, but she had great legs and she had a useful shoe size; she was only a size four. Her small feet meant that she could do shoe work with her leg work and her small feet also made her look taller.'

Julie was attractive and sexy but no classic beauty. She was never going to be on the cover of *Vogue*, but the combination of her outrageous sense of humour, earthy personality and stunning figure bowled people over. Pam said: 'She didn't have what I call a kind of laid-back, model-girl charisma, she had personality.'

Once she joined the agency, Julie threw herself into the four-week course. Pam said: 'She was so enthusiastic. In those days not everyone in the whole world did it, like today, so you took it very seriously. You always started off with keep fit in the morning and then, at eleven o'clock you had your break. Then you would have lectures in deportment, make-up, hair and show work. In those days, to go on to the catwalk you had to learn how to take your coat off, how to model with an umbrella, how to take gloves off and how to use your hands. At the end of the course you graduated at a fashion show. And you started work if you were good.'

Julie grafted and her modelling career took off. Pam said: 'She put everything into it and she was great with the other girls. She was a laugh a minute and they loved her. You could send her anywhere. She was always the good trouper, even then. You never thought to yourself: "Oh bloody hell, she's going to let me down," like you would with a lot of girls.'

Fashion modelling was out for Julie. Instead she did catalogue work and was sent on photographic assignments to model her hands and feet, in shoes, stockings and gloves. On other occasions, she worked at exhibitions and events as a promotions girl. Her catwalk modelling was confined to wholesale clothes – parading in front of professional buyers.

Sometimes she modelled second-hand furs at the local

auctions. Pam remembers: 'The man who owned the fur business used to say to us: "When you are walking towards the customers, pull the coat tight round you. When you are walking back, push the coat back; it makes it look as though there is more fur in the garments."'

One firm where Julie was a favourite was a wholesaler called Eastex who paid house models about £5 a day. Their clothes were good quality, conservative, tweedy and functional rather than elegant, and they specialized in clothes for short women. Julie would arrive in a crocheted mini dress and white leather Courrèges boots with cut-outs on the sides. The girls hated the frumpy suits they were forced to model but loved the steady work and easy life Eastex provided for two seasonal, six-week stints. Eastex loved Julie. Pam said: 'Eastex thought she was wonderful. She was a natural comedienne. She boosted the sales just by being there.'

The buyers would queue to get a place at the spring and autumn shows. They were treated with reverence, showered with gifts and plied with drink and fine food. Most of them came for a day out and had probably decided what they wanted to buy before they got there – 90 per cent of their purchases would be the same as the year before.

Behind the scenes, Julie caused havoc by livening up dull days with a steady stream of jokes and steamy stories. Annie Coates, who was the opposite of saucy Julie, with her straight dark hair, cropped into a short bob, worked with her and seven other girls. 'I really looked forward to going to work. Julie really kept us entertained. You never knew what she was going to come out with next, and she always had a good story to tell about the night before,' said Annie, who did four seasons on the Eastex catwalk with Julie.

Annie, who was nineteen when she first worked with twenty-three-year-old Julie, described her conservatively as outrageous. In the early 1960s ladies rarely used four-letter words but Julie would litter her speech with colourful expletives. She talked like a navvy and got away with it. Because of her sexy, well-groomed appearance, her offensive language seemed quirky, not disgusting.

Some of the younger models, however, were shocked, so Julie wound them up and laughed when they blushed. Annie said: 'There were two or three who were sickly sweet. Julie didn't have much time for that. She used to wind them up, saying things like: "I bet you 'ad sex with your boyfriend last night, didn't y'kid? Come on, admit it."'

On other occasions the more street-wise girls would split their sides as Julie, who had honed her skills as a riveting storyteller, recounted vivid tales of nocturnal exploits and down-to-earth stories about her family. She would mix a few impersonations into her routine, throw in a dirty joke for good measure and watch the team crumple.

The shows were run by a Miss Coup, who tried to keep Julie and the girls in order, and June Rivers – the original Miss Great Britain – whom they nicknamed 'Moon' River. Between shows, the models stripped off, leaving on their underwear and a grey petticoat – except Julie, who stood out in a black petticoat. They sat in a back room lined with mirrors and let Julie entertain them. The place reminded them of school, and Julie was head girl.

Backstage sounded like a Saturday night cabaret at the local pub. The girls laughed and screeched and were always being told to keep the noise down. Julie's *pièce de résistance* was to make the girls crack up just before they walked down the catwalk. Annie said: 'She would always tell a story or dirty joke just as I was about to go out. I remember one – it was disgusting but hysterical – about a little boy who had a dog with a very, very curly tail. The boy was walking down the street and saw the vicar. The vicar says: "That's a very nice dog you've got, Johnny. What's his name?" "It's Porky," says Johnny. "Porky? Is that because he's got a curly tail?" asks the vicar. "No," says the little boy. "It's because he fucks pigs." It probably doesn't sound funny, but when Julie told it, complete with actions and mannerisms, I just absolutely broke up. I couldn't control myself. I just collapsed in this sort of heap and I had to run off the catwalk. I hid behind the dress rail in convulsions.'

A favourite impersonation was Julie's take-off of a couple of rather butch-looking buyers in their sixties. The pair sat in the front row, bickering and drinking free double gin and tonics, and waiting for a chance to touch the girls up.

Annie said: 'One gave me a bit of a grope one day. She beckoned me off the catwalk and said: "Could I just look at that closer, dear?" She started adjusting my skirt for me and feeling this bit of me and that bit of me. They both looked like the actress Margaret Rutherford in her days of playing Miss Marple, and wore tweeds to match. They would argue and be really rude to each other, drink these huge G&Ts and then fall asleep. Julie would wind them up on the catwalk. She would over exaggerate her turns and do sexy wiggles in front of them. They absolutely loved her.'

No one escaped Julie's character assassinations. June Rivers was forever giving the girls advice and harking back to the days when she had been top dog. On one occasion June, now in her forties, brought in the faded evening gown she had worn as a beauty queen. Annie describes June: 'She was a sweet thing, a bit off-beat. She had quite a big bosom and was still voluptuous. She always had her chest out and was very wiggly and quite coquettish. She was forever telling us about the Miss Great Britain contest. She entered the year before they made it official. This dress she wore for the final was off-the-shoulder grey satin with a huge pink satin rose on her bum, which came on and off with a press-stud. When she brought it in, Julie put it on and decided to model it. She strode down the catwalk, chest stuck out, bottom wiggling, doing a wildly exaggerated impersonation of June, wearing this long dress with this rose hanging off her bum. June didn't realise Julie was taking the mickey and just said: "Oh, girls" and giggled.'

Eastex loved Julie because she was such a good salesgirl. They put up with her antics and resigned themselves to the fact that they could not control her. Annie is amazed they were never sacked.

Mostly Julie had fun modelling, but on her way to one assignment she narrowly escaped death. Model Val Martin was driving them both in her sporty Mini Cooper S, when a car pulled out in front of them. She said: 'It was midday and the roads were wet. I went into a whopping skid and crashed into a road sign which came straight through the windscreen and missed us by inches. A few inches to the left or right and either of us could have had serious head injuries. Our faces would certainly have been scarred for life. We were so lucky we just had a few cuts and bruises. The other car rolled over and over. I had to drag the driver out of the car. Two cars passed us but neither of them stopped to help. I've got no idea how we got to hospital. I was shivering like a jelly. All I can remember is that we were wearing black tights which ended up full of ladders and holes, and later I got a bill for the road sign.'

Julie had a hoot modelling, but her real ambition was to appear on television. Lucy Clayton provided local TV station Granada with extras and Pam frequently sent Julie along. She appeared in *Scene at 6.30* as a Manchester girl dealing firearms, and in a satirical short, playing actress Pearl White, fearless heroine of the silent screen. She was spotted as a magician's assistant in *The Good Old Days*, a reconstruction of the Victorian music hall for television, and she had a part in the drama series *Family at War* and the comedy *Nearest and Dearest* as lead actor Jimmy Jewel's girlfriend. But her big coup was a part in Granada's young soap opera *Coronation Street*.

Pam recalls: 'The first job she had on the *Street* was at Elliston's raincoat factory as a factory girl. The fee for the job was three guineas. We would take our 10 per cent and she would get her three guineas minus that. After she did this job, she came back and said: "Pam, I think they'd like me to do something more than just extra work." I don't think I'll ever forget her saying that. She was very excited.'

Coronation Street had been going for six years when Julie made her first appearance as Bet Lynch. On 2 June 1966 the *Heywood Advertiser* ran a headline – 'CORONATION STREET ROLE FOR JULIE'. The copy read:

The popular Granada TV serial *Coronation Street* is currently being given a facelift and one of the new parts has been given to Heywood girl Julie Goodyear of the Bay Horse Hotel, Torrington Street.

Julie, aged 22 [she was actually 24], has been working as a model for some time, but has also been on the files at Granada. When it was decided to inject more life into the series, she was offered the part of Bet, a typical Lancashire mill girl, who will be working at the new factory which is opening in 'the Street'.

This is Julie's first speaking part on television, although she has previously had walk-on parts in programmes, including *Pardon the Expression*. She made her first appearance as Bet last week and she is likely to stay with the series for some time.

The broad Lancashire accent which she uses is authentic, and as she says: 'There is no difficulty with the accent. I'm from the north so it's natural to me.'

Julie says now: 'Nobody was impressed I hadn't done any formal training, so my lack of experience was frowned upon. On top of that I was naïve and didn't have any discipline.' The producers sacked her after six weeks.

She did, however, have a most unexpected admirer in star of the show Pat Phoenix, who played *Street* pin-up Elsie Tanner. Pat, with her deep cleavage and just-got-out-of-bed look, was described as 'the working man's Raquel Welch'. She sent such shockwaves through the nation's male population that she received four marriage proposals a week. A feisty actress, at her audition she told producers who asked her to take her coat off so that they could check her assets: 'I'm not removing it. You'll just have to bloody well guess!' Julie was starstruck and hung on her every word.

Pat was just as impressed and told *Street* creator Tony Warren: 'You've got to meet this kid; she's the funniest thing on two legs, she'll slay you.'

Years later, after Julie became a big star, Pat regretted her enthusiasm. Tony Warren remembers: 'It's one thing to encourage a kooky kid. It's quite another to watch her piles of fan mail growing bigger every day.

'Pat's change of heart was part of an internal struggle. Elsie was getting older, but Pat wanted her to stay young. She should have grown into the next Ena Sharples. Instead she chose to cling to artificial youth while the Real Thing – Julie Goodyear – was getting bigger and more spectacular opportunities.'

At this stage, though, Pat was Julie's great ally and got her a job with the Oldham Repertory Theatre Company as acting assistant stage manager (ASM), a job which required Julie to make the tea and sweep the stage.

Actresses Barbara Knox, who plays Rita Fairclough in *Coronation Street*, and the late Pat Phoenix both trained at Oldham Rep. Kenneth Alan Taylor, who still puts in the odd appearance in *Coronation Street* as Newton & Ridley brewery boss Ces Newton, was assistant producer/director at Oldham Rep the day Julie first arrived. His boss Carl Paulsen (who has since died) summoned him to the auditorium.

Kenneth remembers: 'I was doing something in the office and Carl came to me and said: "Will you come downstairs? I want you to see something." He took me down to the theatre car park and, parked next to his battered mini, was this wonderful white shining Spitfire. He said: "That's the first bit. Now come with me." I followed him into the auditorium and, sweeping the stage with a huge broom, was this blonde girl wearing a white mink jacket. I said: "Who the hell is that?" He said: "It's the new ASM and that's her car." You've got to remember, Carl was running the theatre. He turned to me and said: "There's something very wrong with this business. Why is this kid parking a white Spitfire outside and sweeping the stage in a mink coat?" Other kids would turn up and put a pair of overalls on, and you didn't see white Spitfires in Oldham in those days. It was the equivalent of owning a Ferrari.'

Kenneth remembers Julie being well groomed and the life and soul of Oldham Rep, but never as particularly dedicated. He said: 'Hundreds of kids went through our hands as ASMs but if Julie had never made it and ended up a married housewife with four kids, I don't think I ever would have forgotten her because of her personality. She always made the best of herself. Her clothes were always better and brighter than anybody else's. She always had blonde hair and probably wore a bit too much make-up.

I always thought Julie would probably leave the business. She enjoyed the fun of theatre work. I wouldn't have said that she was a dedicated actress. She liked the fun, she liked the recognition, but it was hard. When you joined you knew it was going to be a hard slog and you had to fight and be 100 per cent dedicated to get anywhere.

'At Oldham you arrived at 9.30 a.m., rehearsed, did a show, then, after the evening performance at 10.30 p.m., the actors went home – except Julie who went out clubbing – and learned their lines. I thought Julie always enjoyed the good life too much and the fun side of it to really make a go of it.'

Julie was earning £3 10s a week. Her duties were about as glamorous as delivering coal. Kenneth said: 'Julie must have wondered what hit her when she was given a broom and told to sweep the stage. She was the dogsbody. She didn't get much opportunity to act because she had to go and get the props, move all the furniture off the stage so we could get on with rehearsals, sweep the stage and paint it once a week with matt-black paint, which was the job every ASM hated. If she was given a part, she would play the odd maid. Unlike Barbara Knox, who played parts right from the word go, Julie never did.'

The organization was autocratic and the cast addressed the bosses as Mr Paulsen or Mr Taylor. It was weekly rep, so the company staged a new play every seven days. Every six weeks Carl chose six new plays and posted a list on the noticeboard. Desperate to get on, Julie constantly breached company etiquette. Kenneth said: 'She was terribly keen. As soon as the list of plays was posted, you sat back and waited patiently to know what part you would be given, even I did. Julie used to come up and say: "Is there anything in it for me? Can I be in this one? What's this play?" She was never frightened of coming forward, never in an objectionable way, that was the lovely thing about Julie.'

Roles were few and far between. Kenneth said: 'She didn't play many large parts. She was one of the slave girls in *A Funny Thing Happened on the Way to the Forum*. Once she played a bunny girl wearing a black leotard with a white powder-puff tail, and stole the show. She just walked across the stage, said a couple of lines and walked off. She had charisma, it was as simple as that.'

The new ASM was more interested in her social life than in dedicating herself to acting. In no time at all she was into her routine, telling naughty stories and hilarious anecdotes. Naturally, the cast loved it. Kenneth said: 'You always waited for Julie to come in because there was always a story. That was the joy of Julie.'

Strangely, she never mentioned her serious relationship

with Geoff when she was telling stories. She talked about her Mum and 'our Gary' but never about Geoff. In fact, she was always talking about other men. Kenneth said: 'She was always knocking around with fellas. They were never around long enough for there to be a favourite. There is one story I remember to do with Julie's sex-life. She'd been out with "Diddy" David Hamilton, the DJ. We were terribly impressed by this. How the hell she met him I don't know. When she came in the next morning, I rushed to her and said: "How did you get on with Diddy?" She said: "Oh, it were all right, we went to a club. Then, after, he drove me to me Mum's, I felt like a fag more than anything else. So I got me cigarette out and me lighter, and I said: 'Hang on, before we go any further, let's have a look at it.' I lit me lighter, and said: "Now I know why they call you Diddy."''

Julie was twenty-four when she met twenty-seven-year-old up and coming DJ and television presenter 'Diddy' David Hamilton. He was already a heartthrob, with scores of women chasing him. At the time he was living in Manchester and working as an announcer for ABC television in the days when continuity announcers were seen on screen. He also compèred a pop-music show for BBC Radio called *The Beat Show*, a show on which top acts of the day, like Billy J. Kramer and the Searchers, played live.

He has vivid memories of the night he dated Julie but his tale is slightly different. He said: 'I can't remember where I met her. She came along to *The Beat Show* as my guest. She stood out from everybody else in this bright red dress she was wearing. She was pretty outrageous even in those days. She had a kind of earthy sexiness, she was so upfront. She really called a spade a spade. I remember being quite shocked. I was quite young at the time.

'We might have gone for a drink in a club. I was probably too mean to buy her dinner. I did drive her home and she did make a suggestion to me that was totally outrageous. She said jokingly: "If I gave you a blow job would you go home happy?" I was so shocked I didn't know how to handle it.

'I think I declined her kind offer if it was an offer; I don't remember my old man coming out, or her cigarette lighter for that matter.'

That was the beginning and end of their relationship. David said: 'I didn't pursue any relationship beyond that because I was married at the time anyway. I was not averse to a bit on the side, being a young tearaway, but she was too strong for me. I thought: "Oh God. She's too hot to handle."'

Geoff Cassidy could take the heat, however, and he stayed in the kitchen. Towards the end of the 1960s the temperature of their relationship soared and Geoff plucked up the courage to ask Julie to marry him. He called Julie and asked her to meet him at the White Hart, suggesting she wore something suitable for a special occasion. Julie arrived wearing a pale pink satin cocktail dress. They took their places at table 14 and ordered the best champagne. Geoff produced a small blue velvet box from his inside jacket pocket. He opened it and presented Julie with a diamond solitaire engagement ring. Julie was ecstatic and said yes to his proposal.

After dinner they came downstairs and settled in the bar. They ordered brandies but kept quiet about the engagement. Audrey said: 'Nothing was said – she didn't make any big announcement – but all of a sudden you noticed this ring on Julie's finger. Julie was glowing that night; she had an inner aura. I think that's what drew your attention and made you notice the ring.'

Following his divorce Geoff had lived at home with his father in Middleton Road. Julie could not officially move in because it would have made things difficult, but she spent as much time there as possible. Once she got her feet under the table, Julie thought a few extra home comforts would brighten the place up. Geoff Nuttall claimed: 'She had the old man out buying furniture. New tellies, radiograms and everything. He bought a Dynatron radiogram in a Regency cabinet, which later he had transformed into a cocktail cabinet. Julie said she wasn't going to live there until it had all this stuff.'

Geoff Cassidy and Julie were total opposites. She was the extrovert beauty queen-cum-model-cum-wannabe-actress with no regular work. He was the quiet, steady, respectable solicitor with a solid reputation and healthy income. It was a fairy tale of opposites attracting, but the reality of their situation was that Julie would now become a solicitor's wife and join the ranks of women who threw cocktail parties and organized fêtes for charity.

The women, not relishing being upstaged by this stunning firecracker, started a whispering campaign. Julie pretended not to care but, inside, she smarted at their bitchy comments and snide remarks. Audrey remembers: 'Because Julie was young and getting on well, there was always nastiness and snobbishness directed towards her. At that time she had everything. She was attractive with a great personality, everything was just falling into place with her career. The women were jealous of her; they thought she was loud and didn't fit in. There was a thing about how a solicitor's wife should be. Solicitors in those days were ultra-staid. Julie was far from that; she was vivacious and flamboyant.

'Julie attended a lot of charity functions and different dos with Geoff. She would make the women look quite frumpish and the men would ogle her. The women would be quite horrible about her. They never said anything to her face – I think she could have coped with that and she could have defended herself – but she knew things were being said about her behind her back. She could tell by the way they all looked at her and froze her out of conversations.'

Julie's raunchy banter and outrageous clothes were fine for the Hart and Oldham Rep, but she was never going to settle in the solicitors' world of starched shirts, polite conversation and Masonic handshakes. Almost three years after they got engaged, the pressure to conform wrecked their relationship. Audrey said: 'The reason they never got married was because Julie wasn't accepted in certain circles. And there's no way Julie would change to be a solicitor's wife. I don't think she could, really.'

Surprisingly, Geoff was not the one to call it off; Julie did. Geoff Nuttall, who was one of Geoff Cassidy's closest friends, said: 'They were going on holiday to Majora. We were in the White Hart one night and Julie told me: "It'll be off when I get back." I didn't take any notice because I thought it was just Julie's usual way of talking, but it *was* off when they came back. On the plane coming home she broke it off and gave him his ring back. She didn't tell him before because she didn't want to spoil the holiday.'

Regulars were staggered by the split. Julie disappeared off the scene and Geoff refused to talk about it. Geoff Nuttall said: 'Geoff was very hard to pin down. He had that deadpan way about him that solicitors had and he was philosophical about it.'

Audrey said: 'Geoff never spoke about her after the split. He wasn't that kind of man. He was very discreet about her. In fact, nobody seemed to talk about it. For a little while we didn't see Julie. Geoff came in but we didn't see Julie. Then one day she floated in like nothing had happened. Julie seemed to start drifting. She didn't seem to use the Hart as much and when she did she'd come in with the attitude of "I don't give a damn". I always felt she did.'

Soon after their separation, Geoff Cassidy began dating Irene Ryan, whom he also met in the White Hart. No one could understand the attraction. 'After Julie, it didn't seem very long before Irene was on the scene. I couldn't understand it. She was so different, so demure and used to do everything right. Occasionally, she would try and do outrageous things like Julie, but it just never came off.'

Geoff Nuttall liked his friend's new girlfriend. He said: 'Irene was a lovely girl. She was very loyal and Geoff was happy with Irene.' About eighteen months later, they became engaged.

Julie then started dating White Hart regular Tony Sibson. Tony was a tanker driver for Lancashire Dairies. Julie told friends he was an accountant. He was tall and looked like Julie's 1990s *Coronation Street* truck-driver lover Charlie. When she first met Tony he was living with his mother. Later, they moved to a little house next to the Black Swan pub in Heywood. It was the early 1970s and Julie had been given a permanent role in *Coronation Street* as Bet Lynch.

For a while the two couples battled it out, making sarcastic comments and exchanging looks when they collided in the White Hart bar. Audrey said: 'They were like cat and mouse. They would meet up occasionally. It was quite embarrassing. No one knew what to say. I don't know who was more embarrassed about it, the two couples or the staff. We were all going hot and cold wondering what was going to happen next. There were definitely vibes between the two women. Irene didn't really stand a chance with Julie. I don't think many women would, truthfully. At the time I just thought they were playing one against the other. But it didn't work out like that at the end. Geoff married Irene and you wouldn't believe it – they had the wedding reception at the Hart.'

Geoff gave Irene the solitaire engagement ring Julie had handed back to him on the plane. Deep down, he was still besotted with Julie, and the night before his wedding, he went to see her. Geoff Nuttall remembers: 'The night before Geoff got married he went to see Julie and asked her if he was doing the right thing. She told him to go ahead. He was hinting that he really wanted to get back with Julie. I don't know what he would have done if Julie had told him not to marry Irene.'

After Geoff and Irene's wedding, friends watched as Julie seemed to go to pieces. Audrey said: 'She seemed to go bananas after she and Geoff broke up, dating loads of different men. People put it down to her getting on in the *Street*, but that was nothing to do with it at all. I'm not saying that wasn't part of it, but I think she was crying out for help really. I don't think the bond was ever actually broken between her and Geoff. I wouldn't think you could ever break that bond. I don't think Julie's ever been happy since they split up. She's tried. But I don't think anything will ever get to that level again.'

Julie's love-life was a mess. She dated dozens of men in

a bid to erase the loneliness she suffered after Geoff Cassidy married Irene. She drove Irene mad by constantly calling their home with a series of minor queries. Barbara Nuttall said: 'When anything went wrong, Julie would ring him up for advice. Irene used to get very upset.'

Tony Sibson hung on, hoping their relationship would be as important as Julie's had been with Geoff. He was bitterly disappointed when she finally moved out of their terraced home. He attempted suicide. Audrey said: 'I think it was a cry for help, not a serious bid to take his life.'

Geoff Cassidy now really seemed to hit the bottle. His career suffered and he was struck off in 1985 by the Law Society for 'conduct unbefitting a solicitor'. He died not long afterwards of a drink-related illness. Julie did not go to the funeral.

Over the next few years Julie lived with schoolteacher Glynn Griffiths, dated policeman John Park, got engaged to Blackpool cabaret comic Jack Diamond and married one of Geoff Cassidy's closest friends, businessman Tony Rudman.

One night, another ex of Julie's, professional footballer Jack Heath, who played in goal at Bury FC, Glynn Griffiths, Tony Sibson and Tony Rudman were lined up at the bar in the Hart. Julie walked in and Geoff Nuttall looked her straight in the eye and said: 'Are you stocktaking, Julie?'

'Piss-off,' she told him, giving a weak laugh.

6

Coronation Street – a New Life

It was 1970 and Julie had landed the part of Bet Lynch in *Coronation Street*. Her stomach was churning as she stood nervously at the bus stop in Heywood on her first morning. Jingling the change in her pocket, she calculated she had just enough cash to get to the Manchester studios and back.

Then a friend of her stepfather's pulled up, driving a concrete mixer, a huge barrel rolling slowly round on the back. He leaned out of the window and shouted: 'Would you like a lift, Julie?' 'Yes please,' she said, hauling herself into the cab.

As Julie and her driver pulled up outside Granada Television's headquarters, Pat Phoenix was arriving in her expensive vintage Rolls-Royce. Both vehicles stood bumper to bumper outside the studios and Julie jumped out – none too lady-like – just as Pat caught her eye. 'She looked me up and down with an expression of total disbelief – and I wanted the ground to open up and swallow me,' said Julie. But as she passed the doorman she heard the clink of coppers in her coat and consoled herself with the thought that she had enough money to buy a butty at lunchtime.

Coronation Street needed an injection of glamour. They had been looking for a sexy new character to rival Pat Phoenix's vamp Elsie Tanner, and Julie had just what they were looking for.

When June Howson took over as producer she offered Julie a three-month contract. June had been a fan of Julie's since she worked with her on *Nearest and Dearest* and *A Family at War*.

Lots of actresses come and go in the *Street*, but long-term survival is about bringing something special to a character. *Street* scripts are pretty flawless – even an average actor can deliver the skilfully drafted lines – but to inject individuality into a part needs a unique ingredient. Julie had what it took and was determined to succeed. Veteran scriptwriter Esther Rose remembers how Julie cracked open the chrysalis that was Bet. 'At first Bet Lynch wasn't much of a part,' she said. 'But Julie really made the most of it.'

Bet was cheeky and quick-witted. She had a reputation for being easy, always fell for rogues who made her feel cheap and misused her and, at sixteen, had already had an illegitimate baby, whom she was forced to give up for adoption. There was certainly a lot of heartbreak behind the smile.

It was a juicy part for an actress who could understand what made Bet tick, and Esther remembers how Julie got to work on her: 'Bet's uplifted bosoms, earrings and tarty clothes were Julie's ideas,' she says. So was hanging on to the name Bet Lynch. When Julie returned to the *Street*, producers wanted to give her a new one, but Julie insisted on Bet. 'I don't know why. It was just right for her,' she says now.

Bet's bolstered 36B boobs and infamous cleavage were usually encased in leopard-skin lycra, revealing skinny-rib sweaters or blouses with plunging necklines. Her assets were mesmerizing, and technicians nicknamed them Newton & Ridley after the fictitious Rovers brewery. If they had to shoot across the bar and thought Julie's chest was too prominent, the cameramen would shout: 'Dip, don't dazzle them Newtons.' Julie just laughs and says, 'Bet's attitude is if you've got it, flaunt it.'

She decided brassy Bet would wear seamed stockings and suspenders. Although no one would see them, the sexy undies made her feel like the cheeky barmaid. Bet's peroxide hair, all tumbling curls or back-combed beehive, was set with big old-fashioned rollers. Her lipstick and nails never matched: 'She always clashed. Bet epitomizes back-street glamour. It's not that she has no taste, it's just that she overdoes the glamour,' said Julie. 'Bet had to look as though she'd nearly got it right. If the nails were puce, the lipstick would be orange, and if the eyeshadow was turquoise the earrings had to be green.'

Julie's first make-up artist, Lois Richardson, helped create the famous Bet look. 'Lois is from Rochdale and knows the Bets of this world inside out,' says Julie. Her plastic earrings became a trademark and over the years Bet has collected 2,000 pairs. They range from pink feathers to tiny toilets and when she wore the tiny loos the seat was up on one ear, while on the other it was down. When the Queen and Prince Philip visited the set in 1982 she wore earrings bearing pictures of Charles and Di.

Now Bet's jewels have become a national institution.

'Within months of Bet appearing in the show, kids were spending their pocket money on earrings and sending them in so I had to wear them,' says Julie. 'They'd tell their friends they'd seen me on television and their friends sent more in and it snowballed. Now they come from all over the world.'

It was not Julie's first time on the *Street*. Four years earlier, Julie had landed the role of cheeky blonde factory worker Bet Lynch. By chance her very first scene was in the Rovers Return, ordering a pie and a bottle of pale ale. But after just six episodes she was fired. Thanks to Pat Phoenix and June Howson, however, on 18 May 1970, episode number 980, *Coronation Street*'s 'Busty Bet Lynch' took a bow.

Every Monday and Wednesday *Coronation Street* was the most watched programme on television, and insiders excitedly reported that Julie Goodyear had the kind of natural scene-stealing personality which would win fans and boost ratings. By the time Julie joined the cast permanently, *Coronation Street* was already being trans-mitted worldwide. Even the natives of the Polynesian island of Oahu, where the top-rated TV series *Hawaii Five-O* was filmed, preferred watching regal Rovers Return landlady Annie Walker spar with husband Jack to the antics of TV cop Steve McGarrett and his sidekick Danno.

Viewers in Thailand, Sri Lanka, Singapore and Sierra Leone were hooked on tales of the Rovers Return pub in Weatherfield. In 1971 a Canadian television station bought 1,142 episodes of the *Street*, a transaction which made the *Guinness Book of Records*.

Julie was introduced as Bet Lynch, the happy-go-lucky friend of recently widowed Irma Barlow, scatter-brained daughter of cleaning lady Hilda Ogden, and given a job at the launderette. A month later she switched to the Rovers Return. For Bet's debut behind the bar Julie wore a fluffy white skin-tight knitted two-piece dress, held together with flimsy, crocheted cord and white patent sling-backs.

Iron-fisted Annie Walker ran the Rovers with the dedication of a drill sergeant. She thought Bet was common, but appreciated that her blonde hair, bosom and quickfire banter pulled in the customers.

In the early days Julie sat in awe of the *Street* stars like Pat, Doris Speed who played Annie Walker and Violet Carson, who played the formidable Ena Sharples. She said: 'When Pat walked into the green room, you bloody knew she'd arrived. I was the new girl on the block, I kept my mouth shut when Pat or Doris opened theirs, and learned my craft. I was hungry to become halfway as professional as they were, so I spent hours just watching and listening. When I wasn't in a scene I was somewhere in the studio lurking behind the flats.

'I called them Miss Speed, Miss Carson and Miss Phoenix. It was a mark of respect. It took six months for Doris Speed to approach me and say, "I'd like a word with you, dear." She told me that from that day on I was allowed to call her Doris, rather than Miss Speed.

'It was difficult at first, a bit like calling your teacher by her first name.'

Julie knew instantly she'd made the right move. She said: 'When I joined *Coronation Street* I felt I'd come home. Not for a couple of years . . . but to stay. It was like a dress that's a good fit and just right for you. It was a mixture of the part, the people, the place – everything about it.'

Friends and family were delighted at Julie's breakthrough. The only person not impressed was son Gary. Julie said: 'He likes *Star Trek*, which is our rival programme on Wednesday nights. Gary said if I could have got a part on *Star Trek*, that would really have been something.'

A regular part in *Coronation Street* meant Julie could start saving. She loved the tiny cobblestone streets, the mill chimneys and corner shops in Heywood but she was still living with Gary, Alice and Bill in a tiny two-up, two-down terraced house in Gregge Street, round the corner from the Bay Horse.

Julie planned to change their way of life by working hard and saving for a new home. She saved spare cash in a savings clock she kept on the mantelpiece in the living room. She knew exactly the sort of place she wanted to buy: 'It's going to be detached, with a big garden for Gary to play in and the windows will be large to let in plenty of light.'

As her success grew, Julie had no desire to leave Heywood for more upmarket areas: 'I don't want anyone to get the idea that I'm getting stuck up because I'm on the telly now. I love the folk round here – that's why I'll stay here in Heywood when I buy the house.' Eventually, she bought a modest semi on Rochdale Road East.

Bet Lynch was an overnight success. Within weeks, Julie's mailbag was bulging with fan letters. She was staggered by her popularity. She said: 'It's been absolutely fantastic. A couple of the other actors told me it would be like this, but I didn't think it would happen to me. After the first few episodes I used to walk along thinking: "Come along somebody, recognize me." Now I get stopped all the time.'

Letters poured in. A lot came from children wanting to

adopt Bet as a sister or asking if she could join their football team as goalkeeper. She also had the usual handful from obsessive fans. Julie said: 'There is one man who keeps trying to make a date. I answer each of his letters with a photograph.'

Bachelor Desmond Ingram was more obsessive than others. The only time love flickered for lonely factory worker Des was when Bet Lynch appeared on his television screen. Twice a week he would rush home from the Leicester clock factory where he worked, have a shave, slap on the aftershave and settle in front of the telly. After the show, he picked up a pen and wrote passionate love letters to Julie or picked up the phone in a bid to contact her. Most of his £14-a-week wages was spent on letters and phone calls to the woman he considered a goddess. He said: 'It wasn't love at first sight, but each week as I watched the programme I found myself falling more in love with her. Already it's costing me over £10 a week in mail and phone calls, which only leaves me enough for my rent and food, but it is worth it. Julie is the only girl in the world for me.'

Julie found such attention distressing and decided to call a halt to it. She turned down an invitation to dinner and told Desmond she was nothing like Bet Lynch. It wasn't strictly true, she was very like Bet Lynch, but he believed her and promised to leave her alone. Producers were delighted with her popularity and Julie's three-month contract was renewed.

That Christmas, Julie realized what fans found so appealing about her and insured her 36B bosom for £1,000. 'I've decided it's my most valuable asset,' she said. 'I want some kind of guarantee that if I lose my bust – either if I lose valuable inches or it gets too big – then I can claim for it. As a barmaid I'm expected to show plenty of cleavage. It certainly helps, having a good bustline. My legs are not bad, but it's my bust that brings in the most comments in my fan mail. Everyone seems to think it's the nicest part of me.'

One night, actor Fred Feast, who played potman Fred Gee, got a flash of her famous bosom. He said: 'She knew men couldn't take their eyes off her boobs and she would flaunt them. Once, after I helped her learn a difficult scene, she said: "Thanks Fred, here's your reward." Then she lifted up her sweater and gave me a flash of her boobs. She's got the best pair I've ever seen.'

Hundreds of adoring fans kept up a non-stop stream of letters and she was popular with the rest of the cast, who loved her humour, although no one wanted to get too close. Kenneth Alan Taylor remembers: 'Doris Speed said to me once: "That girl exasperates me, but she always saves herself with her sense of humour." If she pushed her luck she always had a quip to get her out of trouble.'

In her first year, Julie set the scene for Bet's disastrous love-life. Her first screen lover was Frank Bradley, played by Tommy Boyle. In the summer of 1970 she had a one-night stand with roguish Frank. He returned in September and swept her off her feet by declaring his love and promising they would settle down together. However, Frank proved to be the first of a long line of rats who would use and abuse Bet. Eight episodes later, he disappeared with all her money, leaving her broken-hearted.

Off-screen, her love-life was almost as chaotic as Bet's, but Julie was the one in charge. She allowed no one to trample her feelings and get off lightly. The following year, however, Julie was ready for a new romance.

Blackpool comic Jack Diamond's camp cabaret act was

95 per cent ad-libbed. He came on stage in a gold lamé suit and swapped banter with the audience for hours. He drove a pink Rolls-Royce and owned a couple of Manchester pubs. One was the Oxnoble in Deansgate, a main street in the town centre.

Julie was twenty-nine when she met him in 1971. Alice had been ill, so Julie took her to Blackpool for a spot of rest and recuperation. They saw Jack's name on a billboard and bought tickets for his show at the Norbreck Castle Inn on the promenade.

Jack, twenty-seven, noticed Julie in the front row, caught her eye and started a stream of banter. 'I noticed her blonde hair and figure. You couldn't miss her, the woman was a star even then,' he said. 'Julie was everything a woman should be. She had an electric personality and there were fireworks between us.' Later, they met backstage and a steamy affair started. 'It was a passionate relationship from the word go!' he confessed.

A year later they became engaged and Jack said: 'We went shopping for an engagement ring. When Julie started looking at things over £20,000 I tried to talk her into a tea set!' Eventually, Julie picked out a £1,500 diamond solitaire and the affair was official. Unfortunately, their happiness did not last.

'The first year we were together was fantastic, an absolute riot,' laughed Jack. 'We wined and dined in the best places and really lived it up. Our sense of humour was virtually the same and we spent our time seeing who could make the other laugh the most. On one occasion we were sitting in a restaurant when Julie said: "Don't look now, but the guy sitting behind you has eyes like a basketful of whelks." Of course, I looked and Julie had hit the nail on the head. The two of us spent the rest of the meal under the table helpless with laughter while this poor man carried on eating. That incident sums up our relationship. Whenever we met, it was party time and the laughs would go on until the early hours of the morning.'

Their time together was at a premium. They were both in demanding jobs and were able to spend only weekends and the odd week together. Julie would sometimes take eleven-year-old Gary along and they would spend hours on Blackpool beach or exploring the pier and arcades.

They announced their engagement a year after they met. Granada saw a golden opportunity for publicity and took over. 'People took the *Street* seriously in those days and the *Street* stars were carefully cosseted. Our engagement was totally stage-managed, it was orchestrated by Granada,' complained Jack. 'I would like to have handled it myself, not go through an office as though it was part of a script. Julie and I discussed it and I gave in because I didn't want to get her into any trouble with Granada. I was in a more viable position than hers, so I could afford to give a bit more.

'Bernard Youens [Stan Ogden] made the announcement at the Norbreck Castle. I was a bit resentful of that. After all, it was my bloody marriage! It was on the way to the hotel I realized just how much the *Street* had taken over the public's lives. I was walking out with Julie when this little old lady popped up and started banging me on the head with her brolly. I was trying to fend her off, ducking and diving at the same time and trying to ask her what was wrong. The next thing she started shouting back at me: "What's Annie Walker going to do for a barmaid now that Bet's marrying you?" I couldn't believe it. This little old lady really believed all the *Street* characters were real. She was so upset that I had to tell her I was going to let Julie work part-time after we got married. It was the only way I could stop her hitting me.'

Six weeks later, their relationship was on the rocks. Chain-smoking Jack, who had been engaged three times before, told how he and Julie were ready to commit themselves to marriage and then realized it would never work. They blamed pressure of work. He was on tour in cabaret and Julie was making herself indispensable in *Coronation Street*. Jack said *Coronation Street* was the most important thing in Julie's life. 'The thing people don't realize about Julie is that she is ultra-ambitious. She comes across all natural, but deep down she has a spine of steel. When we first met she only had a bit part in *Coronation Street*. There had been plenty of barmaids before her at the Rovers Return and there was no reason to think she would last either. I knew as soon as things started to go wrong between us, Julie was going to make that part work for her and nothing was going to stand in her way. The first signs were when Granada realized her potential and her part started to become bigger. There were more scripts for her to read and more work for her to do.

'Some actresses would have carried on the way they were and tried to fit in the work with their lives, but not Julie. Work came first and she made sure she buckled down by reading all her scripts and making sure she went to bed early. She was very strict with herself.

'I was working most nights. She was on the day shift. I couldn't expect her to give up *Coronation Street*, it was the chance of a lifetime. But I was a bit resentful because I missed her. When we did meet we tried to snatch personal words between signing autographs. When we met up we would both be knackered and that's when the arguments started. What were witticisms before soon became vitriol. There were some right ding-dong battles. Julie is really patient for most of the time, but she can have a fiery temper. Mostly we were arguing over something or nothing but in the end it got too much.

'One day we just sat down in private and agreed it was not going to work. We were both very civilized about it. It was heartbreaking having to split up. We talked and talked to try and find a way to stay together. We came to the conclusion we did care for one another, but it was a no-win situation. We were both really hurt and both of us cried buckets.

'Looking back, I should have realized that it would never work because Julie is such a professional about her work. Any lover in Julie's life is going out with a married woman because she is already wedded to her career. That is and always will be her first priority. No matter how you feel about her, you cannot deny her professionalism. There is no room for a man in her life. I might have realized that earlier but my emotions were all mixed up because of the relationship.'

Later, Jack collapsed, blaming the break-up of their relationship and pressures of work. He spent Christmas having treatment for a nervous breakdown.

With a failed marriage, two broken engagements and a handful of ex-lovers, most women would have put the brakes on their love-life, but Julie just stepped up the pace. By the end of 1972 she was dating a man twelve years her senior, company secretary and divorcee Tony Rudman, an old friend of Geoff Cassidy's. Back in the Hart, no one could understand the attraction. Geoff Nuttall said: 'I thought Tony Rudman was a bit wet. If Julie spoke to me in a jocular fashion he went into a sulk. I'd known Tony a long time and I'd known Julie a long time, so there was no need for him to be jealous.'

A close friend of Tony's said: 'They weren't suited at all. They were too similar.' Audrey felt the same. She said: 'I didn't have much time for Tony. I couldn't understand what Julie saw in him or what they had in common. I could never work their relationship out. He was too much like Julie, very volatile. I wondered if Julie was getting back at Geoff by dating him.'

They lived together at Tony's place in Jericho, Bury, dated for a year and decided to get married. On 19 February 1973 they drove to Bury Registry Office for a quiet ceremony. For some reason, friends were sworn to secrecy. The first time the public heard about the wedding was two months later, when Julie staged a flashy blessing at Bury Parish Church.

The dress Julie chose was an ostentatious gold gown which friends hated and said was just not her style. 'Her wedding dress was bloody awful,' said Audrey. 'She looked like a fairy on a Christmas tree. When I saw her in that dress I couldn't believe it; she dressed so elegantly before.'

Julie arrived at the church in an open-topped vintage car, a 1920 Vauxhall. The men of the King's Own Royal Border Regiment, who had adopted her as a pin-up, formed a guard of honour on the church steps with rifles and fixed bayonets. It was their way of thanking Julie for a morale-boosting visit she had made to them in Ulster. The surrounding streets were seething with well-wishers and fans. At one stage, a Saracen tank came into view. Julie was staggered. She said: 'I've made hundreds of personal appearances but I've never seen anything like that crowd. You could have been forgiven for thinking it was a royal wedding. Fans surged at us, reaching out with handshakes, slapping us on the back and almost crushing us.'

As her car pulled up thirty minutes late, Julie panicked. She had left her bouquet at the house. Tony instructed a friend to go back, break down the door and fetch her flowers. If he'd known that, later, Julie would be bashing him on the head with them, he might have thought otherwise.

After the ceremony, the happy couple drove to the Hart, where Julie had decided they should hold the reception. The cast of *Coronation Street* were waiting, dressed to the nines and ready to party.

Audrey said it was the reception to end all wedding receptions. 'It was fantastic,' she said. 'The buffet was beautiful. You name it, she had it. Champagne flowed like it was on tap.'

The *Street* cast came in character and raided their wardrobes for their best gear. 'Pat Phoenix wore a black velvet suit trimmed with ermine and came with her husband, actor Alan Browning,' Audrey remembers. 'Doris Speed was in pale blue. Violet Carson [Ena Sharples] couldn't come, but Bill Roache [Ken Barlow], Jean Alexander [Hilda Ogden] and Ken Farrington [Billy Walker] were all there. After that day I realized the *Coronation Street* cast didn't act, they were just their natural selves, apart from Jean Alexander, who was very nice. They really know how to enjoy themselves. They were high-spirited and the atmosphere was really good.'

Julie spent the day in a daze. Wedding number two was obviously a big disappointment to her. Scarcely concealing the bitterness she felt, she said later: 'There were no speeches that I can remember, certainly I couldn't have got the words out that day. And if the guests expected a few words from my husband they were disappointed. Champagne corks popped as the guests enjoyed themselves. But the smile I wore was painted on for the occasion.'

The atmosphere turned sour at 8 p.m., with Julie and Tony looking daggers at each other and, fuelled with endless bottles of champagne, having a huge row. Julie was seen outside the pub in her gold wedding dress, battering Tony on the head with her flowers. 'I've no idea what really sparked it off. One minute they were laughing and drinking, the next there was a huge fight,' said Audrey. But she has her own theory about what caused the argument. She said: 'Deep in my heart I wondered whether she should have had the reception at the Hart. There were too many memories about Geoff Cassidy, and too many feelings and regrets. Tony was no subsitute. I don't think she could ever give the love that she'd given to Geoff.'

Julie never spoke about the row. She just said: 'As the guests sipped their drinks, we slipped out of the room separately. It was to be the end of our marriage! Leaving the Hart, I made for the bungalow [they had bought a home in Bamford, a smart area near Heywood] which was to be our home. Inside, I slumped into a chair and sat there, deep in thought the whole night. At nine o'clock the next morning the doorbell rang. It was the taxi to take us both to the airport for our honeymoon in Paris! I was still wearing my wedding dress and hadn't even taken off the veil. I'll never forget the startled look on the cabbie's face when I said: "Miss Goodyear won't be requiring a car to go to the airport, I'm only the cleaner." I felt shame, anger and bewilderment. I was terrifed in case news of what had happened leaked out. Mum and Dad came round to try and sort things out. Two days later, my husband and I spoke over the phone for the first time since the reception. We met later and decided to rethink our future.'

Later, she changed her story and told a magazine: 'The groom walked out on me halfway through the afternoon – I haven't set eyes on him since!'

Julie theorized that the hoards of people at the wedding had brought home her popularity to her new husband. She said: 'He was unconnected with the world of show-business and therefore totally unprepared for the impact my job would make upon him. That was the real tragedy. I know I must shoulder much of the responsibility for failing to make him aware of this. Sometimes, when I look back, I wonder if it was the shock of that day, when it seemed half of Lancashire turned up to see us at the church, that was to blame.'

However, Tony had known Julie for years. He must have realized how popular she was; there was no way she could, or would, have hidden it.

Ex-fiancé Jack Diamond doubted her explanation. 'It was just another ludicrous match for her, but she realized she had made a mistake and got out – fast. Julie's marriage to Tony Rudman didn't even get started. Julie told me that she decided at the reception it was a big mistake and wanted out. She told Tony immediately after the ceremony. It was absolutely typical of Julie; she was always making snap decisions.'

At least two friends remember seeing Julie and Tony together after the wedding. Photographer Jimmy Rowbotham said: 'I saw them at his mother's house one day.'

A close friend of Tony's remembers: 'I sat at Tony's house with Julie and him. I'm pretty sure that was after the wedding. And I remember him getting angry at all the bull written about it in the papers.'

A year later, Julie and Tony had their marriage annulled, claiming non-consummation.

Julie kept the split a secret from her *Street* colleagues for eight months. She said: 'Back at *Coronation Street*, I faced all the good-natured jibes any newly-wed can expect. I kept up the pretence of being a normal married woman.'

Whatever the true events were, Julie was devastated. Her secret came out when she had a breakdown and was admitted to a psychiatric hospital for a month. Julie's personal life was a shambles, so she turned to the family she loved, the *Coronation Street* cast.

Back on the *Street* it was business as usual. 'Three milk stouts and make sure there's no lipstick on the glasses!' hair-netted battleaxe Ena Sharples would bark at Bet, as she ordered drinks for herself and pensioners Minnie Caldwell and Martha Longhurst. Julie loved these scenes. She had plenty of quips and one-liners which she chucked back at Ena. Using work as therapy, Julie absorbed herself in Bet Lynch. A consummate professional, she never fluffed lines, was never late and rarely corpsed (an acting term for collapsing with laughter). Her co-stars were full of praise. Fred Feast, who played potman Fred Gee from 1976 to 1984, said: 'Julie was very helpful in my early days. We had a good rapport. When I started flicking her bottom with a tea towel as a joke, she thought we should keep it in because it was the sort of thing Fred would do.'

He respected her little quirks, too. 'She had a special place under the bar for her script,' he said. 'We all kept a script for reassurance. Julie kept hers on the draining board by the sink.'

They made sure they had fun. One classic scene, when Fred takes Bet and Betty Turpin to Tatten Park for a picnic, was hilarious. Fred drives Annie's prized Rover to the picnic spot and parks by a stream. He opens the boot to get out the food but forgets to put on the brake. He slams the lid and the Rover slides back into the murky water. With Betty and Bet shrieking obscenities, Fred, up to his thighs in the freezing river, piggybacks Bet to the bank and plonks her down in a cowpat. The three were in stitches in between takes.

Actress Madge Hindle joined in 1976 and played Mayor Alf Roberts's first wife Renee. At the time, Bet lived above Alf's corner shop so Madge and Julie met frequently. 'I liked working with Julie,' she said. 'She knew the script and was utterly reliable. You never felt like she would let you down. She was very, very professional.'

Actor Graham Weston appeared three times in the *Street*, first in 1967 as one half of a circus act who rented the Tanners' house; later in 1978 as a business associate of Mike Baldwin who tried to chat up Bet; and again in 1984 as lover to Elsie's daughter Linda Cheveski. He remembers: 'She was an attractive woman – she ain't Claudia Schiffer – but her humour made her attractive. Julie had a great sense of humour; we would laugh and giggle all the time. She was polite to everyone, even the youngsters who were only in the *Street* for a week, and always knew her lines.

'She was generous, too. After rehearsals she was always near the top of the queue to buy you a pint or gin and tonic. I never heard a word against her. There were others – who will remain nameless – that you could not say that about.'

Richard Shaw, who played Bet's lover, Dan Johnson, in 1981, remembers: 'Julie was becoming the star.'

Richard quickly discovered the effect the show had on viewers. Dan was a scoundrel, romancing both Elsie

Tanner and Bet. On holiday in Rhodes, Richard was spotted in the lobby by a *Street* fan. Furious at his character's behaviour, she gave him what for. 'We were staying in the Astir Palace, a rather nice five-star hotel,' he said. 'I'd just walked into the reception and dumped my bags, when I got belted by this woman. She called me all the names under the sun and shrieked: "Don't you dare mess my Elsie or my Bet around or I'll give you what for" then she clocked me with her handbag. For the first few days I had a massive bump and a stinking headache.'

Viewers were gripped by the romance, which saw Dan ask Bet to move in with him. There were bedroom scenes too, which Richard thought Julie should have played differently. He said: 'There was one after I stayed the night for the first time. They put her in this diabolical black negligée and she wore not a scrap of make-up, with her hair loose. Now show me a woman in a new relationship with a guy and is not up before him to go in the bathroom and put on a bit of slosh. She was not quite a horror but she hadn't done herself justice. I thought it was wrong. Having created this glamorous character, you don't suddenly stuff it down the audience's throats that you are a normal woman.'

Julie's Mum was her greatest critic. A perfectionist, Julie took pride in getting it right. Once she had a long serious scene with Jean Alexander, who played Rovers cleaner and gossip Hilda Ogden. Alice and Julie sat down to watch it. Afterwards, Julie asked Alice what she thought. 'You were good,' she said, 'but she was better! That's why she won the actress of the year award!'

Towards the end of 1980, Julie was almost as popular as Pat Phoenix. Her weekly mailbag could just fit inside a supermarket shopping trolley. In spite of her star status, she vowed to stay down-to-earth. Her wages were spent at Heywood's local shops and she still searched for bargains at Bury market. Julie was often spotted rummaging on earring stalls, looking for outrageous baubles for Bet, or she would help out florist Margaret O'Brien on her stall.

Margaret, a long-standing friend, knew Julie's Mum Alice and her own mother Frances had the same birthday as Julie. She said: 'Julie often helped out if she was in the mood.'

Julie would have made the perfect stallholder. Every time she took her place among the flowers she drew a crowd, which could only be good for business.

Margaret remembers: 'A lad came up once and bought a single red rose and gave it to her. She was dead chuffed.'

Another time, years later, after Alice had died, Julie was back on Margaret's stall. Margaret's Mum, aged sixty-four, had passed away just three months after Alice. Instead of visiting her grave at the cemetery on the anniversary of her death, Margaret made a stunning floral tribute to display on the stall. 'It had sixty-four pink roses, sixty-four red roses, sixty-four white roses and sixty-four yellow roses,' said Margaret. 'Julie arrived and thought it was marvellous. Then a crowd of people gathered round and someone said: "That's absolutely fabulous – who did it?"

'It's something I've done,' Julie grinned and began titivating the bows on the display. Then she turned to the crowd and told them: 'I find it very therapeutic!'

'Everyone thought she was serious,' laughed Margaret.

They were golden days, with heads turning wherever she went. But before long, Julie would find out how cruel life can be.

7

Cancer Battle Begins

Julie had been working hard on the *Street* for nearly a decade and was looking forward to a holiday in the Canary Islands, but she had one thing to do before going home to pack her cases. Queueing up with actresses, typists, canteen ladies and cleaners, Julie visited a mobile clinic in the Granada studios car park, for a routine cervical smear test.

After the nurse finished taking the necessary swab, Julie left the unit and did not give the test another thought. Two weeks later, arriving home from holiday, tanned and fit, Julie flicked through the post and stared at an envelope which made her blood run cold. Inside was a letter requesting she contact her doctor. Julie had been diagnosed as having abnormal cancer cells on her cervix.

Devastated she became aware she could be facing a long battle. She said later: 'Life has toughened me to the point where I don't cry easily. I wept that night, though. It was the only time I was to break down in all those worrying months.

'Letters like that can be misleading; tests can be wrong, so I shouldn't have cried. Women who take a second cervical smear test often find they are in the clear. But panic overcame me, and I vowed to myself not to tell a soul. For the first time in my life I felt real fear. It was a sensation I was to have to learn to live with.'

It was almost Christmas in 1978 and Julie dreaded seeing her GP. She knew instinctively her second test would be positive. She was terrified as she went for test number two. To overcome the fear she felt before taking the life-or-death test, she looked for an antidote to the fear, and found it in her sense of humour. She said: 'No sooner had I walked through the door than a nurse handed me a leaflet on cancer of the breast. "My God!" I thought. "It's spreading already. Bet Lynch is going to become the first bionic barmaid in the country!"

'There were plenty of wisecracks about that part of my anatomy, and suddenly all the jokes surrounding one of the best-known cleavages on television raced through my mind.

'Would it be Newton or Ridley they took away? I studied the leaflet and consoled myself that no one was planning to take away my bust or my legs. I'd still be able to reach the pumps at the Rovers!'

For Julie that Christmas was bleak and without humour, although she tried to put on a brave performance. On 11 January 1979 she received the letter she was dreading, confirming that cancer had been found in her womb.

Julie was thirty-six; her life was at risk, but she still managed a joke. She said: 'If the cancer hadn't been detected, it wouldn't have been long before Annie Walker thumbed through the situations-vacant columns.'

She told very few people about it, apart from *Coronation Street* producer Bill Podmore, a handful of the cast and her immediate family.

Within days, Julie was written out of the *Street* for nine weeks, so she could be admitted to St Joseph's Hospital in Manchester for an operation. And if anyone got curious as to her whereabouts, Jean Alexander, who played Hilda Ogden, told them Julie was having an operation on her bunions.

On the eve of her first operation, actor Peter Adamson, who played one of her ex-*Street* loves Len Fairclough, sat and held her hand. 'We're all with you, kid,' he whispered. As the delegated *Street* representative, Peter waited until Julie came round after the biopsy operation to remove the neck of her womb.

Julie relied heavily on the emotional support of Sister Margaret, a Catholic nun who had helped her mother through an illness. She nicknamed her 'Wonderwoman'. The nun told her cancer was not something to be frightened of, that it needed to be faced up to and treated quickly. 'To say she gave me strength and confidence would be an understatement,' she said.

After the operation, Julie was lying in the recovery room wearing a white, regulation hospital gown. When the anaesthetic wore off the first thing she saw was a picture of Jesus Christ. She said: 'I thought I was in heaven because I saw the Lord's face. Apparently I mumbled: "I'm very pleased to meet you, sir, I'll try not to be too much trouble."

'In fact, the face turned out to be on the crucifix which hung around my nun Wonderwoman's neck.'

Julie left hospital confident that the operation had been a success then, two weeks later, tests discovered that all of the cancer had not been cut out. She would have to have a hysterectomy, or ex-directory as her mother called it.

By February 1979, she was back in hospital waiting for the operation to remove her womb. Filled with pessimism, she had no idea if the surgeons would open her up and discover she was riddled with the disease.

The cast rallied round. Julie said: 'We're one big family. Kick one and we all limp.' No *Street* member was going to be morose about the situation. They pinned a note on the ward door which said: 'Silence, Cup Final in Progress'. Geoffrey Hughes, who played Eddie Yates, turned up with armfuls of tinned baby food, which had Julie in fits of giggles. Madge Hindle, who played Renee Roberts bought her a white nightie, and Doris Speed gave her a frothy pink bed jacket. Pat Phoenix sent a card which said: 'Keep fighting it, darlin'.'

Hundreds of cards arrived from fans, some simply addressed, 'Bet Lynch, Heywood, Lancashire,' and her private room was full with bouquets of flowers.

Before the anaesthetic took effect for the second time, Julie could not resist one last quip. She told the surgeon waiting to perform the operation: 'If you find a bunch of white fivers or any old Stanley Matthews cards, keep 'em.'

The second operation was a success and, five days later, she was given the all-clear. If the cancer had been discovered a year later, she would have been given only a 50–50 chance.

After she left hospital, Julie bought a jogging suit and was determined to get back to peak fitness. To help her recuperate, Julie and her Mum accepted an invitation from a family of hoteliers in Blackpool, who offered to let them stay as their guests.

When she returned to work, hoards of well-wishers were waiting to wish her luck. Delighted to be back home, she made it her priority to organize a champagne celebration to thank the cast for their support.

Julie was genuinely grateful to the surgeons, doctors and nurses who helped her to recover. She was appalled, however, at the derelict condition of the prefabricated smear-testing centre at Christie's Hospital, Manchester, which housed more rats and mice than test tubes.

Originally built in 1944 as a testing block to house laboratory animals, the cytology department was considered low on the priorities list. Consultant pathologist Dr Robert Yule described the building as an 'embarrassment'.

The lab was no better than a Nissen hut. The roof leaked and the ceiling sagged. The walls were cracked and covered with peeling paint. In winter, the labs were more like refrigerators because ill-fitting windows let in bad weather. There were inadequate toilet facilities and cramped offices. Staff working in primitive conditions were expected to deal with 200,000 smear tests from women all over the north west of England. Christie's estimated it would cost £500,000 to build a new lab. Once built it would allow them to deal with more cervical smears, they said, and reduce the death toll – running at 2,500 women a year – from cancer of the cervix.

Julie had been to see the lab and was horrified. 'I couldn't believe my eyes,' she said. Determined to help out, she launched a £500,000 appeal to replace the test centre with a new, purpose-built unit. Excited about her new project, Julie discussed her fund-raising ideas with friends over dinner. Bobby Howarth, the solicitor boy-friend of her old Lucy Clayton boss Pam Holt, was there. Bobby was involved with a health-insurance company called Clinicare. Clinicare wanted to start a cervical-cancer procedure and were looking for a way to publicize the project. They offered to set up a trust for Julie. Bobby said: 'I suggested we set up a properly structured chari-table foundation under Julie Goodyear's name. She thought it was a great idea, but we heard that Sydney Bernstein, head of Granada, had vetoed it. We were cut out. I was a bit brassed off when the Julie Goodyear Trust was launched.'

Julie was determined, however, and the trust went ahead without Bobby and Clinicare.

Three years before Julie set up her trust, forty-nine-year-old housewife, journalist and mother Pat Seed had been diagnosed as having terminal cancer of the abdomen. After doctors told Pat she was dying, she set up a one-woman cottage industry in fund-raising. Within a couple of years, she had sixty-eight branches of her fund through-out the north west and had raised £2 million for a sophisticated cancer scanning unit. The special diagnostic unit at Christie's Hospital was opened on 25 April 1980 by the Duchess of Kent. Pat was worshipped by the public and hailed as a courageous heroine. She was loved in the way people loved the late entertainer and fund-raiser Roy Castle who fought a losing battle against lung cancer.

In August 1980, Julie contacted Pat Seed, and Rochdale MP Cyril Smith, to ask if they would be trustees of the Julie Goodyear Trust. They both said yes but, although their names were on the headed notepaper, they were never legally appointed. 'I think that proved to be a good thing in the long term,' reflected Cyril. Throwing herself heart and soul into the project, Julie came up with endless ways to boost the trust's coffers.

There was a fund-raising event at the Talk of the North Club in Eccles. Lynne Perrie, who was then playing Ivy Tilsley in the *Street*, her brother comedian Duggie Brown and London-based singer Tony Melody were billed to perform. Entrance was £2.50 with profits going to the Julie Goodyear Trust fund.

Julie appeared in a documentary – ITV's *TV Eye* – highlighting the disease, and Whitbread pubs in Greater Manchester sponsored collecting boxes which were sent to 250 pubs. Endless publicity surrounded the project but donations were slow. By mid-November, three months after she had launched her appeal, Julie had raised only £18,000 towards the £500,000 needed.

Manchester was suffering from charity fatigue. Pat Seed's sterling fund-raising efforts drained the market as her fund eventually swelled to £8 million. Cyril said: 'Julie thought all she had to do was announce in the papers that she was opening a fund and the money would flood in. She didn't have the appeal and character of Pat Seed, who was loved in an emotional respect. Julie's *Coronation Street* character is not a character that people love, she's a character that people like.'

Fred Feast went to three functions that Julie organized and said support was disappointing. 'A couple of them were in Manchester clubs – Tramps Nightclub and Foo Foo Lamaar's,' Fred explained. 'Julie was going to be there to sign autographs, supported by members of the cast. On a couple of occasions Geoff Hughes, who played dustman Eddie Yeats, and myself went and I noticed she wasn't getting an awful lot of support from the rest of the cast. There was only Geoff and I there, and on one occasion Anne Kirkbride [Deirdre Barlow] turned up. It didn't seem to me to be the success that they thought it would be. Not a lot of people turned up. I think the public had got fed up with giving money to cancer charities. Julie just hit the wrong time. It was a shame, really, but she meant well.'

Initially, response was encouraging. 'I've had pound notes from pensioners and donations from ten-year-old girls who have held street jumble sales,' said Julie. But donations were slow. To give the charity a boost, Julie organized a raffle. The prize was a Datsun car worth £2,650 which was over the stated maximum raffle prize value of £2,000, making the raffle illegal. It was then decided to legalize the competition by turning it into a game of skill. The trust charged 25p per ticket to guess the mileage the Japanese car could cover on one gallon of petrol. Market trader William Clarke and business partner Rodger Forster, who helped with the trust, took the Datsun to various shopping precincts and public places, selling tickets, but not enough tickets were sold to cover the cost of the car. The lottery was turning into a shambles and something had to be done. Julie handed over control to Clarke and Forster.

Vicky Montague was pronounced the winner at the draw which took place at Rochdale market in March 1981. In a blaze of publicity, Vicky told how she was going to sell the car and give the proceeds back to the charity.

Julie was asked to comment on the gesture by journalist Kay Burley. 'It was wonderful,' Julie enthused.

However, all of Julie's good intentions backfired and, on 12 November 1981, Julie, now aged thirty-nine, and four others – Julie's personal assistant, Janet Ross, twenty-eight; competition winner Vicky Montague, twenty-four;

Bill Clarke, thirty-three; and Rodger Forster, twenty-five – were arrested on a charge of conspiring to defraud members of the public into buying raffle tickets for her charity. It was alleged that the competition had been fixed so that Vicky would win, enabling her to sell the car and deposit the proceeds in the fund.

The five crusaders appeared in the dock at Manchester Crown Court, accused of "conspiring together and with persons unknown to defraud people into buying tickets for a competiton in aid of the Julie Goodyear Trust Fund, by falsely representing that the trust was conducting a genuine and honest competition. The charge alleges that a false winner had been pre-determined and that the car was destined for sale and the proceeds were to be contributed to the fund."

Bill and Rodger admitted the charge, while Julie, Janet and Vicky pleaded not guilty. Julie told police: 'I would not get involved in anything like that – I would never have allowed it to happen if I had known.'

A trial date was set for 1 March 1982 and all five were given unconditional bail. Julie pledged to carry on with the fund-raising and told critics: 'I have had wonderful backing from people who believe in me and I am confident that will continue. I know I have the support of fellow trustees and I will continue my campaign to fight cancer. The money is safe in the hands of the trustees.'

On 4 February 1982, Forster and Clarke were given six-month sentences, suspended for eighteen months, for their part in the fraud. Worried Julie knew that the following month she would be in the dock herself, struggling to clear her name. If she was found guilty, her career would probably be destroyed. Would Granada continue to employ a convicted fraudster?

Three months before her fortieth birthday, Julie was in front of the judge at Manchester Crown Court. Son Gary, now twenty-one, was with her. Julie, dressed in a sober grey dress with a white collar, wore a corsage of flowers at her throat. On the first day of the trial the court was told how Clarke had taped a discussion between Julie and himself in which they were allegedly 'racking their brains to find out who had shopped them to police'. Mrs Helen Grindrod, prosecuting, said: 'The conversation [recorded on Clarke's answering machine] is not a conversation of a woman who is outraged at what had happened – it is a conversation between two people who knew all about it beforehand, a conversation about who had told lies to the police.'

The defence accused Clarke of doctoring the tape and asked if he had added bits. He told the jury he had not. The tape was played to the court, who heard Julie sounding startled when the noise of a dog barking came over the phone. 'I nearly had a bleeding heart attack. They are obviously making us sweat,' they heard her say.

Clarke replied: 'I am falling asleep with no sleep last night and I am just running out of ideas.'

The court then heard how the alleged fraud plot was hatched at Julie's home in Heywood. Clarke said the plan started as a joke but later became serious. He alleged that Janet Ross was present when Julie agreed to go ahead with their plan. Julie claimed she told Clarke: 'No way. You must not do it, I will not have you do it.'

Clarke replied: 'It was her name, her fund. If she had said that we would not have done it.'

Clarke told the court he had been prepared to take the blame for the plot but had changed his mind because of the way Goodyear was behaving towards him. In a bizarre twist, and as reported in the *Daily Star*, Clarke also alleged that Julie had asked him to visit an ex-boyfriend in Weston-Super-Mare, who was attempting to blackmail her, and produced a piece of paper with his name and address written on it. She claimed he had taken it from her home.

Back in court on day four, twenty-four-year-old Vicky, the car winner, gave evidence and told how she had not wanted her name to be on the winning ticket. She said her mother had persuaded her to go along with the plot and had encouraged her to give a bogus newspaper interview about wanting to give the car back to the charity.

Vicky's mother, Joyce, told the court: 'Vicky was very annoyed that her name had been put on the winning ticket. All I was concerned about were the people suffering from cancer. I didn't want to ruin it for them. I told her that no one would benefit personally and that only the charity would benefit and she was persuaded against her judgement.'

Later, Joyce had a change of heart. On the day of the draw Joyce claimed she pleaded with Clarke and Ross to let the draw go straight and said she 'went berserk' when she found out her daughter had won the car.

On the fifth day of the hearing Judge Basil Gerrard stopped the trial and instructed the seven-strong jury to return formal not guilty verdicts on the three women. He said there was no corroborative evidence, saying Clarke and Forster's testimony was the evidence of accomplices in 'this dishonest enterprise'. He added: 'It would be wrong for persons such as these, of good character, who must be enduring quite a lot, to make them go through the hoop for a further four or five days when your decision would have been bound to be not guilty.'

Julie was overjoyed at the decision. Dressed in a navy

suit and white blouse, holding a bunch of sweet peas, she said: 'I'm thrilled and very, very happy. I always knew I was innocent and fortunately the judge has seen that. It has been a long ordeal. The waiting has been the worst. It is a big relief. It has not been a pleasant experience. I'm going to go home now and have a large G&T.' She added wistfully: 'They say everything happens for a reason, but it's hard to see the reason for this.'

Detectives who had investigated the case congratulated Julie on her acquittal. Detective Constable Ray Tulley planted a huge kiss on Julie's cheek and Detective Sergeant Barry Lenihan offered his congratulations too. Afterwards Julie celebrated. Clarke and Forster had nothing to celebrate, though.

The trial had been undeniably stressful for Julie and, to add a cruel twist, her stepfather Bill Goodyear died of lung cancer on 4 September 1982. Grandson Gary was there when Bill finally lost his battle against the incurable disease and although Alice had been unfaithful to Bill, his death hit her hard. 'Alice was on the verge of giving up,' said a family friend, when Julie came to her rescue. 'She persuaded her mother to think sensibly about her life. She told her bluntly: "OK, if you're giving up so am I! I'm packing in the *Street*." After that her mum was a different person.'

The fraud trial damaged Julie's fund-raising efforts and she fell far short of her half-a-million-pound target. 'Mud sticks,' said Dr Yule, reflecting on the poor response. 'There is no doubt the trial did damage us.'

A year after the trial, £420,000 short of her target, Julie donated the £80,000 she had raised to Christie's Hospital. The money was nowhere near enough to replace the whole of the dilapidated building, which is still in use. 'It was a pity,' said Dr Yule, 'It would have been great to have a brand-new lab.' However, it was enough to graft a new lab on to the crumbling structure. The new cytology laboratory was built eventually and Julie unveiled a plaque above the door which said: 'Julie Goodyear Laboratory, 1983'.

When it opened, the unit was analysing 250,000 smears a year and employed fifty staff. Although disappointed, Dr Yule was full of praise for Julie's efforts. He said: 'Without her, who knows where we would have been.'

While the Julie Goodyear Trust fiasco was unfolding, Julie fell in love. On holiday with a girlfriend in Tunisia in 1980, she met a handsome toyboy, six years her junior.

Restaurant manager Andrew McAllister, thirty-two, was taking a break from his job at Bournemouth's three-star Langtry Manor Hotel – once a love nest for royal mistress Lillie Langtry and the then Prince of Wales, later Edward VII.

Julie and Andrew were inseparable during the last week of the holiday and kept up the romance, sending each other flowers, after they got back. At work, lovesick Andrew could not keep his new relationship secret. Manageress Liz Shaw confessed: 'He was wandering about in a daze. He said the holiday hotel was awful and the food was awful but that he had fallen hopelessly in love. He said he'd met a barmaid from Manchester and showed me a snap of them together. I said: "God, that's Bet Lynch!" Andrew said she was a wonderful person. The next day two dozen carnations arrived for him. I couldn't believe it. Men just don't get flowers do they? The card said: "And Yours, My Friend, Love Julie". That's a motto from the Langtry Hotel, meaning "Welcome".'

Three days later, in March 1980, Andrew packed his bags and, as he slipped out of the back door, waved goodbye to the Langtry Manor. He left a note for his boss, saying he would explain everything later.

Then Liz got a call from Julie, explaining why Andrew had done a bunk. She remembers: 'Julie asked me to try to understand and said: "Be happy for us." She was very nice and sounded just like she did in the *Street*. I said I was glad she had a lovely holiday. She said it wasn't often two people got on so well together and so instantly. She could hardly believe what had happened, but she was in love and that was it.'

Pamela Hamilton-Howard, owner of the twenty-bed-room hotel, was not as understanding. She was upset that her assistant manager had disappeared without handing in his notice.

Back in Heywood, Julie claimed she was besotted. 'I'm in love for the first time in my life,' she cooed. She told how she had met Andrew after she and her friend – trying to escape unwanted attentions from the Arab men, and from the ghastly hotel they were in – walked into his hotel for a coffee. At first, Julie said, she was attracted by his kindness, then she fell in love that night as they danced together at the hotel disco. She said: 'My legs turned to jelly. At last I knew what love was all about. It still amazes me.'

Julie confessed that she had made a leap year proposal on St Valentine's Day – the sort of move Bet would have made – which Andrew accepted. 'We don't believe in just setting up home together,' she said. Then, virtually in the same breath, she said that there was no comparison between Julie and her character Bet Lynch, who was impulsive with men. 'She gives too much too soon,' Julie explained patiently, not spotting the glaring similarities between their actions. 'That is why she is not married and I don't think she ever will be.'

There was another surprise planned for Julie that year. Presenter Eamonn Andrews, clutching that big red book containing Julie's biography, planned to ambush her for his television show *This is Your Life*. On 8 October 1980, Eamonn and a film crew met them at Euston Station in London where Julie and Andrew – who knew about the programme – had arrived. Julie had been drawn to London under the ruse of discussing a personal appearance in New Zealand.

Dumbstruck, she was whisked off in a black limousine to Thames Television studios just outside London in Teddington, Middlesex, to record the show which would turn out to be a bit of a sham as Julie and Andrew were no longer dating. Julie, escorted by Andrew, floated through the sliding doors – behind which all the guests waited to come on – into the studio and down the stairs to her seat. She wore a pale blue, full-length chiffon evening gown, with her hair piled on top of her head.

Eamonn asked Andrew about his relationship with Julie. He said: 'Julie told me she couldn't promise me very much, but life would never be dull.'

Alice and Gary took their places next to Andrew, then the *Coronation Street* cast made their entrance. They were all used to the routine, as cast members were a staple diet for the programme.

Actor Peter Adamson told how the cast spent hours thinking of pranks before a show. He said: 'When Pat Phoenix was on, I was waiting to be called on. I said to Julie, who was next to me: "I want to play a trick on Pat but I need a pair of knickers." Quick as a flash, she whipped up her skirt, slipped off her panties and presented me with them. I went on to give Pat a kiss, shoved the knickers in her hand and said: "Here you are love, you left these in my car!"'

When Julie joined the show to pay tribute to Jill Summers, better known as blue-rinse battleaxe Phyllis Pearce, she could not resist a practical joke. Jill looked mystified when Julie leaned forward and pressed a mystery gift into her hand. The secret token turned out to be a pair of false teeth.

No one played pranks on Julie, but she got a big hug from Geoffrey Hughes. When Doris Speed came on, Julie hitched up her frock and knelt at her feet while Doris paid tribute. 'Television is a nervy business,' Doris said, 'and we are grateful to anyone who relieves the tension. Now, Annie Walker may have her doubts about Bet Lynch, but Doris Speed has nothing but gratitude to Julie Goodyear because she has quite deliberately made me laugh and relax on so many occasions before we have played a scene.'

Julie's current *Street* love, actor Richard Shaw – lorry driver Dan Johnson – was next.

Again, Violet Carson, who had not made Julie's wedding reception when she married Tony Rudman, was absent, but a telephone message, recorded at her Blackpool home, said: 'Hello, Julie. Sorry not to be with you but I send my love and hope you will have a thoroughly enjoyable evening.'

Then Julie told a different story about her first performance at the age of six. Originally, Julie had said that she gatecrashed a Carroll Levis talent contest in Rochdale. This time, it seems, she was at the other end of the country. Julie said she was visiting her grandparents in

Plumstead, east London, with her mother and stepfather. They were in a social club when she jumped on stage and gave an impromptu performance of the old music-hall favourite, 'If You Knew Suzie'. 'She brought the house down,' added Alice. 'A man came up to us and said if she lived in London she would become a star.'

Irene Hawksworth, Julie's cousin, told how they shared a bedroom above the pub for a while. 'There was one comfy bed and one camp bed,' she said. 'It was always a race to get the best bed and Julie usually won.' Then Irene went on to tell a story about how she was once laid up in bed with tonsillitis. It was late at night when Irene told Julie she fancied a slice of melon, so Julie knocked up the greengrocer at 10 p.m. just to get her some.

Peter Dudley, who was in the *Street* playing Ivy's husband Bert Tilsley, hid behind the doors with Julie's ex-Oldham Rep colleagues. They came on dressed in the Roman costumes they had worn in *A Funny Thing Happened on the Way to the Forum*, staged in 1967.

In the play Julie was Vibrata, a sexy courtesan. Peter told how he kept calling her vibrator. Then he said: 'Julie had to black up for the part. She had an allergy to the make-up and came out in spots. She looked like a milk chocolate peanut brittle.' His comment brought the house down.

Julie's old teacher Tony Whitehead and schools pals Anita Simpson, Sydney Yates and Peter Birchall, who had shared her acting debut at school, were also invited. A true professional himself, Tony, who was not really interested in Weatherfield antics, had taken time to gen up on his subject. He said: 'Before the show, I watched *Coronation Street* to see if I could see anything of Toni – her character in the school play – it wasn't obvious. Julie had good timing and knew just how to play herself.'

Sue Skelton, Julie's former best friend, also appeared. However, the finale (Eamonn always had a big surprise for his guest at the end of each show) was Sister Margaret, the Wonderwoman who had comforted Julie during her cancer scare. Sister Margaret had been given special permission by her order to appear. 'The religious order to which Sister Margaret belongs does not permit appearances outside the hospital or convent,' said Eamonn, 'but knowing how much it would mean to you, at the last moment we were able to gain special permission and she's here.' It was a tearful reunion which completed the final page of Julie's tribute.

After the show everyone gathered for a party. The famous and old friends were invited to the upmarket White House Hotel in Regent's Park. At first Julie's son Gary was barred from the party for not wearing a tie. Peter Birchall recalls: 'Someone lent him one in the end. I must admit, Gary seemed like a bit of a tearaway.'

Her old friends said Julie didn't spend a great deal of time with them. Her 'best friend' Sue, who hadn't met her for twenty years, said she hardly spoke to her. 'I was disappointed. We made no promises to keep in touch. I thought afterwards we might pick up again but nothing happened,' said Sue.

Teacher Tony Whitehead couldn't get to see much of her, either. 'I was disappointed. We didn't really have time to talk to her because she was busy. She greeted us but she might have forgotten us. I suppose a lot of things have happened since she was in the school play,' said Tony.

Julie spent most of the time with Wonderwoman. As Peter Birchall said: 'At the party we were like spare appendages at a wedding. The attention all hinged on

Julie and this nun. You couldn't get near Julie. The only time I got to talk to her briefly was on the train coming back.'

Andrew McAllister stayed out of the limelight, never mentioning that he and Julie were no longer together. They had separated before filming, but had agreed to keep up appearances for the cameras. By the end of October, seven months after they met, they had separated.

Julie said: 'Andrew was a gentle, tender lover who made me feel little, helpless and feminine. But after we'd lived together for a time and Andrew could find no work, his mood changed. He found himself tied to the kitchen sink and he grew depressed. It didn't help that he was penniless and that I was supporting him. He found it degrading, however much I tried to make light of it. It preyed on his mind. After a time he became like a lodger – brooding and introverted. I realized then that I couldn't marry him. He moved into the guest bedroom and we became like strangers under the same roof. I knew in my heart that it must end for both our sakes.'

Julie broke the news to Andrew that their affair was finished as he lay in bed one morning, sipping a cup of tea. Andrew, not pleased at being dumped, went berserk. Julie explained: 'I suggested it might be better if he tried to find work away from here in a hotel. I told him it was best to make a clean break and stop living a lie. He sprang out of bed and rushed towards me. I'm not sure what happened next but a crystal tumbler shattered on the wall.'

Julie's charlady Edna came to her rescue and called the police. Andrew had calmed down by the time they arrived and, flanked by two policemen, made an undignified exit from Julie's semi. Julie did not press charges.

Later, Andrew was tracked down to a sparse bedsit in Weston-Super-Mare. He briefly told *The Sun* his side of the story. 'I had just endured four hours of Julie's constant nagging when, in frustration, I threw the glass at the wall.' Despite being ejected by police, Andrew said he was still in love and wanted to patch things up, but Julie wanted nothing more to do with him.

8

Following in His Mother's Footsteps

Scandal was soon to hit the Goodyear family and it was like history repeating itself. It centred on handsome Gary, then aged twenty-three, and ironically, like Julie's first scandal, it concerned an unmarried woman becoming pregnant.

Maria Beswick, twenty-two, claimed that Gary was the father of her illegitimate child and said she was going to make forty-one-year-old Julie a grandma.

Her Mum, Mary, was thrilled at the thought of having famous Bet Lynch in the family. But Julie denied that Gary was the father of Maria's baby.

Baby Benjamin was born and there was still no acceptance of paternity from Gary or Julie. Mary Beswick, the new baby's grandma, who also lived in Heywood, was puzzled. She said: 'Gary is definitely the baby's father. I'm overjoyed that Julie will be part of the family.' Both Mary and her husband are deaf and dumb and their comments were made in sign language.

When Maria registered her son's birth, she left the name of the father blank. She said that Gary had told her not to fill it in. Gary kept out of the way but denied he was the father: 'I don't want to talk about it,' he said. According to Maria's brother, Peter, Gary had taken his sister to hospital the minute she went into labour. Benjamin Beswick was born eleven days 'late' at Fairfield Hospital in Bury. He weighed 8lb 5oz. Maria, this apparent show of concern nothwithstanding, was to become another single parent. She brought up Benjamin in her Coronation Street-style terraced house.

Five years later, Maria was asked if she would accept maintenance from Gary or money from Julie. Maria said: 'Gary offered me nothing when Ben was born and I don't want their money now. But if they asked to see Benjamin I would probably agree.'

Gary Goodyear didn't have the best start in life. Born on 28 April 1960 at Fairfield Hospital, Bury, he was fatherless as a toddler. He spent much time with grandparents after his Dad Ray Sutcliffe left for Australia. If Julie was asked about Gary and their early years she would say: 'I am a trained shorthand typist. I worked until two weeks before the birth and I started work again two weeks after, while my Mum looked after Gary. I sold speedboats, washing machines and vacuum cleaners in order to support us. I loved my baby from the start and it was hard to leave him every day. But I just got on with what I had to do.' Others disagreed; they thought Julie was too devoted to her work.

Alice and Bill were mainly responsible for Gary's upbringing and Gary idolized his grandma and grandpa. According to Edith, Alice doted on Gary. She brought clothes for him, looked after him when he was ill, and gave him a stable home life – something she had failed to do properly with Julie. By the time Gary reached secondary school, the pattern was set. Julie would sometimes turn up at parents' evenings but, when she did, gave the impression of being impatient. Usually dressed up to the nines, Julie would arrive with no make-up and wearing plain clothes. Alice Watkinson remembers: 'One parents' evening I was sat waiting to see the English teacher. Julie was sat beside me. She played merry hell. She was getting very ratty. She was not happy about being kept waiting. I said to her: "We'll have to take our turn," but she wasn't happy.'

Gary was known as a quiet lad but by the time he reached sixteen he was giving Julie problems. Rebelling against Julie's tradition of designer clothes and glamour, Gary wore ripped t-shirts held together with safety pins, his hair was spiky with gel and he considered himself a punk. It was 1976, the era of the Sex Pistols, who advocated anarchy, and Gary joined the crowd.

His appearance offended Julie, but her worry turned to horror when she learned that some punks were going out 'queer-bashing' and had got into trouble with the police. Julie was great friends with Peter Dudley, who played Bert Tilsley on the *Street*. He was a homosexual, and the thought that her son might mix with people who beat up gays disgusted her.

Thankfully, Gary grew out of his punk phase and started to conform. He was a handsome lad, just over six feet tall, square-shouldered, with dark hair, a dark moustache and a boyish grin. His looks attracted the girls and he now dressed like a man who never questioned his tailor's bill. Friends describe him as an individual, not a man who lived in his mother's shadow. He didn't brag that his Mum was Bet Lynch, he tried to keep it quiet. 'He'd seldom mention the fact that Julie was his mother rather than boast about it,' said Alice Watkinson.

In his teens, Gary and his childhood minder Edna Barlow's son would go dirt-track riding together. As Gary got older, he graduated from bikes to cars and started racing Formula Fords. To pay for his expensive hobby he worked as a body repairer at Neil Ellis motor engineers in Oldham. 'I work to race,' said Gary who, aged twenty-five, had entered ten races in his Hawke DL17, a seven-year-old Formula Ford 1600 racing car.

He desperately needed a sponsor and wrote 200 letters looking for backers, prefering not to ask Julie although, eventually, Julie did help him to buy a car. He said: 'Part of the deal I struck with her was that I carry her name on it.'

Julie occasionally came to watch him race, but it terrified her. Gary said: 'I crashed once and she hasn't been since.'

Gary joined other celebrities' sons who loved to race. At Oulton Park in March 1985, he raced against Scott Stringfellow, son of the London and New York nightclub owner Peter Stringfellow. Peter funded Scott's team and bought him a new £15,000 Reynard 85. Gary was still driving his old Hawke DL17, backed by his boss, motor engineer Neil Ellis.

After his youthful rebellions and problems with Maria Beswick, Gary settled down fairly quickly. On 4 October 1986, aged twenty-six, he married his long-standing girl-friend Suzanne Robinson, a secretary from Sheffield.

Julie hinted that she did not at first approve of his choice. She said: 'I'm probably the classic mother-in-law.

I don't think anyone in the world would have been good enough for Gary in my eyes, but Suzanne and I get on very well now.'

For Gary's big day Julie wore a lilac suit and matching hat and travelled to Sheffield for the wedding. Her third husband, American businessman Richard Skrob, flew to England to be by her side.

Julie still managed to upstage Gary. Four days before the ceremony three men claimed in the newspapers that Julie was a lesbian. With the storm still raging, Julie brazened it out to attend her son's wedding. The church in the village of Dore was besieged by reporters wanting Julie's comments on the lesbian controversy. Clutching husband Richard's arm, she would only say: 'I love my husband and that's all I want to say on this happy sunny day about anything, except that I wish Gary and Suzanne a wonderful life together. I feel very proud. I have a wonderful son, a beautiful daughter-in-law and a fabulous husband.'

A *Coronation Street* insider was surprised that she went at all: 'We didn't think Julie would go to the wedding after all the tales last week. But she told us in no uncertain manner she was going. She said she didn't give a damn about what people thought about her or what had been written.'

Gary refused to talk about the scandal.

9

Falling for Bill

After her thirteen years on the *Street*, millions of men considered Bet Lynch a sex symbol. Her mailbag was stuffed with letters from fellows describing how she featured in their wildest fantasies. One desperate correspondent regularly wrote in lurid detail, telling Bet exactly what he would like to do to her. Each time Julie opened one of his letters she would shout to the cast: 'Here's another one from Master Bates!'

She received hundreds of proposals and, after a storyline in which Bet enrolled with a video-dating agency to find herself a husband, she was buried under a deluge of offers. They came from solicitors, business executives, doctors and even bank managers, who all wrote serious letters offering her anything from a diamond-studded engagement ring to a dirty weekend in the Bahamas.

But that was Bet. At forty-one, Julie was still single, with two broken marriages and a handful of failed engagements, and still no man to share her fame and fortune.

Julie was about to change all that. By the end of the year she would have two suitors desperate to marry her. The dramas both relationships caused would fill newspapers for weeks, but that would be nothing compared with the bizarre revelations to follow. At least three men would declare publicly that Julie was a lesbian who would fight with her gay lovers.

Two years earlier, on a promotional tour to New Zealand, Julie and *Street* producer Bill Podmore had been at Los Angeles Airport waiting for a connecting flight via Fiji. Julie's attention was grabbed by Richard Skrob, a quietly-spoken American businessman dressed in smart Ivy League clothes. He resembled a skinny version of actor Charles Bronson. They chatted for a while, his flight was called and he headed for the check-in desk. Julie said goodbye and walked back to the bar to join Bill.

A few minutes later the bespectacled forty-year-old widower popped his head round the door and announced, 'I've decided to take a later flight; can I sit and wait with you?'

That was the beginning of their bizarre love affair, conducted over transatlantic telephone lines and in snatched visits.

Richard Skrob was a senior airline executive with the Lockheed company. His wife had died a few years earlier, leaving Richard with two grown-up sons and a daughter, Kathy. When he met Julie in 1981 he was lonely and ready for adventure. The attraction was instant, but Julie spent their airport meeting pointing out all the beautiful women walking past them.

The pair became penfriends, then eventually lovers. They were certainly not ideally suited. Richard was a jet-setter. Julie preferred her annual two-week holiday in the sun – somewhere like Tenerife or Tunisia – as well as the grey cobbled streets of Manchester.

Despite the obvious differences and distances between them something kept them together. Dogged in his determination, Richard would call at all hours, often waking Julie. He'd be ringing from somewhere exotic like Bangkok or Berlin, saying how much he missed her. Julie said: 'He kept in touch by letter, too – trying to say all the things on paper that he so rarely had the chance to tell me face-to-face.'

The situation was not ideal, but Richard was determined and repeatedly proposed to her.

The first offer came when Julie flew to California to meet his family; the next was in Paris, during a romantic weekend. He asked her again after he flew to England to be by her side when she opened the Julie Goodyear cancer testing laboratory at Christie's Hospital. Julie never quite knew how to react.

She said later: 'Because I felt so deeply for Richard, his marriage proposals left me with a terrible dilemma. He offered security and a jet-set lifestyle with his luxury homes and yacht. It was tantalizing, but it would have meant leaving *Coronation Street*. In the end the *Street* won. Funny, isn't it? When it came to the crunch those cobbled backstreets in Salford meant more to me than a millionaire's mansion in an exclusive American suburb.'

Julie's interest in the transatlantic love affair began to wane. With Richard still in the background, she met another man. By December 1983, Julie shocked fans and cast by announcing plans to marry her Granada boss, hard-living Scots director Bill Gilmour.

For twelve months they kept the affair secret but,

inevitably, they were rumbled. As Julie and Bill left the studio one night – Julie dressed in a white fur hat and long cream coat – she snuggled up to her new lover in the back of a taxi and they were snapped by paparazzi. Rather than shouting the customary 'No comment', Julie smiled sweetly and said: 'I'm very, very, happy.'

So was the whole family. Julie's mother Alice, now a sixty-one-year-old widow and still looking after twenty-three-year-old Gary at her house in Regent Street, Heywood, said: 'Julie's gone back to being a giggling teenager. I've never seen her so happy. And Bill is such a great guy.'

Son Gary agreed. 'We are both on top of the world. We are very excited about it all. They are both obviously so much in love.'

Julie added: 'Gary and Bill have met a few times now and they get on fabulously.'

Bill's mother Mima told her son in a phone call from her home in Scotland: 'I am very pleased – you've been on your own too long. Julie's a very gutsy lass.'

Word of their engagement got out after Julie's live-in secretary Janet Ross told neighbours she was looking for a flat and hinted that Bill and his daughter Lindsay might be moving in when she moved out. News of the wedding came as a shock to Richard, who knew nothing about Bill.

Julie and Bill were planning a registry office wedding, followed by a church blessing. Julie wanted a traditional do but Bill was an atheist and they were both divorcees, so marriage in church was out of the question.

Bill and Julie had fallen in love at work as he directed her in scenes with her new *Coronation Street* screen lover. To spice up the action between the two actors, Bill would whisper to Julie between takes: 'Just imagine it's me out there with you.' When the cameras stopped rolling, their eyes met and sparks flew. Bill said: 'My knees were trembling with the intensity of my emotions. I just could not believe what was happening to me.'

The story Bill was directing had Bet dating councillor Des Foster, a rat who lured her into bed then asked her to live with him. Their scenes called for plenty of fumbling – it was written into the script – but none actually took place. The *Street* cast could not comprehend why the couple never kissed or cuddled for the cameras, although it was there in the script in black and white, that they should.

'The closest they ever came to touching was when they sat on the sofa and rubbed shoulders,' said Bill. 'I did a bit of rapid juggling with the action. I didn't want another man kissing my woman,' he confessed.

Although Julie and forty-four-year-old Bill were behaving like a couple of lovesick teenagers, the cast remained in the dark about their affair. The only person who guessed was Julie's screen lover, actor Neil Phillips. Bill said: 'At one stage Neil sidled up to me and said, "I'm never going to get to kiss her am I?" "Nope", I said.'

The only other person who guessed was Julie's best friend on the *Street*, Anne Kirkbride, who plays Deirdre Barlow. When Julie walked in glowing the day after Bill proposed, Anne said it was obvious she was in love. 'Anne burst out crying and threw her arms round me,' said Julie. Then Julie asked her to be bridesmaid at the wedding.

Julie and Bill were painfully aware they had both been losers in love. Sensibly, they decided to take it easy until they were sure their love was real. They proceeded with caution. Julie explained, gently understating the chaos of her love-life: 'Both of us had experienced marriages that had turned sour, caused a lot of pain and left a lot of scars. The thought it could happen again prevented either of us from jumping feet first into a relationship. We went very slowly and very, very warily.'

A year later, they threw caution to the winds. They claimed they were full of love and trust for each other and could not wait to tie the knot.

Originally from Edinburgh, Bill was a handsome man. A girlfriend described him in his younger days as 'better-looking than Paul Newman'. Like Julie, Bill had worked his way up the corporate ladder from the bottom. A skilled photographer, he took a course at an art college in Ealing, west London, where he met his first wife, became a cameraman and joined Scottish Television. He stayed there for two years before joining Granada.

He first met Julie during a short stint directing the *Street* while his marriage was breaking up. Wracked with pain over the split, he was not looking for another involvement. He had promised himself he would never marry again.

Ten years later, he was still reconciling himself to life alone. To dull the pain, Bill spent long nights drinking in the local pub, mulling over his life. He would drink until he could hardly stand, but when the pub closed, he would hail a taxi and look for a nightclub and another bottle of whisky.

Julie spotted him one night drinking alone and took pity on him. She said: 'I sat there thinking what a terrible waste of an enormous talent it might turn out to be. Suddenly I could not stand it any more. I yanked him to his feet and told him he was coming back to my place until he sobered up. That night he slept on the sofa. It was the first of many occasions when he woke up sprawled on my lounge furniture.'

When he woke, he'd get dressed, jump in a cab and go back to his own house. The couple claimed nothing sexual happened between them until after Bill became a more moderate drinker.

Julie said: 'The first time we were able to talk, I realized there was something immensely attractive about this man. The more we got to know each other, the closer we became.'

Bill added: 'The first time I asked Julie out on an official date was just a couple of days away from St Valentine's. I had first-night nerves. Julie did as well because, suddenly, our relationship was on a different level. We were no longer meeting as friends but as prospective lovers. It was like any boy taking a girl out for the first time, the same nerves and apprehension – except neither of us were kids.'

The affair was conducted in secrecy. Those who guessed in the Granada fortress would not dare to say a word. Talking would break an unspoken code of conduct – that cast and crew looked after their own.

The lovebirds were equally cautious. When they went out on the town, Bill chose trusted venues where he knew the boss would not be on the phone to the tabloid newspapers. Their first date was in an Armenian restaurant in Manchester where Bill knew the owner. The candles were lit, the atmosphere romantic, except that photophobic Bill could not bear the glare of candlelight so he blew them out.

After dinner, Bill took Julie to a local club, where they sat chatting to friends before he escorted her home in the early hours. Julie showed the green light and the affair was under starter's orders.

The one blot on the horizon was Richard. Bill knew about Richard and was upset that Julie had not broken off the affair. He took a month's holiday in the Scottish Highlands and sifted through his knotted emotions.

While he was away, Julie decided to do the right thing. After a week wrestling with her conscience, she picked up the phone. It rang in California and Richard answered. Julie said: 'I told him about Bill. He was obviously hurt, as disappointed as any man would be in the circumstances, but said he congratulated us both and told me he had only ever wanted my happiness. It was the most distressing conversation I have ever had.'

Richard was less emotional about being dumped. He said: 'It sounds like Julie has had enough. That's that – there's nothing more I can do about it.'

Bill returned from his Scottish sabbatical refreshed and determined to break his vow not to wed. One night, Bill was at Julie's semi in Heywood. It was a homely scene, one which could have come straight from Bet's living room in the *Street*.

Julie's mum Alice was in the kitchen making a pot of tea. Bill was lying flat on his back in front of the telly. Suddenly, he looked across at Julie, sipping brandy in her favourite armchair, and said: 'Would you like us to live together?'

She replied: 'What?'

He said: 'I am proposing. Will you marry me?'

Stunned, Julie said: 'Are you asking me to be your wife?'

'Will you marry me?' came his reply.

Wiping away a tear and suppressing a giggle, Julie gasped. 'Oh, darling, I would love to.'

You can almost hear the director shout: 'Cut! It's a wrap.'

It was official. Julie was engaged for the fifth time and

planning to marry in the New Year, on 5 January 1984. Everyone was delighted, but there was one man – a shy American airline executive – who was heartbroken. When told about his girlfriend's wedding plans, he said coldly, 'I see no point discussing the marriage. Julie has said all there is to say on the matter.'

A few months earlier, in a last-ditch attempt to get her to say 'yes' to his proposals, Richard told Julie that if she married him they could live anywhere in the world. Obviously flattered, she boasted: 'He suggested we buy a lavish flat in Paris from which I could commute to Manchester and the *Coronation Street* set each week. There is nothing this warm, wonderful man would not have done to be able to place a wedding ring on my finger. But that something special was missing – that extra ingredient that tells you that you have found the man you want to live with for the rest of your life. I was feeling something for Bill at this stage that I have never felt for Richard. Richard was so far away, but Bill was always close at hand. If we were not on the same show then we were in the same building. Richard and I were worlds apart – literally.'

When Julie finally said no, Richard gave up and stopped trying to coax her to leave the *Street* and her Heywood haven.

Julie and Bill got on with their wedding plans. As a director, Bill was used to organizing weddings. He had arranged the *Street* wedding between Eddie and Marian Yeats so he figured his own would be a doddle. He fixed everything. He decided Julie should wear white heather in her hair, fixed a date for the blessing with the vicar and ordered a huge champagne bash for the star-studded reception.

Before the ceremony, Julie still faced one big test before

she could feel easy about marrying Bill. She had to win the trust of his fifteen-year-old daughter Lindsay. Julie confessed: 'I was terrified. It was like an audition – except that the stakes were much higher. Because I knew how deeply Bill cared for Lindsay I was petrified that he might be placed in the position of having to choose between me and her. Bill could see how nervous I was but he wasn't in the least bit worried. He knew we would get on like a house on fire.'

Lindsay was staying with her father for the weekend, an ideal opportunity for a meeting, although Lindsay and Julie had already met a couple of years earlier on the *Street*. For two episodes Lindsay had played a tomboy newspaper girl. Now she was being told one of the stars of the show was to be her stepmother.

Bill called Julie at 11 p.m. to tell her he was missing her, then he suggested she get a cab to his house. When the taxi arrived, the cabbie found an excited Julie hopping up and down on the doorstep.

Julie said: 'The next morning I was lying in bed when Bill walked in with Lindsay. Straight away she jumped on the bottom of the bed, gave me a big grin and seconds later we were chatting away like old friends. We ended up ransacking Bill's wardrobe for all his old denim jackets, which were back in fashion, and sharing them out between us while he stood there with a proud grin on his face. It was smashing – a very precious moment which I will never forget.'

Exactly three days before Christmas, just two weeks after the couple had boasted in print of their great romance, the wedding was off. A war of words now broke out between the two lovers, which added more scars to their already savaged personal lives.

In a story more bizarre than any soap script, Julie began talking about the split and claimed that Bill had been partying hard at Granada. The next morning he got up, had a shower, got on the phone and cancelled their wedding. 'I was pleading with him not to do it, but he continued,' Julie explained in anguished tones. 'I followed him from one telephone extension to another, trying to reason with him, but it was no use. He packed his bags and left. I remember thinking how long he had taken to arrange it all, and how quickly it was all cancelled. I suppose you could call it a brainstorm – everything had seemed so right. Perhaps the strain was too much and he just wanted to get away.'

When asked to comment, Bill seemed surprised that the wedding was cancelled. 'Who says it's all off?' he mumbled. When told it was Julie, he commented: 'If Julie says it, that's fine. That's fine!'

Julie blamed the "brainstorm" on Bill's drinking. 'He turned back to whisky for comfort,' she said, 'and I watched our future go down his throat.'

Bill's drinking habits were legendary. As a Scotsman, he loved whisky, but furious at Julie's comments, he hit back, denying his drinking was to blame. 'I'm not a drunkard and I have never been a drunkard,' he stormed, then added sheepishly: 'I have to admit, I've been drinking today.' He was obviously not completely sober when he made the statement.

When asked if he'd been drinking to drown his sorrows, he hit back somewhat incoherently: 'By Christ, I'm not a drunkard and I have never been a drunkard. All I said was I'm slightly drunk tonight!'

Throughout the trauma, Julie was committed to a heavy filming schedule. The ultimate professional, she had filmed through worse dramas than this, the cancer scare being only one. This time, however, she was not sure she could cope.

Doris Speed, who had been away sick for several months, called her. 'Suddenly I was talking to her and crying and sobbing about what had happened,' said Julie. 'My darling Doris was simply wonderful, as she always is, and told me to try to get in to work and look after the bar for her. I said I'd go in because I would do anything for her.'

The cavalry was summoned. Producer Bill Podmore arrived at Julie's home to escort her to the studio. She said: 'I couldn't speak during our journey. All I could remember were my lines as Bet Lynch. It was a relief to be able to hide behind her character. The only problem was my legs were like jelly – I could hardly stand, let alone walk. As a professional actress you go into remote control – then into wardrobe, and then into make-up. There was no sobbing and no crying. You don't do that when you are working.'

However, Julie's performance was not as Oscar-winning as she made out. One *Street* insider said: 'The first anyone knew was when Julie collapsed after another star asked her what she wanted for her wedding present. She ran off in tears but nobody liked to say anything.'

At the end of the day's shooting, Julie went home to an empty house. Bill's presents lay accusingly under the tinsel-covered Christmas tree. The tears came as she opened Christmas cards addressed to her and Bill, all offering their congratulations. She said: 'I was in shock – I thought it was a nightmare which I would wake up from, but I didn't. I thought he would be there, waiting, but he wasn't.'

The following night she decided to call him. The phone rang at his home in Sale, Cheshire. 'I wanted to know if he was all right,' she said. 'I rang him at 7 p.m. and he said: "Fuck off! Have a good Christmas." I couldn't believe it when he hung up. That was the last time I spoke to him.'

Then Julie reflected: 'Thank God sometimes we don't know what is round the next corner. Here I am – supposed to be a January bride – alone and jilted. Even Bet Lynch never had that one to contend with – and she's taken some hard knocks in her time.

Everyone had sympathy for Julie. The *Street* stars rallied round. Lynne Perrie (Ivy Tilsley) said: 'We all feel so sorry for her. She's a great girl, a true friend and she had been so happy.'

Bill's daughter Lindsay came round on Boxing Day to commiserate. Julie said: 'We cried together for what might have been. I was so proud of her that, at fifteen, she had the loyalty and courage and compassion some people never find in their lives.'

The story broke seven days later, just before New Year, and Julie's Heywood home was besieged by reporters. She made a grand gesture and popped out with a bottle of whisky to stave off frostbite in the hacks' freezing fingers.

While the Gilmour/Goodyear drama unfolded, ex-*Street* star Violet Carson lost her fight for life. Julie said of her death: 'It mercifully took my mind off me. My thoughts and love went out to her sister Nellie, who has loved and cared for her for so many years.'

While Julie was talking openly to *The Sun* newspaper and the press were frantically trying to track him down, Bill had taken off and was walking in the Highlands.

Later, he told his side of the story to model and actress Annie Coates.

Annie had worked for Lucy Clayton's with Julie and had also had bit parts in the *Street*. She'd known Bill well for fifteen years. They all used to drink together in the Film Exchange, a Manchester bar frequented by models and Granada employees.

When Annie and Bill got together after the fuss died down, she sat watching a broken man pour out his heart. On the verge of tears, Bill told how he was on a train headed for Scotland, fleeing the mess caused by their cancelled wedding plans when he caught sight of a newspaper. Annie said: 'The man sitting opposite him was reading a tabloid and on the front page was this huge picture of him and Julie. It was a poignant moment because he was trying to run away.'

Then he made a statement to Annie that was totally contrary to Julie's account built round Bill dramatically cancelling their wedding and offering no explanation. Annie remembers: 'He said that Julie had dumped him!'

Queen of the *Street* Pat Phoenix had announced her decision to quit the *Street*. Headlines were jammed with stories about Pat waving goodbye to Weatherfield. Bill said he would not have been amazed if his romance with Julie had been used to get her back into the limelight.

Over dinner at a Chinese restaurant, Bill's extreme anguish became clear. Annie continued: 'He really believed that, because Pat Phoenix was getting all the attention, Julie used their romance to get the attention back. He said it had worked because the papers were full of stories about him and Julie, and interest in Pat had petered out.'

It was true that, for days, stories of their romance had occupied front pages and at least half a dozen double-page spreads.

Annie said: 'He was in a terrible state, he really was. He was crazy about Julie. He was mad about her, absolutely mad about her. He'd been just as devastated when his first marriage ended. When he got engaged to Julie, he thought he'd found real love at last and was over the moon. When they finished he was enormously hurt. I think it was almost the last straw for him. After that he really started drinking.'

By the end of their meal Bill had drunk too much Japanese sake and whisky.

When Julie talked to the papers, she seemed to be desperately searching for a clue to yet another failed romance. She felt like Florence Nightingale, who had tried to save a poor depressed man from the bottle. She painted a picture in which she sat at home pouring her grief into her wet hanky, worrying about her ex-lover who had so cruelly jilted her. Friends have a different story, however, one in which Julie berates Bill for treating her badly.

Ex-*Street* actress Judith Barker, who played Janet Reed, a woman who had several affairs before settling down to become Ken Barlow's second wife, spent a night in the Old School – Granada studios' watering hole where the stars gather and gossip about work – with Julie.

Judith had known Julie for years; her husband, Kenneth Alan Taylor, was Julie's Oldham Rep boss and also plays the *Street*'s brewery boss Ces Newton. Judith explained: 'It was just after this "engagement" had been broken off. I got the impression from Julie that Bill had dumped her. She was very embittered about it. Bill was sitting at the bar, the worse for wear, and Julie was sitting with me, actress Lesley Nicol, Liverpool actor Andrew Schofield and actor Leslie James.

'She didn't want us to go. She kept saying. "Have another drink. Bugger, you're not going home." She didn't ever want you to go. We were probably being used as go-betweens.

'Gradually, you could sense that Bill was becoming part of the conversation. The more Julie had to drink, the more she was drawing him in. She was doing it in a very embittered way.

'As the evening wore on, the conversation was getting very heavy. Obviously there was some sort of unresolved stuff between them.

'Eventually, he came across and sat on a stool – quite drunk – beside her. We did actually go then. When we left they were deep in conversation. A very kind of aggressive sort of nose-to-nose conversation, obviously trying to sort out their problems.'

According to Judith, Julie and Bill's relationship had an element of fantasy in it. 'Their engagement was bizarre,' she claimed. 'Everybody involved in the *Street* knew it was really crazy. We all said: "What is she doing – it's ridiculous".'

Her colleagues assumed the engagement was the result of a drinking spree. 'We thought she probably said what a good idea it was and they both went along with it. She sort of painted a really domestic picture of them both going shopping and going to the bank, and saying it was shut and they'd no money for the weekend. It was almost like that was what she was longing for and I think probably still is. But there is no way she was going to live a normal domestic life. I can't imagine she ever would.'

Back at Granada the big question, of course, was: Would Bill Gilmour work on the *Street* again? The thought of the couple bitching at each other before cameras started rolling was a real problem. Julie said: 'I hope Bill will be as professional as me when we next meet on the *Street*.'

But Granada TV chiefs were seriously considering transferring Bill to another studio. A spokesman said: 'As far as working together is concerned, we will have to assess the whole situation when everyone returns to work.'

When asked to comment, Bill would only make a two-fingered gesture and said he would never tell his side of the story.

Meanwhile, speculation was rife as to whether Julie would be sacked for selling the story of their break-up to *The Sun*. Peter Adamson had been booted out after selling *Street* secrets to the *News of the World*.

However, Granada did not see there was any similarity. A spokesman said: 'The two situations are quite different. We approved of Julie selling her story.'

The dramas and headlines began to subside then, on New Year's Eve, a newspaper story appeared in which Julie really was the heroine. It said: 'Jilted *Coronation Street* star Julie Goodyear stopped an elderly neighbour jumping from a bedroom window with an impromptu dance act. Julie – busty barmaid Bet Lynch – kept up the routine in Heywood, Lancs, until the woman was rescued by relatives. And yesterday the woman's granddaughter, Michelle Siddy, said thank you. Meanwhile Granada TV bosses dismissed rumours that Julie's ex-fiancé, Bill Gilmour, would be sacked.'

Four weeks later, Bill was taken off the show and switched to a new series of *Bulman*, a show about a down-at-heel former police inspector. The move avoided any unnecessary embarrassment for 'jilted' Julie.

Bill made it clear that the move was not down to his broken engagement. He said: 'I have know for some time that I was coming off *Coronation Street* to work on this programme. I could be working on *Bulman* for a year.'

A Granada spokesman added: 'It was always planned for him to be involved with the new series.'

Some of the cast were relieved Bill had gone. They were worried in case bitter rows broke out as Bill tried to direct his ex-lover.

10

A Woman's Woman

Julie had a broken heart to mend. Two weeks before Bill was moved from the *Street*, she jetted off to Florida for a romantic reunion with abandoned lover Richard Skrob. 'It was idyllic,' she beamed when she was spotted arriving back at Heathrow. 'We just shared the sun, sea, coral reefs – and each other.'

Julie said Richard had called her to commiserate over her shattered wedding plans. She jumped at the chance to patch up their neglected romance. 'Forgiving isn't a word we even spoke about,' said a tanned, fit-looking Julie after seven days of Florida sunshine. 'As far as Richard is concerned, there is nothing to forgive. He was very distressed for me. Naturally, we spoke about Bill and the unhappy experience of Christmas. But being in the sunshine does heal wounds. Our relationship has endured the adversity. Talk of marriage is premature but we plan to see each other again very soon.'

Comparing the two lovers, she batted a back-handed

insult in Bill's direction. She said: 'Bill and Richard are as different as chalk and cheese. Richard is a gentleman. The contrast is vast. All Bill and I had in common was work.'

Richard sent a £15,000 Mercedes to cheer her up. Julie burst into rehearsals one day, shouting: 'Come and look at this!' The cast instantly guessed who had sent the expensive gift.

'Does this mean the American affair is back on?' asked Fred Feast.

'Looks like it,' said Julie, leaving her colleagues with their mouths gaping. The romance was simmering again.

The publicity surrounding Julie Goodyear made the public curious. They knew her Heywood address at Rochdale Road East because it was printed in the paper during her trial and acquittal. Hoards of sightseers turned up to check out Bet's abode. Once a coach full of day trippers from Sheffield sat munching sandwiches as they stared at her modest semi.

Others went further to satisfy their curiosity. A teenager who came from Julie's ex-husband Ray's old home town of Blackley, actually broke into Julie's house.

Julie was out, but her Mum, Alice, came home while the girl was still in the house. At first, she hid under the table, then she left her hiding place and found Julie's dog. When Alice saw the seventeen-year-old intruder, she was giving the dog a cuddle. Alice burst into tears with shock and called the police.

The teenager was arrested. She admitted stealing a tie pin and pill box, worth £20, from Julie's home. She told police that she was looking for her mother, who had moved from Salford to Rochdale, but could not find her house. She did not explain how she came to be in Julie's house, which was in neither Salford nor Rochdale.

At her trial, she admitted failing to surrender to bail, claiming she was in a hospital casualty department. Her solicitor, Mr David Foster, described her situation as 'dire'. He said she was in breach of three conditional discharges and a probation order, then asked for a deferred sentence. The judge sentenced her to six months' youth custody.

The experience left Julie shocked, but the break-in was tame compared with the jottings of killer Arthur Hutchinson. Later that year, Julie's name was discovered among his possessions.

In September 1984, murderer Arthur Hutchinson was sentenced to life imprisonment after being found guilty of a grisly triple murder. Among his prison notes Hutchinson listed women who could have been targets for robbery or rape. Alongside their names were descriptions like 'well-preserved', 'lives alone' or 'widow'. Julie was included in the list.

As all these dramas unfolded, Julie finally agreed to marry Richard. He promised her anything she wanted and agreed to take second place to the Rovers.

In January 1985, Julie, almost forty-three, without telling the cast, slipped off to the Bahamas for a secret wedding. It was Julie's third attempt at a successful union.

Alice had been briefed to stay silent about the event. All she would say while the couple were on honeymoon, was: 'She seems to be happy and having a good time. I expect she is lying on a beach soaking up the sun right now, and I don't blame her. People keep asking about a romance but I am not saying a word.'

Julie also refused to comment. All she would say later was: 'He is a gentleman and treats me like a lady. He came into my life out of the blue. I've never met a man like Richard before. He treats me with such kindness and respect and, to be truthful, I've rarely inspired that kind of reaction from men.'

Julie shrugged off reports that she was leaving the *Street* to join Richard. When she told the cast over lunch that she had married again, she warned them: 'That doesn't mean you are getting rid of me.'

Her relationship seemed ideal. Julie had her freedom, her job and a man. They had a plush flat in Paris, where they met whenever possible but, within months, the marital seams had started to split. A report appeared saying that Richard was still grieving for his first wife, Karla, who had died of cancer four years earlier.

Then, when Julie got back to work in the *Street* after the honeymoon, she was thrown into the limelight by a series of challenging storylines.

Weatherfield's first lady, Annie Walker, had retired. Son Billy Walker had sold the pub to the brewery and Bet had been mooted to take over the Rovers as landlady. If she got the job, it would be an historic occasion. No single barmaid had been promoted to landlady before and she would have to work hard to prove herself.

Julie also got a ticking off from the *Street*'s producer Bill Podmore who, according to a Granada source, had hauled Julie over the coals, saying her love-life was overshadowing her role as Bet. A *Street* insider said: 'Julie is under incredible pressure and it is beginning to show, even though she is as hard as nails. When Julie returned home from her honeymoon in Barbados, she was immediately plunged back into the show's limelight as the new manager of the Rovers. The gruelling work schedule has meant that she and Richard have not been able to see each other. Their only contact has been by phone.'

Colleagues said Julie had gone from a bundle of fun to a bag of nerves.

A year later, on Boxing Day, Julie left the country to be with Richard. She arrived at Richard's Los Angeles home in the suburb of Uplands to begin celebrating their first wedding anniversary. She knocked on the door, Richard opened it and whisked her off her feet, carried her to the bathroom, switched on the jacuzzi and threw her in. Later, he gave her a beautifully wrapped box – her anniversary gift. Inside was a Hollywood version of Joseph's technicolour dreamcoat – a multi-coloured sequined outfit, fit for a soap star. Richard had bought it in central LA for Julie to wear at the anniversary villa he had booked in Puerto Vallerta in Mexico.

She seemed happy with their unconventional marriage. She said: 'We manage very well – how often we meet is our secret. Some people might think our marriage is unusual but that depends what standard you are going by. We all get on very well together as a family and there hasn't been any problem. I get on with my neighbours out here too although this is hardly *Coronation Street* and people are not in and out of your door all the time. I have found the people here absolutely charming. I have met them so often now that they know I am an actress in England. At first they didn't.'

However, some neighbours still seemed unsure as to who Julie was. Mrs Ginny Becker, an old friend of the family who was close to Richard's first wife Karla, said: 'I've never met the lady or even seen her here.'

Mrs Becker did not even know her neighbour had married until two months after the event. She said: 'This is a quiet, old-fashioned neighbourhood and people keep themselves to themselves. But I have certainly not noticed this lady visiting or been introduced to her.'

Julie and Richard boarded a plane for Mexico. To record the anniversary celebrations, they took top photographer Alan Olley with them.

When they arrived, Julie opened her suitcase and brought out her anniversary cards. Bits of confetti floated to the floor, a reminder of their wedding day. It was an old ploy. Richard's romantic streak was stirred. While Julie unpacked, he arranged to dine by candlelight under the stars. While the Pacific rolled gently on to the beach and the champagne flowed, the couple looked longingly at each other.

Alan was there, sharing the intimacy. He said: 'I was amazed. Nothing was too much trouble for Richard – he really seemed besotted with her. I found their physical contact quite incredible. It was non-stop. They held hands all day and were always kissing each other. Sometimes she'd turn to him and say, "I am the luckiest woman in the world" and he'd lovingly reply, "Yes, and I'm the luckiest man in the world."'

Although Richard is generally shy and quiet, he was extremely protective towards Julie and went out of his way to make sure everything was just right for her.

Julie would sigh: 'Forget women's libbers. I love being pampered. Give me more!'

It was January 1986. Julie arrived back at Heathrow and climbed off the plane with a couple of male escorts. She grinned: 'I met these chaps on the plane when they came up and said they were great fans.'

A few months later, there were rumours that the marriage was over. These were nothing compared with what was to come.

Julie's personal life was about to crash. A bizarre

ménage à quatre would be revealed, which would expose a ruthless side to Julie, which fans and supporters could hardly believe existed. The stories would accuse Julie of having a lesbian relationship, of stealing another woman's husband, of using Richard Skrob for a 'lavender marriage' (a marriage of convenience to hide her gay secret) and destroying the lives of her lovers.

At first the reports seemed incredible. But as more intimate and lurid details came to light, backed up with photographs of the star dressed in suits and ties, jackboots and braces, her arm around butch-looking women, the story picked up credibility.

The story began to unfold on 9 June 1986. Splashed on the front page of *The Sun* was a report from cabbie's wife Helen Ford, who claimed that Julie had stolen her husband.

The Lancashire mother in her mid twenties was distraught after her husband Duncan, twenty-nine, had dumped her for Julie. However, she soon recovered from the shock and declared: 'I was very upset at the time. Before she came along I thought we were happy. I've nothing against her because she did me a good turn. She's welcome to him. I have another man now and I couldn't be happier.'

Duncan, it seems, was not as happy as his ex-wife. Four months earlier, an ex-business partner and friend of the out-of-work cabbie, known only as Barry, witnessed astonishing scenes at Julie's Heywood home.

One night he arrived to pick up Duncan. It was midnight. Julie appeared, wearing a dressing gown, and threw Duncan out into the street. The twenty-five-year-old Heywood-based cab driver said: 'Julie rang my office, shouting for me to go to the house. When I got there, she came to the door and asked me to get Duncan out. Eventually he came out fully clothed. She was very angry and he was upset. Julie disappeared and came back with holdalls and hangers with his suits on. She threw the whole lot into the garden. Duncan opened one of the holdalls, got a can of lager out and had a drink in her garden until police arrived and asked him to go.'

Police confirmed that they had had a midnight 999 call from Julie in February. The report was disturbing because the incident happened just one month after Julie's romantic first-anniversary celebrations. On the occasions when Richard came to visit, Barry said Julie would throw Duncan out. When Richard returned to the States, Duncan would move back in.

Barry confirmed: 'I would regularly drop Duncan off at her house at the end of his driving shift. He was living there.'

After the story appeared, Duncan was spotted in Julie's back garden and grunted: 'I'm only the bloody gardener here.'

The row died down, but a week later Julie was back in the headlines, not over her love-life but because a *Coronation Street* stunt had gone horribly wrong. Filming a spectacular blaze at the Rovers, Julie had refused a stand-in and was almost asphyxiated by smoke.

The scenes saw cellarman Jack Duckworth replacing fuses in the pub's antiquated fuse box. Bet showed complete faith in his abilities and told regulars who watched the lights and pumps go off for the umpteenth time: 'Worry not, booze artists. Cometh the hour, cometh the man with the power an' the knowledge! Superspark'll soon have the ale flowin'.' When the lights went down yet again, Jack replaced the five amp fuses with thirty amp ones.

At the end of the night, Bet retired with a paperback to her frilly, pink satin boudoir, unaware that the overloaded fuse box was starting to smoke. By the time the tinder-dry cables ignited, Bet was fast asleep.

The fire was spotted by Kevin Webster and his girlfriend Sally who had been at an all-night concert in Sheffield. They raised the alarm and, within minutes, Percy Sugden, Terry Duckworth, Ken Barlow, wife Deirdre and daughter Tracey were all in the street.

The commotion woke Bet, who rushed to her door and staggered blindly into a smoke-filled pub, crawling on her hands and knees, desperately searching for an escape route. All exits were blocked by fire and she staggered back to the bedroom and fell to the floor calling for help.

It was an historic moment. After twenty-six years of watching regulars supping pints in the snug, viewers saw the Rovers destroyed in a spectacular blaze. Sally Whittaker, who plays Sally Webster, said: 'It was just the most exciting thing that had ever happened. This wonderful building, that everyone in the country knew, was about to burn down.'

Realism nearly cost Julie her life. The staged blaze suddenly roared stronger than expected and Julie was overcome by fumes. An ambulance was called and she was rushed from the studios to nearby Salford Hospital. Reliving her experience, Julie said: 'It was bloody frightening, I can tell you. I felt lousy for some days afterwards. But I suppose I was lucky really.'

In her handbag, Julie carried a Polaroid snapshot of herself looking drawn and smoke-blackened. She said: 'I knew that using a stuntman wouldn't look right. They had firemen on the set, who pointed out the danger, but once the blaze started, it became much more fierce than we had expected. It was so fierce that a flight of stairs in the scene unexpectedly collapsed. The cameras were covered in asbestos to protect them from the heat. I knew I was in trouble when they started to melt. The smoke and fumes just seemed to smother me. I thought I was a goner. There's black smoke and white smoke in fires. The black smoke is really toxic fumes. The intention was that only white smoke should come anywhere near me, but the problem happened because the fire got so fierce.'

Julie was treated for the effects of smoke on her throat, nose and lungs. She was released from hospital and told that she would have to film the scene again.

On 18 June 1986, she was seen on screen in her nightdress as firemen fought desperately to save her life.

While the scorched interior of the Rovers was being gutted and renovated, Julie's public image was also being torched. The soap queen saw her carefully manicured veneer go up in plumes of thick black smoke.

Three months after the first Duncan Ford story appeared, the out-of-work cabbie decided to tell his side. Details of a sordid love triangle between Julie, her Scottish personal assistant Janet Ross and Duncan emerged, with hovering husband Richard Skrob in the background, oblivious to the sexy goings on, jetting in for dutiful tri-annual visits.

In a story more suited to the pages of a sleazy magazine, Duncan told how he had met forty-four-year-old Julie three years earlier when he arrived at Granada studios in his cab to take her home. According to mustachioed Ford, Julie lured him back to her house, invited him in for coffee and, in the middle of a passionate kiss, issued a four-letter ultimatum. 'You can either fuck off home or get up those fucking stairs,' she told the stunned driver who was standing in her kitchen.

'Right, I'll go home,' said Duncan who could not have been more terrified if he had been told to drive Ena Sharples to the shops for a new hairnet. Insulted at his rebuff, Julie gave him a swift right-hander across the face. Obviously used to having his face slapped, Duncan said: 'It was one of the hardest clouts I've ever had from a woman.'

What the cabbie's attraction was is not certain. Duncan could not boast the appearance of a virile super-stud. With his thinning hair, pinched face and scrawny body, he could not match some of the handsome lovers Julie had dated. However, Julie seemed determined to have him.

'After she hit me, I thought I had written off all business with her,' he said. He was wrong. The next day, ignoring her Mercedes in the garage, Julie was on the phone requesting that he drive her to work. Duncan began to weaken. He said: 'On Monday, I drove her home from work. She said, "I've been at the champagne again". She had said that on the Saturday when she hit me. I was coming to realize that it was her way of suggesting she wanted to make love – a code-word. I told her to stop messing about.'

However, married Duncan, fifteen years younger than Julie, was coming round to the idea of being a soap star's toyboy. He vowed that if Julie came out with the same line the next day, he would stay the night.

It was Wednesday evening and Duncan had settled into a routine of picking Julie up from the studio and dropping her at home, turning down her advances then going back for more the next day. When Julie sighed yet again from the back seat, 'I've been on the champagne again,' Duncan thought: 'Right, we're on.'

Julie couldn't make love to him fast enough. Within moments, the mismatched pair were cavorting in a steaming bubble bath. Then Julie allegedly made a confession which stopped the passion in mid-flow: 'I'm a lesbian!' she said. Then she told Duncan that her gay lover was butch-looking Janet Ross, her personal assistant, who was in the kitchen cooking the three of them a meal.

'At first I refused to believe it,' he said. 'After all, we were giggling in the bath at the time and Janet, who was cooking tea downstairs, must have been able to hear us.'

Then Julie went on to confess that Janet was not her first female lover. She said an affair with another woman, which lasted four years, had finished after the girlfriend deserted Julie when she discovered the star had cancer. After the woman had left her in the lurch, Julie slept with Janet. Her excuse for the affair was that, for a year, she had been imprisoned by the media, who wanted details of her illness, and Janet was her only comfort. 'What was I supposed to do,' Julie told Duncan. 'Kept in for twelve months and seeing no one but Janet.' Conveniently, Julie forgot to mention her other lovers, Bill Gilmour and Richard Skrob.

Duncan seemed unperturbed, even curious about the tantalizing arrangement, and moved in. After all, isn't it a male fantasy to be in bed with two women? However, a steamy threesome was not on the agenda.

From the minute he waved goodbye to his wife Helen and her five-year-old son David, and arrived, clutching his holdall, Duncan was caught in a cat-fight. He fought hard to emerge as the triumphant tom. He immediately made moves to mark his territory and insisted that he be the only one to sleep next to the soap star. He said: 'I can see now that both Janet and I were fighting for Julie's love. It was an incredible love triangle – a man and a lesbian fighting over the star. Janet just couldn't hide her jealously over me being the one Julie slept with. Julie tried to blame Janet's moods on premenstrual tension but the truth was written all over Janet's face.'

Julie seemed to enjoy the fireworks. She lit the blue touch paper and retired.

Considering that Julie was supposed to be a lesbian, none of her passion for men had dulled. Duncan described her as a wild, passionate lover and revealed, in explicit detail, her sexual habits. 'In bed she was no innocent,' he recalled. 'She could easily jump on top of you. That first night she showed no shyness at all in undressing in front of me and making love. She was a real, full, passionate woman.

'She started off by telling me that I was getting a "forty-year-old virgin",' said Duncan. 'She said she could go without sex easily and that she had not really had sex since the birth of her son Gary when she was a teenager.' With that thought in the back of her mind, no wonder Julie 'went like a train'.

Duncan continued describing their sexual antics. He said: 'We had it in bed, on the settee and once we even had it in the garden during the day. We just threw a blanket on the ground and made love fully dressed, although we both knew we were taking a hell of chance of being seen.

'At the end of our romance she bought a Rolls-Royce – a two-tone job, gold and brown. She said she wanted to have me on the back seat. Unfortunately, we never did get around to that.'

However, their romance did have problems. Duncan recalled how one night Julie produced a gun and threatened to blow off his manhood. She had been given the pistol by Richard for protection. After a blazing row with Duncan, she grabbed it and fired it at the ceiling. Trembling, Duncan said: 'Thank God, the gun only had blanks in it. Julie pointed it at the ceiling and fired it, saying: "This is to say fuck off!" The air was filled with smoke. Then she pointed it at my manhood and said, "The next one I'll get you with." I turned sideways to protect my investments – but she didn't fire.'

They had been arguing over Duncan's possessiveness. But there was an upside to the fight. Afterwards they had a steamy sex session to make up. While Ford and Goodyear were in bed, Janet haunted the couple, popping up every so often to remind them she was still there.

At the time, Duncan had no feelings about Janet but, later, guilt set in and he began to feel a bit of a heel. 'You could see what it was doing to Janet,' he said. 'She resented my even being there. Other times, Janet would watch the two of us cuddling on the settee and snappily say, "I'm going to bed now." The whole scene was bad news.'

Duncan told how he dabbled in Julie's lesbian-orientated social life. Twice he escorted her to Manchester gay clubs. Julie claimed they were the only venues where she would not be mobbed.

One place did not appreciate the heterosexual lovers smooching on the dance-floor and they were almost beaten up for being too straight. Duncan said: 'I was dancing with Julie with my leg between hers and it wasn't going down too well with the "locals". She went to the toilet and while she was sitting on the loo the door was

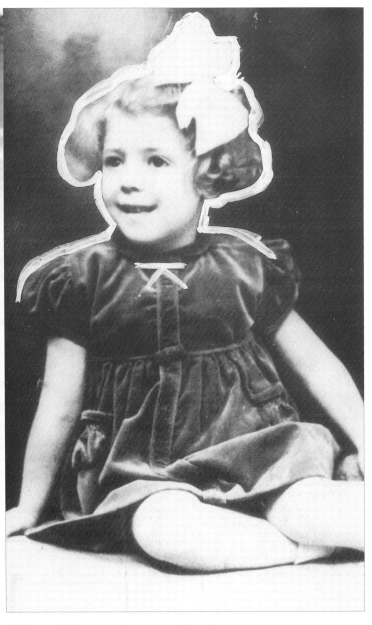
Julie, aged five, was already performing.

Top: Julie, in school uniform, cuddling her mum.
Above: Julie dressed in her best frock for a Sunday School outing.

Top left: Julie at 14 (*right*), on holiday in Torquay with her best pal Sue Skelton.

Top right: Julie, teenage beauty.

Above: 15-year-old Julie stands out in the Queen Elizabeth School photo (*second row down, third from left*) – May 1957.

Below: The original Avro magazine feature showing Julie before, as "Julie The Shorthand Typist", and after, as a "Vamp". The caption cautions: "To subdue the wolf whistles we must point out that Julie is now Mrs. Sutcliffe

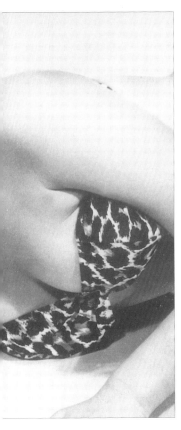

Top: At 17, Julie worked as a typist for the aviation firm Avro. This stunning shot appeared in Avro's in-house magazine, and Julie became the factory pin-up.

Right: Julie winning the Britvic Beauty Contest. "What a laugh it turned out to be. I had to drink a glass of the stuff in every one of the fifteen pubs along the Golden Mile in Blackpool."

Top: In 1958 Julie, the youngest in the cast (*bottom left*), was awarded the Head Master's Dramatic prize for her part in the school play 'We Must Kill Toni'.

Above: Later, at Oldham Rep, Julie (*top, far left*) makes the most of her role as slave girl in 'A Funny Thing Happened On The Way To The Forum'.

An early test shot. In the sixties, Julie signed with the
Manchester branch of Lucie Clayton's modelling agency.

Julie and 'Coronation Street' creator, Tony Warren, pose outside Buckingham Palace after the presentation of the MBE to Tony by the Queen in December, 1994.

Above: Julie and Ray split and divorced in 1963. Julie had more affairs and one broken engagement before announcing wedding plans to Jack Diamond in 1973.

Left: Aged 17 and pregnant, Julie married 23-year-old draughtsman Raymond Sutcliffe, a fellow Avro employee.

Top: Julie stunned friends by announcing her engagement to Geoff Cassidy's pal Tony Rudman. The marriage was blessed at Bury Parish Church (*son Gary Goodyear sits between Julie and his new stepfather*). Tony and Julie rowed at the reception and later separated.

Right: Friends claim Geoff Cassidy was the first "real" love in Julie's life.

Top: Street director Bill Gilmour planned a fairytale wedding to Julie, but three days before Christmas 1983, Bill cancelled all plans.

Above: In 1983, the same year as her shortlived engagement to Bill Gilmour, Julie became engaged to Richard Skrob. They married in 1985.

Gary Goodyear and mother, Julie, kiss at Gary's wedding to
Suzanne Robinson, October 1986.

Kissogram "Outrageous Toy Boy Tony", Tony Sipes, was 22 when he first met 47-year-old Julie. They split after details of their affair came out. Tony committed suicide a year later.

Above: Julie could afford a mansion but prefers to live in her modest semi in Heywood.

Opposite top right: Julie and her mother were always close. Julie was shattered when her mother became terminally ill with cancer.

Opposite below: Appearing on TV, Julie urged women to have regular cancer check-ups.

Above: Beside the sea in Blackpool – Julie cuddles baby Gary.

Below: Joyful Julie holds a laughing Gary by Ray and Julie's Hillman Minx.

kicked in by a few angry gay women. Meanwhile, four or five men had surrounded me and asked if I was married to her. I told them where to go and when Julie came back in a couple of bouncers ushered us out.'

Eventually Duncan became curious about Julie's gay sex-life and started probing for details. 'I once asked Julie how she did her lesbian stuff,' he said. 'But she would only say. "That's a very cheeky question."'

Ford's story marked the beginning of a battle between two tabloid newspapers, *The Sun* and the *Daily Star*, to expose Julie's lesbian love-life. While Ford talked at length to *The Sun*, scapegoat businessmen Bill Clarke and Rodger Forster – the men who pleaded guilty during the Julie Goodyear Trust fraud trial – talked to the *Daily Star*.

In his story, Clarke went further into Julie's bizarre sex-life than Ford and described how the woman who appeared twice a week as Britain's sexiest landlady had had a string of female lovers, including a senior TV executive, Janet Ross, her sister Joanne and a black girl.

He told how she loved to dress as a man, choosing collar, tie and three-piece suits, wearing them with leather boots. He also said her closest non-sexual relationships were with gay men, but occasionally she had sex with straight men, explaining to Bill: 'I have always wanted to find a man who could turn me on as much as a woman can. That's the way it's really supposed to be isn't it? I just want to be normal like everyone else. In my position it would be much safer.'

Rodger added: 'She'd got a helluva lot to lose if her secret came out and she knew it. But she just couldn't help herself. I felt quite sorry for her, really. There she was, the big public star with that randy man-hungry image who, in real life, wanted to make love to women.'

Julie would often call Bill and Rodger and ask them to make up foursomes with her and Janet. But Janet's presence did not stop her chatting up other girls. Bill said: 'Usually, Julie liked ultra-feminine girls. She would march up to them in nightclubs or even public places and proposition them straight out. Occasionally, she would choose the wrong ones. How some very nasty scenes stayed out of the headlines I'll never know. By the time Janet Ross came on the scene, five years ago, she was into more butch, very masculine women. Janet wasn't the first, but she was the longest-lasting and most serious. Julie and Janet were like man and wife – in that order.'

In his kiss 'n' tell, Bill Clarke said he and his business partner Rodger Forster were intimate friends with Julie for two years. He said they paid weekly visits to an assortment of British gay bars and clubs with Julie and Janet Ross. Taking the men into her confidence, Julie told them about her inner turmoil over the stark contrast between her public image and her private preferences.

Bill and Rodger, who were living together in a mobile home in Lancashire, first met Julie in early 1980 when they hired her to open an event they were staging. They became friends. From the outset they suspected Julie was sexually attracted to women. Any doubts were soon scotched by Julie herself. Bill said: 'She invited me and Rodger out for a meal to a little Italian restaurant in Manchester. Julie turned up with a pretty, well-dressed redhead who turned out to be her latest girlfriend.

'Virtually as soon as she sat down, she told us straight out that she was gay and that she had always preferred girl lovers to men – though she had had a few of them, too. From that evening, every time we saw her over the next two years, she openly displayed her lesbian activities and talked constantly about them.'

Rodger added: 'She waited until her girlfriend went to the toilet, then said to me: "I'm trying to get it to bed." Then she started going on about how she was gay. When the girl came back, the discussion carried on as if we were talking about the price of fish. After that Julie and her gay life were discussed openly with us.'

Bill said Julie used them to pick Janet up in the first place. She told them she'd seen a girl she really fancied in a gay club in Blackpool called Lucy's, and asked them to take her back there. For two weeks the three of them kept visiting the club until, one night, Janet walked in with her sister Joanne and a gang of lesbian friends.

Within minutes, Julie was by Janet's side and the two women spent the rest of the evening holding hands and chatting in a quiet corner. Two weeks later, Julie invited Janet to move in.

In the months that followed, the two men shared cosy moments with the star and her girlfriend and watched while they petted, kissed and cuddled, like any two ordinary lovers. They witnessed Janet's anguish as Julie chatted up other women and taunted her with tales of her infidelities.

Bill listened while Julie boasted of her conquests. He said: 'Julie grabbed my arm when we were in a gay club one night and pointed out a gorgeous-looking black girl. She boasted: "See her, I've had her. She was great."

'She would stand there, surveying the talent, then move in – and if Janet was there as well, tough luck.'

On one occasion, Julie seduced Janet's sister Joanne. Rodger said: 'Joanne stayed at Julie's house one weekend and Julie told us – and Janet – that she had seduced her. For months after that Janet and Joanne didn't talk to each other. They were jealous of each other. Julie just laughed it off. If Janet was having a bad time, Julie didn't care.'

Bill produced photographs of Julie cuddling with Janet's sister Joanne as proof of the affair. The clothes Julie had on were a million miles from Bet Lynch and the elegant dresses she was known for. She wore a masculine jacket, shirt, tie and riding boots and Joanne wore a similar outfit.

Janet had a much softer look than her sister. Both had cropped hair. Janet wore no make-up, masculine clothes and a gold star of David which hung from a chain round her neck.

Clarke alleged they were husband and wife and that, despite Julie's feminine appearance, she was the dominant one. He also said she played the part of the unfaithful husband and claimed the couple had terrible rows over Julie's infidelities. He said: 'It was Julie trying to pick up other girls or boasting about girls she had had sex with – she used much more blunt language – that usually started the rows with Janet.'

Julie was starting to lead a double life. By day she would dress like a TV star and behave like one too. In public she was the perfect lady. At night, she would change into her true gay self.

In public, she ate nowhere but the classiest restaurants and clubs and dressed in £500 gowns. In the gay clubs – she liked them to be particularly seedy – she seemed to think the rougher and scruffier the better. She felt at home in the dingy clubs she visited in Ashton-under-Lyne, Preston and Blackpool.

'I used to get embarrassed going into those places,'

squirmed Bill. 'But not Julie, she loved it. She would stand there dressed in her men's suit and boots, with a brandy and Babycham in her hand, eyeing up all the girls. I suppose it was because she was free of all the public pressure to be man-hungry Bet Lynch, that she could at last show her true feelings. And they were gay.'

Reporters caught up with Julie at her home as she left for a meeting with Granada bosses who wanted the truth about the publicity. They asked her to comment on the gay revelations. Speaking from the back of her gold and brown Rolls-Royce, wearing a low-cut white dress with a jewelled motif on one shoulder, she said, totally non-plussed: 'What has appeared in the paper is interesting. In fact it is fascinating.' But did she deny it? 'Let's say some of the facts are not as accurate as they could be,' she said coolly, then added: 'You're trying to make me sound more interesting than I really am.'

Later, after a carpeting from Granada bosses, Julie issued an angry statement which said: '*The Sun's* last story about me claimed I had stolen somebody's husband. I didn't respond to that because everybody knew that was nonsense and I'm not going to respond to this either. I can't understand why anyone should want to spread such malicious stories about us, the cast of the show generally, above all in this particular week.'

A week earlier, Julie and most of the *Street* cast had attended the funeral of the programme's former star Pat Phoenix. Julie was heavily criticized for arriving in a huge show-stealing hat, upstaging Pat at her own funeral. It seemed to be a case of the queen is dead; long live the queen.

As the week wore on, Julie broke her silence and said: 'I am a normal person, leading a normal life and I just do the things normal people do. I'm a lady. And that's the way I want to come out of this attempt to discredit me.'

Granada's managing director David Plowright backed her. In an unprecedented statement, which seemed to be as much concerned with the *Street*'s reputation as Julie's, he said: 'This invasion on her private life is an unfair and malicious attack. This is yet another unfair attempt to denigrate a member of the cast of *Coronation Street*. Thankfully, these efforts to damage the popularity of the *Street* and the affection in which it is held by millions of viewers always fail.'

What neither David nor Julie explained was why anyone would want to ruin her reputation. None of the other *Street* stars faced this kind of vendetta; why should Julie be singled out? As Britain's top female singer Kim Wilde once said: 'I've read kiss and tells about people I know and from my experience they pretty much deserve what is said.'

While Julie ran the gauntlet, Julie's 'Girl Friday', Janet Ross, went into hiding. The thirty-three-year-old personal assistant was found five days later and said the story was 'vicious lies'. 'In all the years I was in that house', she said from her bolt-hole in Blackpool, 'there was never any physical contact between us. I would go to court with my hand on my heart and tell them that what has been said about us is total and utter rubbish.'

However, Janet, who then gave up 'secretarial' work and got a job as a precision engineer in West Lothian, Scotland, did reveal that they led a bizarre life.

When Janet accompanied Julie on personal appearances, her job was to light Julie's cigarettes and fetch her brandy and Babychams. She waited hand and foot on Julie, even washing her silver Mercedes car, and she was on duty twenty-four hours a day, seven days a week, with time off only when it suited the soap star.

In addition to her personal duties, Janet acted as a skivvy, moving Julie's furniture around on a monthly basis so that the carpet did not wear. Her salary was just £60 a week. Janet said: 'In the end I had to leave because I wanted a private life and I couldn't have one working for Julie.'

After the furore, Janet left Heywood and moved to a three-bedroomed council house in Livingston, near Edinburgh. A steelworker's daughter, who once worked as a coach-builder, Janet said she played for the local ladies' darts team but had no friends. Dressed in a leather jacket, jeans and red lace-up shoes, she confessed: 'I know I look butch. I often wear shirts and ties.'

Talking about her own and her employer's love-lives, she said neither was bothered about sex: 'I didn't have sex in the four years I worked with Julie but it didn't bother me. We did once share a bed in a hotel because we had both been booked into the same room. Julie wore a frilly negligée and I wore striped cotton pyjamas. We just went to sleep. There was nothing physical between us – there never has been,' she insisted.

Despite Janet's denial, Julie must have been sweating over her future in the *Street*. When Peter Adamson was aquitted after being tried for indecency, he sold his story for £50,000 to cover legal expenses. Furious, Granada fired him. Julie's critics were wondering if she would also get the bullet. If she did, how would Bet be written out of the show? Would Lancashire's lustiest barmaid be found hanging from one of her own earrings or would she be found at opening time, impaled on one of her own beer pumps?

Meanwhile, the show must go on. Back at the *Street*, the cast read the story in the *Daily Star* and dreaded facing Julie. What could they say to a woman they had known for fifteen years who had just been exposed as a lesbian? As if that pressure wasn't bad enough, they had an extremely heavy schedule. The day after the story appeared, it was the producer's run.

For the producer's run, the actors would don their best clothes and run through the two episodes about to be filmed. The whole crew – technicians, cameramen, writers, director – would watch as the cast rehearsed the latest scripts. Producer Bill Podmore would sit taking notes and, after the run-through finished, would instruct the writer and director as to any necessary changes.

Everyone was nervous before producer's run, even Eileen Derbyshire, who plays Emily Bishop, and has been in the soap for twenty-six years, since episode three. That morning Julie was not expected until 11 a.m. Conversation in the green room was all about the exposé, with the actors asking: 'Why today? She's going to be nervous enough as it is.'

Kenneth Alan Taylor was making a rare appearance as brewery boss Ces Newton that day. He fully expected Julie to sneak in unnoticed and hide herself in a corner refusing to talk. At 11 a.m., right on time, no doubt thinking in Bet Lynch mode, Julie made a brazen entrance. Ken was astonished by what he saw. He said: 'Julie had on a cream, man's suit and a cream trilby hat. She said: "If you've got it, flaunt it. If they think I'm a dyke then I'll dress like a dyke". The fact she appeared not bothered defused the situation and the cast breathed a huge sigh of relief.'

Bill Clarke claimed at least two *Coronation Street* actors

knew about Julie's gay secret. He said Chris Quentin, who played Gail Platt's first husband Brian Tilsley, and Johnny Briggs, who stars as smooth-talking factory boss Mike Baldwin, had different reactions when they found out. 'Johnny Briggs was taken aback, but Chris accepted the situation,' said Bill.

Fred Feast told how he was introduced to one of Julie's female lovers. He said: 'Julie and I had been working late and she was putting on a stunning evening dress to go nightclubbing. As I left to go to my digs, she said: "On your way out, you'll see a good-looking fella waiting for me in the foyer. Tell him I'm nearly ready." When I went downstairs all I could see was a black woman in a man's tuxedo. I asked her, "Are you waiting for Julie?" She said, "Yes."

When I challenged Julie about her, she admitted: "That's the way it is, Fredface."'

Later, Julie confided in Fred about her affairs with girls and men. She told him of her lengthy sex sessions with Janet. 'If Julie needed to relax, she and Janet would stock up on food and enjoy each other,' said Fred. 'Sometimes their curtains stayed closed for four days. No man ever did for Julie what women did.'

Other colleagues and friends were astonished by the lesbian revelations and could not quite connect the stories with the Julie they knew. Kenneth said: 'She certainly wasn't gay in the Oldham Rep days. When they first started saying she was, I thought, "This isn't the Julie I know." I would have said she was 150 per cent heterosexual. I remember her telling me once she did it in a big plastic bag with a fella. I said: "Why Julie?" She said: "Because I'd never done it like that before."'

Audrey Brogden had seen Julie in the Hart with a butch-looking woman wearing a pin-striped trouser suit and had assumed her masculine attire was a fashion statement, although the woman's appearance was so masculine that one of the elderly bar staff referred to her as 'Sir'.

Geoff Nuttall remembered being introduced to a tall woman by Julie in the Hart one night, whom she referred to as 'Bill'.

Tony Rudman, Julie's ex-husband, was more candid. He said: 'I know from my personal experience – since our divorce – that she had lesbian girlfriends. If you go back ten years [1976] I saw Julie regularly necking in the local pub [White Hart] with a woman who was as butch as they come. She made no secret of it. They'd sit and kiss and cuddle for us all to see. Then they'd go out into the car park, get in some beat-up old Dormobile van the other woman had, and drive off into the night.

'It didn't just happen once – and I'm talking from my personal experience, from what I witnessed with my own eyes – but regularly. If you went round the pubs and clubs of Heywood, where she lives, then nine out of ten people you ask know she is gay. She's never really tried to hide it from the locals. Well, she couldn't, considering how blatant it was.'

The gay story was gaining credibility and was being picked up by all forms of media. Millions of viewers watched as Julie was left speechless after a *faux pas* by television presenter Fern Britton. During an interview for Southampton-based TVS television, Fern intended to ask Julie when single Bet would get a new boyfriend. Instead she said: 'When is Bet Lynch going to get a new girlfriend?' She quickly corrected herself and said: 'I mean boyfriend.'

After an awkward pause, Julie roared with laughter at the slip-up and quipped: 'Shame on you – is that an offer?'

The lesbian controversy sparked many a pub row. Drinkers were divided in their opinions. Could sexy Bet Lynch be gay? Some thought so, others were convinced she was not. If she was gay, where did that leave husband Richard Skrob?

In a defiant show of unity, Skrob flew in and was snapped wining and dining with his wife at the Portland, a top Manchester hotel. 'We're just a couple of lovebirds,' cooed Richard, dismissing the lesbian tales. 'You can see us in all our happiness tonight.'

The couple ate a sumptuous dinner of oysters and steak, washed down with the best champagne. Later, Richard admitted that their lives were not all lovey dovey: 'Like any couple, we've had our snags in the past. And we'll weather anything that comes our way in the future.' What the snags were, he declined to say, but Duncan Ford's statement shed some light on the mystery.

He explained how Julie came home after her honeymoon with Richard, devastated that her third marriage, like her second, had not been consummated. It seemed odd that Julie should marry *two* men unable to perform after months of presumably satisfactory courtship.

Ford insisted: 'Julie told me her marriage was a disaster. She said Richard slept on the settee all through the honeymoon. He had never made love to her. During the day he left her alone. Once she offered him a champagne cocktail – her way of hoping to lead him to love, but he had said, "Perhaps later" . . . and went scuba diving.

'That night I took her upstairs and made love to her in her bed. She said straight afterwards, "Do you realize you have just consummated my marriage?" And she sang a song to a famous pop tune. It went, "Isn't it queer, I married Richard, but Duncan is here . . .".'

Richard knew Duncan was staying with Julie and seemed unperturbed. Duncan said: 'Julie told him I was a friend sharing the house until my divorce came through. When he rang and she wasn't in, he would just chat to me about the weather. There was no jealousy, no tension. He never questioned my being there. He was just weird.'

When Richard occasionally visited his wife at her Heywood semi, Duncan would be told to move out. Presumably, the order was to save him the heartache of being shifted to the spare room.

Duncan said: 'Richard slept in her bed, which infuriated me. As far as my conscience was concerned, she was married to me, not him. But Julie said that every time Richard went to bed with her, he just went to sleep. She despaired and could not work out what he wanted from their marriage. She told me that before they married she told him about her past – the lesbian affairs and all. So he had no reason to treat her like that.'

On three occasions during their two-year marriage, Julie and Richard flew to exotic locations in a bid to sort out their lives. Duncan said: 'A few days before these trips she would go off sex completely, as though she had a conscience for Richard. But when she came back and he had failed her again, she went at it like a rabbit.'

Julie told Duncan details about a trip the couple took to Spain, with her mother Alice, in May 1986. On the first night Julie, dressed in a sexy negligée, waited breathlessly in the master bedroom for her husband to pounce. 'I took my drink into the bedroom and thought, "Think of England – it's going to happen this time,"' Julie explained to Duncan.

Richard did not appear. Hours later she went looking for him and found him in the spare room.

Julie decided to divorce Skrob after twenty-one months of non-marriage. On 22 May, Duncan listened as Julie phoned her husband to tell him the news. He said: 'She told him, "We have a non-marriage and you will be receiving divorce papers. You'll get the shock of your life." All he kept saying was, "Don't be silly, Julie.". But she went for irretrievable breakdown. Her lawyer gave her a list of grounds – non-consummation, desertion, mental cruelty and others.'

In January 1987, Richard signed the papers confirming his marriage had been one big non-event. Afterwards, Julie finally admitted her long-distance marriage had been a sham. She blamed the publicity, not the 7,000-mile distance between them, her engagement to another man or her lesbian affairs, for the break-up. Julie, who was now forty-five, said: 'The full glare of publicity put a great strain on it. I just felt I had to give Richard his privacy back.' She added: 'The marriage is over. It was my decision. There is no one else involved. Pressures of work kept us apart.'

Glossing over the fact that the couple had pledged to meet every weekend but only stayed in touch by phone, she added: 'Of course we had problems. Who doesn't? But we never had a chance to put things right because of the distance between us and the glare of publicity.' She sounded surprised her marriage of convenience had failed.

Later, she said Richard had promised to move to Manchester to live with her but stayed in California: 'As a gentleman, I think he could have kept his word.' She added: 'When you phone your husband and an answering machine replies, "Hi there, Dick is unavailable", you know you're on a hiding to nothing.' She did not say how many times Richard had called her to find her answering machine switched on or a strange lodger answering the phone.

Richard denied wanting to move to Lancashire. He said: 'The weather is terrible. Us southern Californians are used to having good weather and orange juice running through our blood.' His comment sparked a bitter war of words.

Julie hit back: 'I agree with his term regarding orange juice running through him. No blood. Just orange juice!'

After the divorce, Julie decided she was not marriage material. Asked if she would give it another go, she said firmly: 'No. I think three times is enough for anybody in their right mind.' Asked if she thought three weddings a bit excessive, she quipped: 'Ask Liz Taylor, I don't think she'd say it was. Mind you, it is a lot for Heywood. Why did I do it? For a day out in the frock,' she half-joked, although one can imagine Julie carried away with the fantasy aspect of the wedding – the spectacular dress, the adoring crowds, the sumptuous food, the attention – then realizing that life is not a Hollywood movie.

Two years later, in December 1988, Richard died, the victim of a rare form of leukaemia. He had married a few months before he passed away and his forty-nine year-old widow Jeanette talked of the bitterness he took to his grave. She said: 'He fell madly in love with Julie and wanted to live the rest of his life with her.'

Jeanette blamed Julie for the problems during their transatlantic marriage. She said it was Julie who should have moved to California: 'Richard was a very successful businessman with a brilliant career. Why would he want to move to Manchester? He loved California and the thought of moving never entered his head.'

She also said that Richard knew he was sick and his

whirlwind romance with Julie was a desperate bid for happiness. Neighbours agreed that his marriage to Julie was out of character. One said: 'I had known Richard, his late wife and their three children for more than twenty years and I could never have imagined something like this happening to him.'

Jeanette was sad that Richard had suffered such heartbreak. She said: 'What gets me is that Julie had all that time available to make him happy. Yet I had only a few months of marriage before he died.'

Julie had never mentioned his death but once it was discovered she issued a statement through the Granada press office, which said: 'Of course I knew that Richard had died in 1988. It was very distressing because we had remained friends. I didn't talk to anyone about it. I carried on working. It would not have been appropriate for me to have attended his funeral as he had remarried following our divorce in 1987. My deepest sympathies were sent to his family.'

11

Toyboys are More Fun

After nineteen years at the Rovers, Britain's best-known soap siren was settling in to middle age. Julie still got sacks of fan letters and was not worried about the odd line or two appearing on her face.

After all, other British soap stars, like Joan Collins who played ruthless Alexis Carrington in the American family saga *Dynasty*, and actress Kate O'Mara who played her sister Caress, looked stunning as they headed for their sixties.

Coronation Street bosses would prefer stars not to have plastic surgery so Julie could not have a face lift like Joan. Still, both Collins and O'Hara, high-profile women, had a lot in common with Julie. Both suffered broken marriages, Joan four and Kate two. Both were single and both dated toyboys. Kate later married for a third time to actor Richard Willis, eighteen years her junior.

Storyline-wise, it was a quiet year for Julie on *Coronation Street*, which gave her time to concentrate on other avenues. It was September 1989 and Julie was about to follow in Joan and Kate's stilettos into the world of toyboys. *Street* actress Liz Dawn, who plays Vera Duckworth, threw a riotous fiftieth-birthday party at her home in Prestwich, Lancashire. Julie turned up with a Greek toyboy, who spoke very little English. Julie introduced him, but when he took off his overcoat Liz was shocked. All he had on underneath was a skimpy leather G string trimmed with spiky metal studs, a bow tie and a smart pair of shoes.

The hairy-chested hunk shook hands with the open-mouthed *Street* stars and said things like: 'Is nice we meet.' When he turned his back Liz nudged Julie and said: 'You've got a great catch there, Chuck.'

Other stars at the party were Brian Mosely, who plays mayor and shopkeeper Alf Roberts; Bill Waddington, who plays busybody Percy Sugden; and Sally Whittaker who plays Sally Webster. Their eyes bulged as Greek Tony playfully kissed Julie and sipped champagne beside her on the sofa.

At the end of the night the couple left and Julie fell about laughing. She'd just pulled one of her best practical jokes. Her hunky Greek 'boyfriend' was in fact a twenty-two-year-old hired strippogram who billed himself as 'outrageous Toy Boy Tony'.

Toy Boy Tony, real name Tony Sipes, earned £500 a week from Manchester-based agency Naughtygrams, owned by Janice Percy. He was blond, short, (about 5ft 7ins), with spiky hair, rippling muscles, a great sense of humour and a huge acting talent. Tony was extremely popular with women, particularly petite blondes, and received sacks full of fan mail from admirers.

He chased fame as keenly as he chased fair-haired

girlfriends. In his spare time he would walk round Manchester Arndale Shopping Centre to see if anyone recognized him. He also had his stage initials – TBT – monogrammed on his clothes and he always carried a Filofax stuffed with contact numbers.

Julie had called Naughtygrams on the afternoon of the party looking for a handsome young strippogram who could act. A couple of weeks earlier she had been on holiday to Greece, and appeared via satellite on Liz Dawn's *This is Your Life* tribute. The stunned cast watched as Julie congratulated Liz surrounded by four G string-clad hunks. Now she wanted it to look as though she had brought one home. She said her escort would have to pretend to speak no English. He should be clad only in a smart coat, smart shoes, a G string and dickie bow and she would wear the same robe she wore for her *This is Your Life* television appearance. The agency called Tony, who snapped up the job then panicked because he had no smart shoes, only designer trainers. In the end his Dad lent him a pair of brogues.

After the party, Tony drove Julie and housekeeper Janet back to Heywood. Then he surprised Julie by asking if he could come in and put his clothes on. She said: 'That's the most original chat-up line I've ever heard.'

Janet made them a drink then went to bed. As soon as she had gone, Julie pulled off the blue kaftan she was wearing and undid her bra. Tony said: 'We ended up making love and I left at 6 a.m. completely exhausted. The next night Julie told me she had fallen asleep in her dressing room for the first time since she joined the *Street*. She said all her pals were saying how wonderful it was that she had a young male lover.'

Tony became a regular visitor to Julie's house, and they

rang each other every day. If Julie could not contact him she got Janet to call Naughtygrams to ask, in code, if he was available that evening. Janice would pass a coded message on and Tony would recognize the signal to call. Julie even had long phone conversations with his parents at their home in Chadderton on the outskirts of Manchester. They did not seem to mind their son dating a woman twenty-five years older than himself. Despite flaunting their relationship – Tony escorted Julie to a VIP opening of a Manchester club – she swore him to secrecy about their affair.

Julie lavished gifts on her young stud. She took him shopping locally and splashed out on clothes. Tony said: 'She is a very generous lady. She took me to places where she was a valued customer and bought me shirts and jeans.'

They also appeared arm in arm at the Royal Variety Show, where Julie was thrilled when rock queen Tina Turner asked to meet her. Tina is a big fan of *Coronation Street* and Julie. Julie admired the singer, who escaped her violent husband Ike to become one of the world's biggest stars.

Backstage the two performers chatted for a long time, then Tina suddenly said: 'I didn't realize you had such great legs.' It was a massive compliment, coming from a woman regarded as having the best legs in the business.

A couple of days later Julie went on a shopping spree, searching for clothes that would show off her shapely limbs. She chose mini skirts and figure-hugging dresses. 'She blew £1,000 in less than an hour,' said Tony. 'Julie looked fabulous in some of the gear – much younger than forty-seven.'

Tony spent most nights at her house, but disappeared

on Saturdays while a beautician spent four hours giving Julie facials, massages, tone-ups and manicures. She had a special beauty room with a large wooden bench and a mirror surrounded by light bulbs, like in an old stage dressing room.

Julie even met Tony's parents, Jean and Eric. Jean, who was seven years younger than Julie, was staggered when the star asked if she thought she was too old for her son. She recalls: 'I said my husband and I were open-minded and that sort of thing didn't bother us so long as they were happy.'

They first met Julie when Tony brought her to a family lunch at the Town House in Oldham. Jean remembers: 'During the meal, Julie took a fancy to a leopard-skin dress one of the waitresses was wearing. Suddenly she disappeared and after a few minutes returned wearing it. She had slipped the girl £30 for it after promising her she would try to wear it in the *Street*.'

Julie dated Tony for a passion-filled two months, until a story appeared in the papers about their romance. At the thought of another scandal – Tony was younger than her son – Julie went berserk. She called Tony and summoned him to her house and gave him a grilling, accusing him of leaking details. Tony denied he had talked.

Tony had everything to lose and nothing to gain from revealing their relationship. He dreamed of becoming a star and many thought he had the talent to fulfil his ambition. He was developing a comedy stand-up routine, which he planned to launch on the club scene. There was talk of getting scriptwriters to pen gags for him. Tony wanted to quit stripping at pubs, clubs and office parties.

With Julie on his side a career could be launched with no problems. She was introducing him to the right people, he was mixing with the stars and, even if she did not give him a leg up, he would have the contacts to help himself. Everywhere he went people would ask: 'Are you Bet's toyboy?' And he loved the recognition. When the story broke Julie refused to talk about their affair, which devastated love-lorn Tony. He could not believe she was going to ditch him and couldn't understand why she had turned against him.

The break-up hit him hard. He broke down and cried. In the following months he grew irritable, emotional and sensitive. Finally, he wanted revenge, and in April 1990 he sold his story to the *Daily Star* for £500. The headline read: 'THE NIGHT BET FLASHED HER NEWTON AND RIDLEYS AT ME'.

Tony carried on working as a strippogram, but any hopes of TV fame vanished. Julie's career carried on as normal.

She was invited to 10 Downing Street by Prime Minister Margaret Thatcher for a top girls' night out. Julie left the party arm in arm with entertainer Cilla Black. At the beginning of the year Mrs T had visited the *Coronation Street* set, but she refused her favourite whisky, offered by Bet. 'I'll just have a bitter lemon – I'm on duty,' said Mrs T. The Iron Lady was welcomed by regulars, including Peter Baldwin, who plays salesman Derek Wilton, Liz Dawn (Vera Duckworth) and landlord Alec Gilroy, played by Roy Barraclough.

There was a moment of nostalgia as she was shown round the set. Above the corner-shop door was the name Alfred Roberts – the name of her own father, also a grocer. 'That brings back memories,' she said. 'But we were never licensed. My father would never have sold intoxicating liquor.'

Maggie stayed two hours and watched a scene being filmed but confessed she was often too busy to see the series. 'Now I'm going to video it,' she said.

She told love rat Ken Barlow, actor Bill Roache, who was cheating on wife Deidre with sacked town hall worker Wendy Crozier, that the *Street* had a part to play in everyday life and in setting standards, and she hoped there would be a moral outcome to his current storyline.

By June 1990, Julie had spent twenty years pulling pints at the Rovers Return. Earlier that year she and screen husband Roy Barraclough were awarded honorary membership of the Society of Licensed Victuallers.

The tributes came in thick and fast. *Daily Express* columnist Jean Rook wrote: 'For twenty golden years, men have fantasized about pulling Julie Goodyear like a pint. They foamed at the mouth over barmaid Bet Lynch, of the brass bedknob hairdo above Britain's best-loved bust. They still lick froth-flecked lips over Bet Gilroy, of the pump handle legs and the Boadicean bosom.'

The Sun's television critic, Gary Bushell, honoured her. He calculated that Bet had pulled more than 20,000 pints and said:

In her time Elizabeth Theresa Lynch has sported the most outrageous earrings, the highest heels, the tightest skirts and the lowest-cut dresses on television. But the Bet Lynch story isn't just a case of thanks for the mammaries – she's also got the biggest heart in soapland . . .

Landlady Annie Walker, the grand old dragon, was dead against employing this buxom bit of a girl. But her son Billy knew better and Bet's rise to stardom was assured. It was her flirtiness, her hectic but ultimately miserable love-life, that brought Bet centre-stage. Male viewers felt they could pull her as easily as she pulled pints. Women identified with her many heartbreaks and the never-say-die way she would pull herself together again.

She had fifteen screen flings before marrying podgy publican Alec Gilroy in 1987, starting with long-distance lorry driver Frank Bradley in 1971. But Julie's acting skills quickly established that Bet was much more than an over-made-up face.

Colleagues queued to pay homage. Veteran scriptwriter Esther Rose reminisced: 'Julie was the nearest thing the *Street* would allow to a sexy young piece – all suggestion, but no leg-overs. There was no doubt from the beginning that she was a very good actress.'

Former *Street* producer Bill Podmore said: 'Julie is the queen of the soap. She has all the glitz and glam to keep her wearing the crown for a long, long time.'

The soap's creator Tony Warren said: 'She has an amazing quality of her own that she's handed over to Bet. It's a battered resignation cheered up with real warmth.'

Rochdale MP Cyril Smith said: 'Julie Goodyear has made the role her own and she does it with great style. Her terrific personality and outgoing good humour shine through in the character of Bet.'

Compliments poured in: 'Julie Goodyear has become television excellence in human form,' said *Woman* magazine.

However, Julie was modest about her achievements, and said: 'What I've got is five per cent talent and 95 per cent staying power.'

Fans found it easy to approach her. Once when she was sitting on the loo in a public convenience, a hand pushed a pencil and a piece of paper under the gap of the locked door and a voice said: 'Bet, while you're doing nothing, would you just sign this?'

A perfectionist, behind closed doors Julie would turn on the television and pick holes in her performance. 'It's usually too late to do anything,' she said. 'But I store it up and try to do better next time.'

She confessed that, now she was Weatherfield's *grande dame*, she studied the younger actors so as not to get complacent. She said: 'I remember I used to watch Pat Phoenix and Doris Speed. Now I still lurk round the studio just watching the youngsters act, remembering my own hunger to get there when I started.'

Immortality for Bet was something she longed for. Amazingly, she had played the-tart-with-the-heart for twenty years and was still not bored. How could she find her dull? The similarities between them were enormous.

She said: 'I love Bet's strength, her sense of humour, the marshmallow centre inside that tough exterior, the way she gets back up every time she's knocked down. Though, God knows, they've tried to get rid of me. They nearly drowned Bet in the park lake, then they tried to set fire to her along with the Rovers. But they'll never be rid of me. The *Street* is my life. If they want me out they'll have to drag me off in a van.'

The only other parts she says she was attracted to were Cilla Black-type 'people' shows. A 1960s pop star, Cilla abandoned her singing career and carved a niche for herself with two top television series, *Blind Date* and *Surprise Surprise*. *Blind Date* brought young couples together with hilarious consequences and *Surprise Surprise* reunited long-lost family members. A down-to-earth Liverpudlian with a fast line in chat, Cilla had an effortless talent for teasing the show's guests while putting them at their ease. She brought her Mersey humour to the shows and expertly juggled her roles as star and background presenter.

A top presenter's job was not on the cards, so golden girl Julie put all her effort into Bet. She did confess that she had a few changes to make. Her show-stopping figure, a size 10 when she joined the *Street*, was now closer to a 14. 'I've been dieting like hell since I realized my Aunt Florrie was right when she told me, when I was sixteen, "You've a nice little waist but, I'm warning you, when you turn forty, you'll thicken up."

'I hate dieting – if they took me to a health farm, I'd be under or over the fence for chips and peas. But you can't go on playing high comedy if you're a plank from neck to hip, and I plan to survive.'

Julie had done more than survive. She proved again and again that she could turn her hand from comedy to tragedy. With a fistful of awards, there was no doubt she was an excellent actress. Whatever else people said about her, no one could fault the sometimes hysterical, and other times heart-rending, performances she turned out.

Like a lot of the *Street* stars, she had become institutionalized and typecast. To leave the *Street* needed a huge effort, and many knew they could never manage it. Julie said she wanted to stay, but was she just scared to leave?

Six years earlier, Kenneth Alan Taylor had offered Julie a step into the outside world. He begged her to look at a play written by British actress Diana Dors. Diana, a screen siren in the 1960s, wrote *Not Waving But Drowning*, a moving tale about a failed woman singer. She would have loved to have played the part herself, but she was seriously ill and did not expect to live.

Di's adoring husband, Alan Lake, who committed suicide after her death, asked Ken to look at the play his wife had written as therapy during her illness. Ken remembers: 'It was a wonderful play, but I knew then that Di was terribly ill. I could see there was no way she was ever going to work again.'

The couple asked if he could stage it and Ken thought instantly of Julie for the lead. The play was a gift, a chance for Julie to prove she could survive outside *Coronation Street*. But she no longer had the nerve. Ken said: 'I tried to persuade her to do it but she said: "No. I've lost my bottle as far as the stage is concerned." She also said, which I found odd. "I think if I went on stage – let's be honest, I know as soon as I walked on I'd get a round of applause – I think it would finish me. I'd just break down. I don't think I could cope with all that."'

She turned it down and carried on playing Bet.

In September 1990 Julie took a holiday. She flew to the Italian resort of Saint Agnello to join a girlfriend. A few days later, she was joined by self-employed decorator Kevin Lawn, a man who had left his wife and kids and wanted a sex-change operation. He caught up with Julie at the plush Hotel Villa Garden. Julie, now forty-eight, denied that there was any romance between them. 'It's all rubbish,' she insisted. 'I'm just friends with Kevin. He's not my boyfriend at all. I've got quite a few friends. I'm not bothered about their religion, their politics, colour or their sexuality. I'm just interested in them.'

In fact, Kevin had moved in with Julie a month earlier, in August.

Lawn, thirty-four, cut an odd figure with his streaked blond hair and Dame Edna Everage-style glasses. He was not keen to be associated with Julie. When he spotted *News of the World* reporter James Weatherup chatting to her, he went berserk and sent him crashing to the ground. He pinned him down, screaming: 'You print one fucking word about me, bastard, and I'll kill you stone dead.' Holidaymakers watched in disbelief as he then chased photographer David Thorpe.

Later Kevin told *The Sun* what went on behind the scenes. In the Hotel Villa Garden bar one night, Julie ignored Kevin. Worried, he mentioned it the next day, expecting an explanation or reassurance that everything was OK. Instead, Julie shouted: 'Right, that's it. You can fuck off if you're going to behave like that,' and stormed from the room.

Penniless, Kevin packed his bags and spent three days hitch-hiking home. Julie was still in Saint Agnello when he called her from Manchester. He was expecting a volley of abuse; instead, Julie asked him to return on the next flight, which he did.

When Julie first met Kevin he was a transvestite, keen to have a sex-change. One of his favourite frocks was a yellow number which he wore with Bet Gilroy-style make-up. Lawn took hormones and was proud of his 36in breasts. However, one month before the operation Julie talked him out of it, saying: 'Don't do it. Don't have the operation. It would be a shame. It would be a waste.' She took his hormone tablets and flushed them down the toilet.

Eighteen months earlier, Kev, had left his pretty, common-law wife Debbie and kids Corina, fourteen, and Nadine, ten, after a row about his kinky habits. He frequently dressed as a woman, which Debbie coped with as long as he kept the practice nocturnal, but when he began to dress in frocks and high heels during the day she felt the situation was out of control.

Kevin, from Knutsford in Cheshire, met Julie in Manchester's New Union pub on 15 June 1990. At the time he had no idea who she was. Julie was dressed in a New Zealand All Blacks rugby shirt, black mini-skirt and black high heels. She had her hair in a ponytail.

Kevin was dressed as a man. He spotted her with a group of friends and thought she looked nice. He walked nearer to her table for a closer look. He caught her eye and wobbled his glass, offering her a drink. She accepted and invited him to sit down.

The first thing he said to her was: 'I'm a transsexual and I like dressing as a woman. I'm not gay, I just want to be a woman.'

Julie did not bat an eyelid. She just said she did not believe he had real bosoms, so Kevin lifted his pink sweatshirt to show her.

Julie quizzed Kevin about his sexuality. She wanted to know why he was so keen to change sex. They chatted like sisters for about two hours before Julie told him that to have the 'snip' would be a terrible waste.

At the end of the evening they were like old friends. Kevin got up to leave as he had work the next day, but Julie told him firmly: 'You're not going anywhere. You're taking me home to Heywood.'

They jumped into Kevin's clapped-out seventeen-year-old Ford Capri – Julie owned a white convertible Mercedes 350SLC, complete with personalized number plate – and started the ten-mile journey to her house. On the way they passed Granada studios. Julie told Kevin it was where she worked. He still did not twig that Britain's most famous barmaid was sitting in the front of his old banger. He thought Julie was probably a secretary or something.

Back at Julie's semi, they sat chatting until the early hours, when Kevin said he had to go. Julie offered him the spare room but Kevin knew he would never get to work so he made his excuses and left.

Before he went, Julie managed to slip a piece of paper in his wallet. On it was written 'Julie Goodyear' and her phone number. She was thrilled when Kevin rang and invited him over. He turned up wearing a blue and white striped jumper, three-quarter-length ladies' beach jeans and a pair of white trainers. His shoulder-length hair was in a bouffant style.

Julie didn't even blink. She just said: 'You'll do.' Nervous, Kevin asked what she meant. She said she was taking him out for dinner. They went in his car – Julie explained that they would be recognized if they went in hers. It was only then that Kevin thought to ask what she did. When she said she was Bet Lynch in *Coronation Street*, Kevin was dumbstruck.

He said: 'I didn't believe her at first, which she found funny. Because she wasn't wearing her Bet Lynch wig, she looked completely different.'

They arrived at a country-mansion-style posh restaurant near Rochdale. Kevin was embarrassed because he felt out of place. The waitress showed them to a corner table and Julie sat with her back to the other diners so that she would not be recognized.

She ordered a mixed grill for Kevin and told him not to worry as he struggled with the neatly laid out rows of cutlery. 'Don't worry,' she said. 'Copy me. You'll learn. Just relax and have a good time.'

Kevin was curious about her celebrity status and asked

what it was like being Bet. Julie told him: 'Monday is my day off so I'm not famous today. But I get a lot of people pestering me. Sometimes, I wish they would leave me alone.'

They sat chatting and had been in the restaurant for almost an hour when a waitress came over to the table and said: 'I hope you don't mind, Miss Goodyear. I just wanted to say I hope you and your new affair will be happy.'

Julie was stunned and furious. Kevin thought her remarks were hilarious. Julie snapped: 'It's not funny. She thinks you're a woman and I'm a lesbian. I'm not a bloody lesbian, you know.'

The next day they had dinner at Julie's house. It was nothing fancy, just chicken legs and salad washed down with a bottle of Mateus Rosé, Julie's favourite wine. After dinner they chatted and Julie put on a John Lennon record. They sat drinking and by the end of the evening Kevin was offered the spare room. This time he accepted. 'I was falling in love with Julie,' he said. 'She was the kindest, funniest, most unpretentious woman I'd ever met. She didn't have any hang-ups and didn't make me feel like a freak. She understood me and, for the first time in years, I realized I enjoyed being a man, even though I still liked to dress as a woman sometimes. I felt loved as a man – and she made me realize I did not want to go through with my sex-change operation.'

The couple must have sounded like Hinge and Bracket during their frequent girly chats. They got on like a house on fire and Kevin began staying three or four times a week. They went out for dinner and Kevin got a kick out of behaving like a gentleman. He opened doors, lit her cigarettes, carried her shopping, the kind of things men do for women. 'It was a revelation to me,' said Kevin.

After they had been friends for three months, Julie invited Kevin to move in. He still enjoyed playing macho man but, two months later, told Julie he had urges to dress as a woman. She said: 'If that's what you want to do, do it. Each to their own, love. It doesn't bother me.'

A few days later, Kevin brought some of his wardrobe round to Julie's. That night he said he was going to dress up. Julie said it was fine. 'I put on my clothes, eyeshadow, mascara and lipstick,' he said. 'I was nervous when I went back downstairs but Julie didn't bat an eyelid. I'd already told her my name as a woman was Kay. She said, "Sit down, Kay, I'll get you a cup of tea – or would you prefer a drink?" She wasn't at all put out.

'We talked like women do, about what we'd done during the day, who we had seen, what nice clothes we'd seen in the shops. At the end of the night I went back upstairs and we went to our separate beds.'

Kevin's 'urges' became routine and each time he dressed as a woman they went through the same ritual.

Another night it was Julie's turn to dress up. It was November and Julie had bought a black lycra catsuit. She teamed it with a black studded neck collar, bracelet and belt which she had bought for a video shoot. In the raunchy outfit she looked like high-kicking secret agent Emma Peel from the cult television series *The Avengers*. Kevin said: 'She looked really sexy and I gave her my leather biker's jacket.'

Kevin remarked that her outfit looked like bondage gear. Julie laughed and thought it would be funny to go to the New Union pub and pretend she was a dominatrix. The pair started plotting what to say and do and were rolled up with laughter. They found a dog's collar and clipped a lead on to it.

Kevin walked her into the bar holding the dog lead. He got the drinks, came back to the table and Julie said, in a stern voice: 'Sit, boy' and 'Drink, boy'. Convulsed with laughter, she kept turning her face to the wall. Then she said: 'Fetch' and Kevin trotted to the bar to get more drinks. While he ordered her brandy and Babycham, a dodgy-looking man walked up to Julie and asked what rates she was charging. 'He thought she was a prostitute,' Kevin told *The Sun*.

They left soon afterwards. The joke had gone cold and Julie was worried about being recognized.

Kevin was amazed that Julie preferred the modest life to the high life. He thought that, despite her riches, Julie would rather eat at the local Chinese or Indian than posh places. But Julie was as happy upstairs as she was down. Partial to a bit of glamour, a favourite haunt was one of Manchester's glitziest hotels. Julie was a popular face and always had time for the customers. If they got chatting about the *Street* she would do her Bet Lynch voice and have them in stitches.

One night, Julie went on an incredible champagne bender at the top hotel. During the fizz-filled session, she let slip that she had been involved with a lord! She offered no more details but was proud of her fling with a peer.

Her indiscretion came out during a bubbly binge which went on for an incredible *eight* hours. During the marathon drinking session, Julie and one of the senior managers cracked nearly every vintage bottle of champers in the hotel cellar. Julie had arrived that evening dressed in a stunning evening gown. She always dressed up when she visited the hotel. One spectacular dress she wore there was covered in feathers.

She met up with *Street* colleague and one-time hotel

resident, Jill Summers, who plays battleaxe granny Phyllis Pearce. They had dinner together before going to the bar and it wasn't long before the high jinks started. Ex-manageress Ann Astley remembers: 'When Julie and this guy got together they both reckoned they were a couple of champagne buffs who could taste the difference in various brands. By 6 a.m. I reckon they had been through just about every vintage bottle of champagne and pink champagne in the cellar.'

Jill left the pair at midnight after swigging a few whiskies. Julie, who booked in for the night, swayed to her room as dawn broke.

Kevin was not involved in such sprees. He said: 'We'd often spend evenings at home, with her learning her *Coronation Street* scripts and me doing the crossword. 'I used to think she looked really sweet in her half-moon reading glasses on a gold chain. And she wore Van Cleef & Arples aftershave instead of perfume. On Saturday morning we'd go shopping at Bury market.'

She did once take him to a Bedfordshire health farm though, for a two-week Christmas break. Geordie soccer hero Paul Gascoigne, who then played for the premier north London club Tottenham Hotspur, was also there. Kevin was staggered when Gazza, a big star in his own right, stopped him and asked if he would get Julie's autograph. He was too shy to ask himself. Kevin said: 'He wanted if for his Mum and asked me to get it. "I'm too embarrassed, man, but me Mam will love it. She's a big fan," he said.

'I got Julie to sign a photograph of herself. It said, "With all my love, Julie Goodyear". I gave it to Gazza the next day and he gave me his autograph for my two daughters.'

Besotted, Kevin began planning a wedding. He spoke to the Reverend Peter Hughes of Knutsford Unitarian Church, who agreed he would marry thrice-divorced Julie in church. Kevin asked his best friend Steven Clarke to be best man.

Before they married, Kevin wanted Julie to meet his daughters and took her to his home in Knutsford. Neighbour Gail Wilbraham, thirty-five, has vivid memories of the visit. She said: 'The kids couldn't believe it. Julie was smoking a cigarette in a long holder.'

Everything was going swimmingly, then, a month after Julie's relationship with Kevin was revealed, Toy Boy Tony committed suicide. It was almost a year since details of their fling had been divulged and they'd split.

Tony's body was found in his fume-filled car by a police patrol car in Coal Pit Lane, Oldham. The engine of the car was still running. The twenty-three-year-old had parked round the corner from his home in Chadderton and gassed himself. A doctor pronounced Tony dead and his parents Eric and Jean and his eighteen-year-old sister Donna were informed. Eric said Tony's death had nothing to do with Julie. Friends and family were devastated and no one could understand why Tony had taken his life. Donna Keigher, boss of Saucygrams, the agency Tony moved to after his row with Naughtygrams, said: 'Tony was full of laughter and brought pleasure to a lot of people. I saw him a few days ago and he seemed quite happy.' Julie was not available for comment.

Grieving Eric searched frantically for clues to his only son's death. He broke into Tony's electronic Filofax and read his diary but found no secret worries which might have pushed him to despair. Salesman Eric told an inquest at Oldham that Tony had no health, money or job worries. 'We were very close,' he said, 'and he would have approached me if he had any problems worrying him. All we can think of is a young girl he had a strong relationship with – but that should have been no reason for doing what he did.' Tony left no suicide note.

A few months after Tony's death Julie's relationship with Kevin began to cool. Kevin claimed that Julie was a stern mistress who ruled her home with a rod of iron, laying down rules that even he found difficult to live with. He said, 'She got annoyed if I moved anything in the house. One day she came home early from work and I had just got out of the bath. She flew off the handle and told me I was never to have the first bath. I apologized.'

Kevin told of other rows they had. Once he sat on a sitting-room chair and moved an ashtray so that he could reach it. Julie exploded: 'Don't sit on that chair or put anything on it. It is a valuable antique.'

Kevin was aware that it was her home so he obeyed the strict house rules, which included telling him to go to the spare bedroom to watch TV, even if she wanted to watch the same programme.

If the phone rang, she asked Kevin to sit in the kitchen. She also liked Kevin to greet her at the back door when she came home from work. Once he arrived back early, and tired out, went to bed. Julie came in late and he was asleep – but not for long.

'She came upstairs, woke me up and said, "Don't ever do that again. You are meant to greet me at the back door when I come in." '

On other occasions, Julie would sit on the sofa. 'She'd say, "Tea" if she wanted a cuppa, and I'd lay a little silver tray with her special china teacup, matching teapot and vase with a single flower in it.

'Or she'd say, "Bath wants running" which was my cue to draw her a bath. She seldom said please or thank you. Sometimes she didn't bother to speak – she'd just hold out her brandy glass and wave it around if she wanted a refill.'

Julie could also be gentle and kind. Kevin told her he used to collect fish, so she bought him a £180 tank and two guppies she nicknamed Arthur and Martha. The next morning Kevin found her crouched on the floor close to tears. One of the fish had jumped out of the tank during the night and died.

Kevin had a friend called Graham who had AIDS. Graham was a fan of Julie's and asked to meet her. She agreed and they met at the New Union pub on 4 November 1990. Graham and Julie got on very well and she invited him to come back to her house. When they got there she insisted on letting off all her fireworks a day early in Graham's honour.

But her moods could change; one minute she would make wild fantasies come true for those close to her, the next she would make life a misery.

Kevin began to sense that Julie was ready to move on. It was Christmas Eve and he was about to hand over her presents when she said: 'I've got something to tell you.' Feeling sick, Kevin said: 'You don't need to tell me. I know it's over.'

She opened her presents and said: 'It was, until you gave me these.' Kevin had bought her an amethyst ring and a gold gate-link bracelet. Before the expensive gift Julie was ready to issue marching orders, but she was not that heartless; it was Christmas Eve, after all. She told him he could stay. Then, on Boxing Day, they had a row and Julie gave the presents Kevin had bought her to a stranger in a local pub.

Distraught, Kevin went to stay with his mother, but he and Julie eventually made it up and went on holiday to Gran Canaria. It was March 1991, and although it started well, the romantic break was no second honeymoon.

On the flight Julie was in splendid form, laughing, joking, signing autographs and chatting to the stewardesses and crew. Kevin had only ever flown three times, so Julie arranged with the captain for him to visit the cockpit. 'It was brilliant,' he enthused and returned to his seat raving about the experience. Julie decided she would have a look, too. She had been gone about twenty minutes when the captain announced they were about to land. Shortly afterwards Julie's voice came over the tannoy.

She said: 'Kevin, I love you, Julie.' The passengers cheered and Kevin sat with a huge grin on his face.

They had been drinking on the plane and by the time they reached the hotel they were quite drunk. The bellboy showed them to their room. He proudly opened the door to show his guests in. Julie took one look and commented: 'Look at this place! I've seen better council flats!'

She stormed down to the reception. When the manager came to the desk, she shouted, 'You don't know who I am, do you? I'm on TV all over the world!'

The manager was not impressed and did not mince his words: 'Madam, you no like hotel, you fuck off.' Kevin froze; he thought Julie was going to clock him.

It was 1 a.m. and there was nowhere else to go. Julie stayed in the bar while the manager showed Kevin the huge, luxurious El Presidente suite. Walking on eggshells, Kevin fetched Julie and took her to approve it. She looked around and said: 'I suppose this will do.' They had got off to a bad start but, in the end, they had a great holiday – until the day they were leaving.

Kevin was taking a bath when the phone rang. Julie was sitting on her bed next to the phone but told him to answer it. Leaping to his feet, Kevin slipped in the bath and broke his arm. He thought it would be a good idea to pop into the medical centre opposite the hotel for treatment but Julie did not agree. She told him: 'Wait until you get home and go to Bury General.'

They flew back to Manchester. On the journey, Kevin was in agony. Back at home, he went to hospital and they confirmed he had, indeed, broken his arm. They bandaged him up and he was in plaster for six weeks.

After the Gran Canaria dramas, Kevin knew he was on the way out. He left for good the day after Julie's forty-ninth birthday party on 29 March 1991, which he helped to organize.

Julie seemed to be enjoying herself but the minute the last guests left she walked over and told him off. Kevin was speechless. He was clueless as to what crime he had committed.

Julie offered no explanation. She turned on her heel and went to bed. Kevin packed his bags, knocked on Julie's door and said goodnight. There was silence; Kevin knew the death warrant had been signed on their friendship.

He sat up all night thinking it over. When Julie came down in the morning he told her he was leaving. She said: 'If you go now, there is no coming back.' He knew, but he picked up his bags and left.

12

Reconciliation

'All I know about my father is that he was a British soldier during the Second World War. I don't know whether he is alive or dead, a millionaire or a tramp,' Julie would explain patiently when asked about her real Dad, George Kemp. 'He obviously doesn't want anything to do with his daughter, no matter how famous she might have become.'

When reporters finally tracked down the retired electrician in October 1991, less than a mile from Julie's home, he said: 'She knows all about me and I find it strange she hasn't talked about me.' For some reason gentle George had become a skeleton in the family closet and it seemed Julie wasn't going to be the one to unlock it.

The World War Two veteran told how he was hurt that Julie had not given him public recognition. He also told of his heartache at not being invited when Julie appeared on *This is Your Life*. 'It upset me a bit,' he said. 'Some people said I should have put my oar in and told the truth but I thought: "What's the point?" '

Family friends were not so generous. One said: 'I was absolutely disgusted at the *This is Your Life* programme, because George was never mentioned.'

Over the years it was obvious Julie knew of George, for when she married Ray Sutcliffe she put George's name on the marriage certificate, but George was not invited to the wedding.

Julie had not seen her father since she was seven and Alice stopped her visiting him. For years George wanted to rekindle a father/daughter relationship despite what had happened all those years before. He thought he would never hear from his daughter again, when one afternoon, in December 1983, the phone rang and it was Julie. She was contacting him for the first time in thirty-five years with the news that she was marrying Richard Skrob.

'Out of the blue she rang me late one night,' said George. 'She told me she was coming to see me the next day and I asked her if she wanted her tea with us. "That's the first time anyone has ever asked me that," she said.'

Julie came round the following afternoon and parked her Merc outside. She sat herself down in front of the fire and started chatting like she had been doing it all her life. 'She was breathless and flustered,' said George. 'I think she was afraid of being recognized by the neighbours.'

George had often wondered what had happened after the visits stopped and how she had been treated by Bill. His worst fears were confirmed when he heard about her unhappy childhood. Julie broke down as she talked about being left alone in The Bay Horse. 'She said she was often left alone for long periods,' said George, who was distraught at the thought. 'Once they moved to The Bay

Horse it got worse. She told me she was often locked in her room above the pub for hours on end. It was because Bill and Alice were terrified that some of the regulars might molest her. She didn't go into detail about it, but she said it frightened her.'

On Julie's first visit she left her best gear at home. 'She was looking really down-to-earth, as if she had just got up,' George remembered. 'It didn't seem like we hadn't seen each other for so many years. Maybe it was to do with the fact that we were used to seeing her on the TV as Bet.

'We got on really well. She sat between my wife and myself to watch TV. In the end she was only here a couple of hours and she didn't bother with any tea.'

Her whirlwind visit left the couple reeling. 'George didn't know what to make of it,' said Ada. 'She was telling us all about the wedding.'

George added: 'I think in a roundabout way she was asking me to give the marriage my blessing. But I didn't. I told her, "Why don't you go and live with him, because you have made so many mistakes before." I don't think she liked that. She also told us she would give us some photographs of the wedding, but she never has done.'

George was baffled as to Julie's reasons for keeping him under wraps and it was one of the things he asked about at their reunion. Julie told him the stories about not knowing him were just newspaper talk, then she added that he would be pestered and pestered if the truth got out and it was best to keep it quiet. George did not understand. He said: 'But I am her Dad, so why try to hide it?'

At their first meeting George said Julie told him she had found him after visiting a clairvoyant, which he found surprising considering she lived so near.

However, their two-hour meeting ended in tears as father

and daughter said goodbye. They promised to keep in touch.

At Christmas George and seventy-six-year-old Ada were invited to Julie's house a couple of times. The first time was Christmas Eve. 'She sent her lady companion to pick us up in her car,' said George. 'When we got to the house we had some drinks, which her friend served. She didn't join us because she was driving. Julie showed us round and I remember she was proud of the fact that she could do all her own plumbing and things. She showed us the taps she had changed on her bath. She was quite a little handywoman. The taps were shaped like swans and gold-plated. She seemed to be very pleased with them. She took us into the garden, where she had a greenhouse she was very proud of. She liked to do a bit of gardening. When she came to our house she brought me one of her plants.

Julie didn't put on any airs and graces with us, but we were a bit upset about the way she treated the lady companion who lived with her. She ordered her about. We felt a bit embarrassed for her, but the lass didn't seem to mind. I must admit Julie knew how to put people in their place.'

George and Ada never really felt easy in Julie's house. They never quite knew why, they just felt out of place.

Eight years after Julie first got in touch with George, he was 'discovered' by reporters and a newspaper story appeared after George admitted that he was Julie's father. He got a phone call from Julie after the paper hit the stands. She was shrieking at him. She accused George of selling his story. He denied it because it wasn't true. She said she could prove he had made money from the papers.

Careful checks show no payment was made, either to George or Ada, for any quotes appearing in newspapers.

George tried a few times to contact Julie but his calls

were never returned or else the message came back that she was too busy to see him.

George said: 'She's gone back into her shell and I don't suppose she'll ever come out of it again. That's Julie for you. Leave it at that.' He did not want to pester his famous daughter.

He kept up with her on-screen and off-screen life by reading the papers. First came her divorce from Skrob, then the affairs and lesbian allegations. George was stunned. Ada said: 'He would read the papers and just shake his head. I don't think he could believe that he was reading about his own daughter.'

In 1992 George was diagnosed as having cancer. He insisted Julie was not to be told. Ada said: 'He respected her wishes right up to the end. George said he didn't want to bother her with his troubles.'

Two years after the cancer was diagnosed, George, aged seventy-six, lost his fight and died. Julie saw his obituary in the local paper and called Ada to confirm that the report was true. When Ada answered the phone Julie said: 'So, he's gone then, has he?'

Ada said: 'I told Julie about the funeral arrangements, but she said she doubted if she would be going because of the press interest.'

Julie had last spoken to her father when they rowed about a newspaper finding him. Julie and her ex-husband Richard Skrob never spoke again after their final bitter exchanges. Many things had been left unsaid.

13

Queen of the *Street*

Britons love a villain. For nearly ten years Julie's private life had been sliced open, dissected and pinned out on a slab for the public's inspection. The lurid and shocking sex scandals attributed to her would have toppled a Conservative MP in a week. But the adverse publicity inflicted only minor scratches and bruises to her popularity and she escaped virtually unharmed. In some ways, Bet was more popular than ever.

At the end of 1991 Weatherfield's leading lady was named a trendsetter by top designers and models. The autumn catwalks clanked with sequins, lamé and outrageous jewellery. The hair was bouffant, the make-up exaggerated. International designers Chanel, Dolce & Cabbana and Rifat Ozbek produced bar-girl collections and style pundits claimed the influence came from *Coronation Street*.

A report in ultra-trendy style magazine *The Face*, a publication not known for praising soap stars, said of Bet:

'As a fashion icon she became a legend, popularizing outrageous jewellery and accessories before Chanel, and wearing tight body-hugging leopard-skin catsuits long before Katharine Hamnett.

'It was Bet – not Ivana Trump – who first displayed the hairdo of the 1990s, the extravagant piled-up beehive.'

There was a picture of Bet dressed in a plunging leopard-skin dress next to US socialite Ivana Trump, who wore a glittering lamé blouse. Both sported peroxide beehives and gold jewellery. The similarities were striking, although Ivana's carefully coifed look was courtesy of top designers while Bet's was probably Bury market. To complete the feature there was a picture of Elsie Tanner next to mini-skirted supermodel Linda Evangelista dressed in Dolce & Cabbana's fringed halterneck two piece, supposedly inspired by barmaid fashion.

Two months later, at the end of January 1992, *Woman* magazine readers voted Julie top female soap star. Bet romped home as winner, bagging nearly half the votes in a national poll. Australian soap star Craig McLachlan, from *Neighbours*, was voted best male star.

It was a boost Julie welcomed. She had been off work battling a mystery virus since Christmas. Despite being inundated with cards and flowers from all over the world, Julie was still under the weather. 'Unfortunately I've developed a tummy bug, but Bet will be back,' she assured fans.

On 8 January 1992, after the festive break, Julie was due to resume filming but she sent a note to producers saying the illness had left her exhausted. *Street* sources suggested Julie was boycotting the show because she was disenchanted with the time off given to Roy Barraclough over Christmas. 'Julie thought that Roy had been singled out for special treatment,' a source close to the cast was reported as saying.

A Granada spokesman said: 'This is absolute nonsense. Roy has had several breaks to work in the theatre. It is not additional time off.'

Roy's character, Alec, had been written out back in November 1991, to allow Roy time for theatre projects. The story scriptwriters came up with to explain his absence was another *Coronation Street* winner. Alec waved goodbye to the Rovers and was living it up on a Caribbean cruise ship. While he played castaway, Bet reeled in old flame Des Foster. It was the first time she had cheated on Alec since their wedding in 1987.

Decorator Des had first slipped between Bet's sheets eight years earlier when he was called in to paint the Rovers. He ditched her after she asked him to leave his wife, but she still carried a torch for him. Her parting words were: 'Look me up if you're ever passing.'

He did, but the affair took a dramatic turn when boozy cellarman Jack Duckworth stumbled on the cheating pair. Staggering home late after a snooker game at the British Legion, Jack thought he had spotted a burglar when a Ford Capri pulled up outside the Rovers.

However, it was not a villain out to steal Bet's earrings – it was Des stealing her heart again. Jack threatened to shop Bet to Alec, saying: 'So this is what the boss's wife gets up to while her old man is away.'

The storyline was a Christmas cracker, with over 20 million tuning in.

For New Year the public was treated to Bet's belated twenty-first birthday celebration. For 252 months Bet had been pulling pints, slicing lemons and opening bottles of milk stout. She could walk along the optics blindfolded and still pick out the gin. Granada's daytime television star Judy Finnigan was drafted in to host a spectacular party held at the Manchester studios. A raucous girls' night out was arranged, with sixteen barmaids reunited for the occasion. A studio audience was shown a series of hilarious clips culled from old episodes which had Julie in stitches. She sat giggling as scenes she hadn't seen for years were screened. They showed the one of her in hotpants tap-dancing on the bar with rebel barmaid Lucille Hewitt, and another clashing bosoms with busty bar girl Margo as the furious pair rowed.

After the clips, an Andy Warhol-style screen, pasted with pictures of the *Street*'s stars, went up to reveal a mock-up of the Rovers bar. All sixteen girls, including Julie, stood, raised a glass of champagne and wished the public a happy New Year.

After the official tribute came the party. Actress Vicky Ogden – man-eating barmaid Margo Richardson – stood in on the show while Bet was in Torremolinos. She stayed for only eight episodes, but was still excited at the chance to reminisce with the cast. She remembered saying her lines without batting an eyelid when the pressure went off on the beer barrels. 'It happened while I was performing,' she said. 'A technician had to duck under the bar and I suddenly became aware of somebody fiddling between my legs. I had to stand there looking cool, calm and collected while some spark snagged my tights with his spanner.'

Most of the barmaids had turned up. There was Cheryl Murray, who played Mike Baldwin's assistant in 1977 and was relief barmaid for a month in 1983; Sandra Gough, who played Irma Ogden, Stan and Hilda's daughter, Bet's best mate and part-time barmaid; Sue Jenkins, who spent three years behind the bar as Gloria Todd from 1985; and a host of regulars like Beverley Callard, who plays Liz McDonald, a former barmaid who replaced temptress Tina Fowler; Sally Whittaker, who played Sally Seddon, now Webster, and who spent three months behind the bar; Helen Worth, who plays Gail Platt who helped out for a day in 1986 when the Rovers reopened after the fire, and, of course, seventy-one-year-old Betty Driver, who plays the *Street*'s longest-serving barmaid, Betty Turpin.

Actress Jennifer Moss, who played tearaway Lucille Hewitt in the 1960s, was unhappy. For almost fourteen years she stayed at *Coronation Street* and two clips of her were shown, including the one of her go-go dancing on top of the bar with Bet, but her name was not mentioned in the tribute.

Jennifer, who left the show in 1974, said: 'I was pulling pints behind the Rovers for six years – even before Bet Lynch. Neither Julie nor Judy Finnigan, who both know me, bothered to mention my name, even though that whole go-go dancing scene was really about me. I was the one who organized it and I had to take the flak when Annie Walker found out. To be snubbed twice in one show is too much.'

A *Coronation Street* spokesman said sharply: 'We cannot mention everybody's name. As for the go-go dancing scene, it was played for Julie Goodyear, who was appearing on the tribute. Anyone else in the shot is incidental.'

At the end of February, the stars faced a sad occasion. They had to say 'farewell' to ousted Granada chief David Plowright, who was leaving after losing control of the station in a bloody boardroom battle.

Julie starred at the affair, packed with 1,000 showbiz people. She burst out of a huge cake wearing a jazzy £1,200 sequined bodysuit trimmed with feathers, flown in specially from Hollywood. Plowright looked stunned as she planted a kiss on his forehead and serenaded him with 'Thank Heaven for Little Girls'.

Bill Tarmey (Jack Duckworth) and Liz Dawn (Vera Duckworth) paid tribute by crooning 'On the Street Where You Live.' Champagne flowed and the sky lit up with a spectacular display of fireworks. A banner across the street read: 'THANK YOU – YOU MADE TV WORTH WATCHING'.

Plowright had been responsible for Granada classics like *Brideshead Revisited* and *Jewel in the Crown*. He also helped the *Street* to fight off competition from the BBC soap *EastEnders*, which was launched in 1985. He turned the show round and made it a success for the 1990s but was booted out after he refused to sanction more cuts in spending and jobs. Julie and Bill had headed a star-studded petition to try to get Plowright reinstated, but failed.

After the Plowright bash and Bet's twenty-first, came Julie's fiftieth birthday. To celebrate, she agreed to be interviewed for television by top journalist Sue Lawley. Sue, poached by Granada from the BBC for a salary of £350,000, had a hard-hitting, high-profile chat show and spoke only to VIP guests.

Julie was questioned at a top Manchester hotel and insiders said Sue, a skilled interviewer, teased out hitherto unspoken details of Julie's private life. The two women spent hours in front of the camera and the finished report was said to be explosive. But then the programme was axed, along with Lawley's series.

Reports claimed that Julie was upset by the tough grilling she received from no-nonsense Sue. A source said: 'Julie hadn't expected the third degree, didn't enjoy it and felt gutted at having her private life prised open. Afterwards she told executives she didn't want it shown.'

Sue said she was pleased with the programme: 'I'm happy to say the interview was fine leaving me. It was lively and strong. It would have made a very good, strong piece of television. It's sad that it is never going to see the light of day.' She admitted she had quizzed Julie on her love-life, but said the *Street* star had 'given as good as she got'.

She was careful to avoid 'no go' areas and added: 'We laughed a lot. I think Julie is a great woman.' Sue said the show had not appeared because it clashed with general election coverage and, as it was centred on Julie's fiftieth birthday, was not considered topical enough to screen.

The one-hour special on Julie was set to follow a series of weekly interviews with top-ranking guests. Programmes on Prime Minister John Major, superstar musician Eric Clapton and Queen Noor of Jordan had already been shown. Millions would have tuned in to watch Julie bare her soul but Granada pulled the plug and the tape hit the cutting-room floor.

The whole of Sue's series followed. 'It was difficult to maintain an independent journalistic agenda,' she said philosophically. 'The fashion for people pouring out all on TV is fading a bit.'

A source added: 'Sue couldn't get guests who would agree to her style of questioning. She tried to do interviews which didn't plug books but going for the jugular meant the demise of those shows.'

The minor drama blew up at the beginning of May and

then, later that month, Roy Barraclough announced he was divorcing the series and leaving Bet. He wanted to get back to his first love, the theatre. He said: 'I'll miss Alec like hell. Being in the *Street* had been a joy and privilege. But now I think I'd like to take things a little easier.'

One would think Roy was leaving to appear in Shakespeare or an Alan Bennett play, but the stage role Roy had lined up was a pantomime – *Mother Goose* at Wolverhampton.

If Julie was disappointed at losing a husband, she did not say so. Anyway, there was a *Street* wedding to look forward to. Lonely café owner Alma Sedgwick was finally marrying *Coronation Street* tycoon Mike Baldwin, a one-time lover of Bet's.

On the day, crews battled to get the couple to church on time as Manchester was snarled up by a religious demonstration. A parade of five thousand Young Christians brought traffic to a standstill.

Alma, played by Amanda Barrie, and Mike, played by Johnny Briggs, were dressed in their wedding finery when they had to abandon their chauffeur-driven car and run through crowds to the film location.

A coach carrying sixty extras for the reception scenes was forty minutes late. To top it all, there was a power cut. Engineers had to use a portable generator to supply the film lights.

Landlord Alec was best man and Bet was at his side. Needless to say, Bet tried to upstage the bride by dressing in a stunning white suit and glittering diamanté jewellery. It was the last special occasion Bet and Alec attended together. In September, Alec left after trying desperately to persuade Bet to join him for a new life in Southampton. He was offered the job of a lifetime there, running the entertainment programme for a cruise line. In their parting scene Alec made an anguished bid to persuade his wife to accompany him but Bet stayed behind at the Rovers.

Julie was obviously considering her future. For over twenty-two years she had put heart and soul into Bet Gilroy, née Lynch. At fifty, it was time to start planning a new future.

Five months after the never-to-be-seen interview with chat supremo Sue Lawley, a report appeared saying Julie wanted to host her own chat show. A source said: 'She is confident she can chat to anyone – even John Major – as well as showbusiness celebrities.'

Granada were in a real dilemma, said the source, then added: 'Only Julie could come up with a scheme like this.'

If she was granted a chat show, Julie would not leave the soap, but would be written out of the *Street* to meet any new commitments. The only other soap star to work on two major projects was *EastEnders* actress Wendy Richard, who plays grumpy housewife Pauline Fowler. She had time out to record the comedy series *Grace and Favour*, a follow-up to 1970s hit *Are You Being Served?*

The wheels were in motion, the seed of new challenges sown and Granada bosses had to think hard. If they gave Julie her own chat show, some of the magic she brought to Bet would be destroyed. She would no longer be known exclusively as the Rovers landlady and viewers would probably feel confused watching Julie as herself. They had a lot to discuss. And while bosses mulled over her future, Julie got on with her life.

She heard about twenty-three-year-old cancer victim Beverley Read, who was in so much pain that she told her family she wanted to die. Beverley was suffering from incurable liver cancer which had spread to other organs.

For her the battle was nearly over, but she did not want to give in without a fight so she set up the Beverley Read Trust Fund to raise money. The cash would be donated to cancer research and the liver transplant unit at Addenbrooke's hospital in Cambridge. She raised more than £11,000 in just nine weeks.

A huge fan of Bet's, one of Beverley's final wishes was to meet Julie, herself a cured cancer victim. In November 1992, a newspaper stepped in and arranged for Julie to fly to Beverley's home near Norwich in Norfolk.

It was an emotional meeting. Julie said: 'I told Beverley I loved her and gave her a big cuddle. Her face lit up and we had an instant and very special bond. I know how much this day meant to her and it meant an awful lot to me. The memory will live with me for ever.' Then she coaxed the rest of the cast into donating old costumes for a charity auction, with the proceeds to go to the fund. Julie gave a green costume top and two pairs of earrings and helped to collect sixty-five signed photographs. Mavis donated a floral blouse, Rita an angora jumper, Gail a maroon blouse, and Alf an extra-large pullover.

No one could fail to be moved by Beverley's story. Eleven months earlier, Beverley had started to feel sick and suffer bouts of tiredness. Specialists diagnosed liver cancer. The consultant thought it was on one side of her liver only and could be cut out. But surgeons found the whole liver was affected. Beverley was then taken into the operating theatre for a liver transplant. When she woke up she found her family in tears and was told the transplant had not been performed. The disease had spread to other parts of her body.

A month later she was told she had fibrolamella carcinoma, a rare form of cancer. The news was broken that she could be dead within two months. Her doctor advised her: 'Get into debt, go on holiday or just sit and watch the trees blossom.'

Her mother Pauline, forty-four, and stepfather Telford took Beverley and her boyfriend Richard on a Caribbean cruise. On holiday twenty-four-year-old builder Richard proposed. They married in her home town of Bungay and lived together for a week after the wedding, then, as Beverley's condition deteriorated, she went back to stay with her mother. Living on borrowed time, she had already survived eight months longer than expected.

Julie was understandably moved. After their meeting she said: 'She has a wonderful fighting spirit and is a wonderfully courageous woman.' Julie's commitment to Beverley was touching and showed the caring side of her nature.

The following month *Coronation Street* staged its annual birthday party and Julie stole the limelight. The show was thirty-two years old in December 1992 and the cast were shocked when Julie turned up with gay black footballer Justin Fashanu on her arm.

Justin, assistant manager and striker for Third Division club Torquay United, was, at thirty, twenty years younger than his escort. She had first met him seven years earlier when the former Dr Barnardo's boy was playing for Southampton and she turned up to watch a game.

When Justin 'came out' he faced hostility from other players and fans, but Julie was 'a real brick'. He said: 'She was a warm shoulder to cry on and I loved her for it. She had been through so much in her own life that she could understand how desperate I felt.'

It was in 1981, after signing for Nottingham Forest for £1 million, that Justin discovered a gay club in the city.

By early 1982 he had slept with his first man. He met Julie three years later.

He said: 'She was a great fun lady and we got on so well together. But after a while I went over to the United States to play and lost contact. When I returned to play for Manchester City I met up with her again. I was sitting at a table in a local club with a group of friends and sent over a bottle of champagne. Julie called me over and made me feel at home straight away. We were flirting with each other like mad and at one point she stroked my thigh and said: "You've got lovely footballer's legs."'

Then Julie and six friends went back to Justin's hotel room and ordered a plateful of bacon butties. Julie, who had her hair in a bun, let it down and they cuddled on the sofa. Their friendship blossomed and, in 1989, they became lovers.

They were at the Midland Hotel in Manchester having dinner when they first slept together. Justin said: 'I'll always remember that night. We ordered some food and ate it in the room and then it just happened. It was so natural. Afterwards I was fabulously in love and Julie was glowing.'

Justin thought he could never be happy with a woman. He had lived with a girlfriend, but stopped having sex with her after he became a born-again Christian. Justin said: 'I stopped having sex with my girlfriend and that's when I started to have homosexual feelings.' He added, 'I've enjoyed my relationships with men, but then along came Julie. I think she is very attractive and very sexy. She is very much a woman.'

He was unconcerned by the age gap. He said: 'I enjoy her experience of life. It is mixed with a youthfulness of spirit and physical beauty.'

Apart from his affair with Julie, Justin had boasted of sex with top male footballers, pop stars and TV personalities. He also said he had had an affair with a married MP he met in a London club.

The unlikely lovebirds used Julie's semi as a base, but the couple found that with Justin's Jaguar XJS with its personalized number plate A9 JSF parked outside, it was difficult to keep their affair secret. So they switched their meeting place to the far more public Queen's Suite at the Midland Hotel in Manchester.

Julie thought thirty-year-old Justin was adorable and said: 'We laugh a lot together, which I think is very important in any relationship.'

Justin credited Julie with rekindling his interest in women. He said: 'I know we are depicted as the odd couple, but we are perfectly matched – in and out of bed. Julie never complains about my performance. And Julie makes love like she is as a person – incredibly warm, giving and interesting. I have never made love to a woman like that before. It is totally fulfilling. I didn't think I had it in me to love a woman so much.'

Once their secret was out, the couple were often spotted together. Julie helped Justin to score as she cheered him at a Torquay match. United were playing at home against Third Division Shrewsbury. Julie sat in the directors' box wearing a blue and yellow Torquay scarf, yelling: 'rubbish!' as a player was booked. Then Julie jumped up, punched the air and hugged chairman Mike Bateson as Fash headed a ball in the twenty-sixth minute and striker Sean Joyce slammed it in the net.

At half-time she walked round Torquay's Plainmoor ground, blowing kisses to the 2,000-strong crowd and prompted a cheeky chorus of: 'Get your tits out for the lads!' and a mass humming of the *Coronation Street* theme tune. After her tour Julie told the Devon club's chairman Mike Bateson: 'It's a lovely little ground but it's not like Manchester United.' That day Torquay had their first win in four matches.

When the final whistle blew, Julie raced to the Torquay dressing room and cracked open a bottle of vintage champagne. She poured it all over Justin in the team bath. She laughed as she posed for a 'team' photo, chuckling: 'By 'eck, this picture is going to get the rest of the cast going!' Then added: 'After being in the baths with all those naked footballers Christmas has come early for me.'

Two months later, after he moved to Scottish Premier League side Airdrie, Justin left Julie, telling her: 'Sorry, love, you're just too old for me.' He added: 'Life can be so cruel at times. I love Julie more than I've ever loved anyone and all the ingredients were right – except her age. If she'd been ten years younger, I'd probably have married her.'

The problem was that bisexual Justin dreamed of having a big house he could fill with kids. Julie was fifty and had had a hysterectomy, so starting a family together was out.

Justin called Julie at home to break the news. She knew something was up straight away and invited him round. The minute Justin arrived he told her he thought their relationship had reached an end. She asked if he was getting hassle about their relationship. He said no. Then she asked the killer question: 'Do you think I'm too old?' Justin had to be honest and told her that, because of the age gap, he didn't see a future.

Julie broke down and sobbed. Justin broke down too. 'It was so, so sad,' he said. He added: 'My relationship with Julie was a wonderful experience and one I don't regret having one bit. Unlike her *Street* character, she is fabulously feminine. 'I'm sure we can stay friends because what we had was something very special. What I think Julie needs is a middle-aged man who is young at heart. Not someone like me who is still trying to sort out his own life.'

Julie was furious and, no doubt stung by his comments, accused him of living in a fantasy world. She said sarcastically: 'I can tell you why he makes me laugh at lot – he gets vast sums of money out of newspapers for totally fantasizing about me. That has got to be funny.'

Away from Justin and back on the *Street*, Julie was playing godmother and agony aunt. Young Suzanne Hall, who played dimwit Curly's fiancée Kimberley, was having a tough time with her co-star. Curly, played by actor Kevin Kennedy, seemed reluctant to make friends with the actress whose character was the love of his life.

As a warm-blooded courting couple, kissing was called for, but Kevin would always hold back. A kiss with pretty Suzanne seemed the last thing he wanted. Even when the script had 'kiss' written on it, Kevin had to be prompted. 'The director usually had to say, "You have to embrace now",' Suzanne explained. 'I thought the viewers would think we were more like friends than a courting couple. Kevin and I did our job and that was it. I felt sometimes that he didn't particularly like me. I don't suppose there was any love lost between us. I thought it was something to do with me.

'In the end I looked on it as a job and went to work and that was it. I used to learn my lines in my dressing room on my own, or with my husband Brian at home.'

Suzanne made valiant attempts to thaw the ice but her

friendly gestures were ignored. Suzanne said: 'I tried to warm to him by sending him a birthday card and Christmas card, but it didn't seem to work.'

Millions of *Street* fans were hooked on the romance which was to see unlucky-in-love Curly, assistant manager at Bettabuys, marry Mummy's girl Kimberley. They had been engaged once before, but had split up, and Suzanne left the show for a while. She was later invited back and, eighteen months later, Curly and checkout girl Kimberley signed up with a lonely-hearts agency. The computer matched them together and they met outside a library, with Kimberley cooing: 'Ooh, Curly . . .' They rekindled their romance, slept together and planned to tie the knot but the screen happiness was a million miles from their real-life freeze-out.

Suzanne's problems made her miserable. Julie picked up the vibes and stepped in to help, offering words of comfort and encouragement. 'She is terrific,' enthused Suzanne. 'Like a godmother-type character you can go to if you need anything, or approach and talk about any problems.'

Kimberley eventually split with Curly and Suzanne left the show. Before she went, she wanted to say goodbye to Julie. She knocked on Julie's dressing-room door and walked in. Julie said with a grin: 'Look what you've done.' She was halfway through wrapping a bottle of champagne and had already written a card which said: 'To Suzanne . . . Rovers always return. All my love, Julie.'

Suzanne left and has not yet returned, but Julie's connections with Kevin Kennedy's private life were not yet severed.

Julie continued on the *Coronation Street* treadmill and was about to get a big pay rise. Four years earlier, the *Street* had gone from two episodes a week to three, adding another half-hour show on Friday nights. Julie, who reportedly earned £100,000, got a £50,000 pay rise. Now bosses decided to repeat the three shows during the day. ITV chief executive Andrew Quinn announced: 'From September 1993, ITV will screen a network repeat of each episode of the *Street* in the following daytime schedule.' Senior cast members expected their salaries to double. It was speculated that Julie would earn £300,000 pre-tax, but the double-your-money pay bonanza hit the deck. The cast had already received a pay rise when the show went out in an omnibus edition. However, only two ITV regions still screened it, so TV bosses could claim the stars were already overpaid.

The cast was assembled and told: yes – the show would definitely be repeated three times a week in the afternoons; but no – there wasn't a penny in it for them. A *Street* source revealed: 'There were several very irate members of the cast there who thought they were getting a raw deal. Initially, the gut feeling was one of revolt or mutiny – but in the end common sense prevailed.' The stars swallowed the pay snub and got on with their work.

Later that year, in June, fifty-one-year-old Julie was spotted holidaying in Sweden with another toyboy, thirty-eight-year-old sports administrator Olle Wannerberg. The pair spent two nights in Julie's £300-a-night suite in the upmarket Sheraton Hotel in Gothenburg, south Sweden.

On the first night they stuck a 'Do Not Disturb' sign on the door and emerged fourteen hours later. Julie and Olle then walked around Europe's biggest shopping mall. Julie wore no make-up and looked frumpy in denim shirt and jeans, but splashed out hundreds of pounds on new outfits.

Julie had met Olle on holiday in Majorca three months

earlier, after being dumped by Justin. Olle had no idea she was famous, as *Coronation Street* is not shown in Sweden. When she was snapped by a photographer and asked about Olle, Julie buried her head in her hands and said: 'I really don't want to talk. We are having a very nice break together but want to be left alone.'

When she got home, Julie stayed mum and no details of their relationship were released.

In August 1993, accolades were heaped on Britain's top-rated soap, which scooped three major awards. *TV Times* magazine, the television viewers' bible, voted Julie number-one soap actress. Lusty Bettabuys manager Reg Holdsworth, played by Ken Morley, was voted best soap actor of all time. And the *Street* was voted number one in the mag's Silver Anniversary poll.

Ken had been in the soap only three years, while Julie had clocked up twenty-three. She was universally recognized as a superb actress and it was surprising that she did not win the top award. In any case, there was no love lost between Ken and Julie. Once, when they were filming Reg's wedding to Maureen, Ken Morley got a reception he had not bargained for.

They were shooting the scene in a small Manchester hotel. Bet was talking to her truck-driver lover Charlie, played by John St Ryan, as Reg passed behind them. Each time Ken passed Julie, he goosed her bottom. Julie turned to John and hissed through clenched teeth: 'If he does that just once more, I'm going to belt him.'

They filmed another take and, to everyone's amazement, Julie swung round and socked Ken so hard his glasses spun sideways round his head and he staggered across the room. The director looked at Julie and said: 'Why on earth did you hit him?'

Julie blazed: 'If he dares grab hold of my bum once more I'll hit him again – so hard he won't get up!'

Another drama was brewing with a different cast member. The private life of Kevin Kennedy was about to cause Julie some problems. Kevin, who plays Curly Watts, was being harassed by twenty-two-year-old George Cooper, his ex-wife's toyboy lover. George gatecrashed a private Granada function, claiming he did not know it was by invitation only, and stood in a corner having a drink. When Kevin walked in with his new girlfriend Claire and spotted George, he stormed over and swore at him, saying: 'What the fuck are you doing in here?' George knocked Kevin's hand off his chest then security came over and asked him to leave.

Now Julie stepped in. George was staggered by her intervention and said: 'I couldn't believe it when Julie came over and told the security blokes to leave me alone. She stroked my hand and asked me what was going on. She said she would sort things out. One security bloke said I'd better go, but Julie told him to leave me alone.

'They called a taxi for me and, in the end, three security men put me in. Julie Goodyear was absolutely brilliant. I reckon she got me out of a nasty scrape.'

Later that year the police were called in by Julie to solve a mystery involving missing jewellery. Julie was spending a week at the Holiday Inn Crowne Plaza hotel in Manchester, close to Granada's studios, while workmen redecorated her home in Heywood.

While she was there, two diamond-encrusted gold rings, worth £51,500, went missing from her £299-a-night fourth-floor suite. The rings were in a box of jewellery full of valuable items, but nothing else was stolen. The theft was discovered by Julie's assistant when she opened the

jewellery box. The incident was confirmed by hotel manager Shaun McCarthy and Greater Manchester police,
who gave brief details. Julie did not want to comment, but
Granada said: 'The matter is in the hands of the police.'

It seemed almost sensible that Julie should instal a direct
line to the local police as she seemed constantly to require
their assistance. Two months later, the police came to the
rescue again after Julie's personal assistant Pat Claffey
disturbed an intruder at Julie's home. Pat was struck in
the face by a man she discovered lurking at the back of
the house. Pat, in her forties, had gone to the garage to
get Julie's car ready when she spotted a man. When she
asked what he was doing there, he punched her in the
face. Pat reacted fast and grabbed him. A source said:
'There was a brief scuffle and Pat says she gave as good as
she got with this bloke and sent him packing.'

The man was traced by police and warned: 'Stay away!'

14

Charlie is My Darlin'

The unpredictability of hosting a chat show is a million miles from the security of pulling pints at the Rovers. However, the nation's best-known barmaid had enough confidence to give it a whirl.

After a long hard fight, Granada finally agreed to give Julie the chance to front her own talk show. Grabbing at the challenge, she prepared to throw herself 100 per cent into the project. Or as one newspaper put it: 'by 'eck, that Oprah Winfrey had better watch her chat-show crown . . . Julie Goodyear is chasing it.'

Chasing rainbows more like. It's one thing to be a good listener. It's quite another, when you are used to learning lines from a script, to think at lightning speed, teasing information from people that will entertain the watching public and a studio audience. But Julie was sure she had the right qualities to make it work.

'She has strong opinions and is certainly prepared to voice them,' said a Granada insider, when the announcement was made on 31 March 1994. 'She's going to make a few people sit up and take notice.'

'This is something completely different for me,' said Julie. 'It promises to be a very exciting show. I am thrilled to have been given the opportunity to be involved.'

The Talk Show, like Oprah's, was to be a 'people' show with the public discussing topical issues. Oprah is famous for persuading guests to open up and confess their intimate, salacious and sometimes horrifying life stories on screen. Her biggest coup was when Michael Jackson – nicknamed Wacko Jacko because of his eccentric behaviour – agreed to an interview. Other shows saw child-abuse victims and relatives of murder victims pouring out their hearts, while contrast was provided by saucy strippers and viewers with outrageous hobbies. *Oprah* has everything – laughter, tears and juicy well-researched stories.

What makes the talk show the most popular in the US, and pulls a healthy viewing figure for Channel 4 in the UK, is Oprah herself, who has the kind of non-judgemental, gentle manner which enables her to chat successfully to everyone. To top it all she makes it look easy, which it is not.

Granada wanted to produce a similar style of programme. Executive producer of the show, Jane Macnaught, said: 'We were looking for a show with a new approach and broad-based appeal. We were delighted when Julie agreed.'

Eee by gum, there was going to be trouble at t' mill. Granada were right, though; people would sit up and take notice, although not in quite the way they had planned.

Once the decision was made the television factory's wheels started turning and a new image for Julie was planned. Julie was to drop the satin-and-sequin look loved by Bet and slip into a whole new wardrobe of quiet, understated, elegant clothes. Her hair, usually piled on top of her head like an ornate crinoline, would be teased into a classier style.

There was a lot at stake with this series. If Julie was successful, it could put her in superstar league, certainly as far as money was concerned. Julie already received an estimated £150,000 a year and with a hit chat show she could double her pay packet. It would also get her out of the Rovers rut and away from the bar which had been her home for twenty-five years.

Whatever the future, Julie was not going to be given an easy ride. Just after the chat-show announcement appeared in the papers, an old flame popped up to cash in on Julie's fame. Never mind being crowned Queen of the Street and – she hoped – of Chat; Julie was in danger of being inaugurated Queen of Sleaze.

'EX-COP'S PASSION FOR STREET STAR', announced the strap line on the front page of the *Sunday People*. 'MY SEXY NIGHTS WITH TV JULIE', screamed the following headline. Underneath the bold black type and a picture of Julie, dressed in a white dress revealing her mountainous cleavage, was written in red type: 'Exclusive story pages six and seven'.

At the sight of the *People*'s splash, Julie must have choked. The pathetic story was after all eighteen-years-old. Julie had not dated ex-Detective Inspector John Park since 1966, when she was twenty-four and he was a nineteen-year-old rookie. Now she was fifty-two, for heaven's sake. Still, it made compelling reading.

John, a self-confessed alcoholic, talked openly from his squalid £60-a-week bedsit, which he shared with girlfriend

Liz on Blackpool's golden mile. He told how he first met Julie in the 103 Nightclub in Bury, three miles west of Julie's home in Heywood. Within weeks, he said, they were having a passionate affair.

Their maiden night of passion happened after John drove Julie home in his Ford Capri and dropped her at her Mum's house. 'She invited me in for a cup of tea, but I found myself staying the night,' he said, sounding somewhat surprised. He continued, 'I felt very uncomfortable but we had the most incredible sex. She is the sexiest woman I have ever known. We just didn't want to stop. Next morning I was really embarrassed, but her Mum was great. She popped her head round the door and said: "What do you want for breakfast?"'

John claimed that during their romance they made love everywhere. 'We loved the open air, my car, the fields and once we did it in a park,' he boasted. He added that they also stayed with John's Mum Freda. 'I used to let her and John sleep together upstairs,' said eighty-one-year-old grandmother Freda, who added: 'Julie treated me like a mother.'

John claimed he acted as Julie's bodyguard as she became increasingly famous. He said he accompanied her to all the showbiz and charity events and said he and Julie were so close they were virtually living together. Eventually, he said, Julie asked him to marry her. 'She was the only woman who has ever proposed to me,' he preened. 'But although she was wonderful and great company I knew in my heart marriage wouldn't work.' They split in 1969 after dating for three years – a year before Julie landed a permanent role in the *Street*.

White Hart landlady Audrey Brogden remembers Julie bringing Park into the pub. They ate in the restaurant, but

Julie did not request her favourite table, number fourteen, which she had shared with Geoff Cassidy. Instead they sat at table number seven. John made an impression on Audrey, but not a good one. She did not like him and thought he was a bit of an idiot.

Like several of Julie's other boyfriends, including Geoff Cassidy, John liked his booze too much. When he told his story, forty-seven-year-old John, who at one time had been known in the Manchester police force as 'Starsky', and who won a Chief Constable's commendation for excellent service, was a pathetic drunk downing a bottle of Scotch a day. He had already ruined his life with booze, losing a long-suffering wife and two kids after a divorce, and he had retired from the force on medical grounds after a fifteen-month suspension. After twenty years' service he was given a £500-a-month police pension and spent most of it on drink.

A year earlier, desperate Freda had contacted Julie and pleaded for help. She left a message on Julie's answering machine explaining the situation but Freda claimed Julie did not call back. At the time a friend said: 'She remembers going out with John. It was some time ago and she's sorry to hear he has now hit hard times. She remembers the relationship with affection, but it was a long time ago and she has not been in touch with John in the recent past.' And who could blame her, since John sounded like a miserable scrounger who had "burnt his bridges."

No one took much notice of Park's revelations and Julie got on with preparations for her chat show – working title *La Chat*.

Julie decided not to talk to other chat-show hosts although their invaluable experience might have helped prepare her for the challenge of hosting her own show. Instead she relied on the advice of her director. Julie was paid £2,000 to film a pilot during her summer holidays, and it was scheduled to be screened in August.

For the first time in years Julie agreed to be interviewed, but only in order to promote the show. She must have felt confident about the project, even though a month earlier, in July, a negative story appeared saying the chat show had been axed. Granada issued an official statement saying: 'No decision has been made at this stage. It's up to the ITV Network Centre in London.' But another unnamed Granada source was quoted as saying: 'That's the official line. Unofficially, though, it's off for good. *La Chat* simply will not happen.'

The damaging report did not put the mockers on Granada's plans to screen the pilot, although it would be seen only by northern viewers in the Granada region. It also did not stop Julie going ahead with a round of interviews to promote the show. 'It is one of the scariest things I've ever done because I have no character to hide behind,' she told one interviewer. 'It just had to be me – and that was the toughest thing of all. But my audience will be ordinary people, the kind of people I relate to. That's why I believe in it. I want the people to have a voice, you see.'

To another interviewer she said: 'People talk to me because I'm a good listener, that's why I so desperately wanted to do this talk show. It was my idea and I fought very long and hard to bring it to the screen. I wanted to give ordinary people a voice. Get them discussing various topics of the day. I'm just in there moving it along and asking the questions people at home would want to ask.

'People talk to me quite naturally anyway, and I wanted

to see if they would talk to me in a studio situation. I did not do this as a journalist, I did it as a humanist. The very reason people feel able to talk to me is that I am not a journalist. I am not asking any questions I have not been asked myself and I think the audience will respond to that.'

It was a big build-up with fragile foundations. As soon as the show was aired, critics came down on it like a ton of breezeblocks. *Daily Star* columnist Carole Malone, who had previously interviewed Julie over an eight-hour dinner, said: 'As one who has had to sit through forty minutes of the bilge that masquerades as *The Julie Goodyear Talk Show*, let me tell you, folks, that Jules is to chat shows what I am to the aerobic workout. To say she is useless would not be emphasizing the point enough.'

An audience of 160 guests were invited to take part in the pilot. The majority were Julie Goodyear fans, plus around 20 per cent culled from professions like psychiatry, social work or journalism. To add weight, media personality Nina Myskow and king of the public relations men, Max Clifford, joined the audience. Each was paid £25 for taking part, plus travelling expenses and overnight hotel accommodation, if needed.

A full rehearsal took place the day before the pilot was filmed, giving Julie a chance to polish her technique. The following day VIP guests met Julie in the green room. She flirted outrageously with one tall, blond guest. She even sent Alison Sinclair, her public-relations lady, to tell him: 'Julie says you have the loveliest eyes of any man she has ever seen.' Later Julie sauntered up to the thirty-six-year-old man and told him: 'I'm a tiger in bed.' Guests were then ushered into the studio, where a warm-up man told jokes for twenty minutes to fire them up. During breaks in filming he kept the crowd buoyant by cracking jokes.

The themes for the show centred on romance, revenge and kiss and tell. Behind the scenes, waiting to go on, Julie was shaking like a half-pint jelly. She sat in her dressing room surrounded by buckets full of flowers sent by Granada's cleaners and commissionaires, and half wished she had never pushed for *The Julie Goodyear Talk Show*. Later, she said: 'Everyone was rooting for me. And that's what almost made me go to pieces, because I thought, "My God, now I've got to prove I can do this." They gave me my call to go on and I just thought, "This is it kid, there's no character to hide behind here, no Bet to help you out. It's down to you."

'I remember seeing my floor manager, who'd brought in his new-born baby to give me a kiss for luck. I took that kiss, stepped out from behind the curtain – and *wow*! The rush of love was incredible. I knew then it would be OK. My fate was in the hands of people who loved me.'

It was true, she did have a friendly audience, but it is also worth taking into account that any studio audience gets a rush when the cameras start rolling and they realize they are going to be on television. It is exciting for people to take part in any televison recording.

Julie made her entrance from the back of the auditorium, gliding down the stairs between the rows of guests. But from the moment she appeared in her expensive navy-blue Georgio Armani trouser suit, her peroxide hair teased into a chic French pleat, her fate was sealed. Julie was about to prove how difficult it was to be a chat show host. One impartial audience member, who took part in the show, commented: 'The general standard of debate wasn't just lowbrow . . . it was piss-poor. Julie was fine delivering rehearsed lines, but when it came to thinking on her feet and asking people intelligent questions she just didn't have it.

'There was a bunch of lads brought in to talk about why women should stay in the kitchen. One of them was allowed to develop this theme for many minutes and it was utterly boring. Julie should have put him down very sharply, very quickly, very wittily, but she didn't.

'There was another guy – a British John Bobbitt – who had had his willy sawn off by his partner. Julie conducted an interview with him. He told his story in a dull monotone saying things like: "Then she cut it off and there was blood everywhere . . ." Julie said: "Ooh, really? Oh no, chuck."'

Willing her to succeed, the audience did get behind her, though, and gave her a boost when she hit the odd rocky patch. The audience member said: 'During a take Julie got something terribly wrong. She turned to the audience and said: "Oh Christ, it really isn't my day." There was a bit of applause to bolster her up, but by that stage she had really given the game away.'

For the rest of the show Julie struggled to take control, often referring to notes she held in her hand. The audience member began to analyse what was wrong: 'Julie was not intimidated by the camera, or by the delivery, but seemed intimidated by the idea of thinking on her feet. She was fine delivering rehearsed lines, but when she was talking to me she actually had question cards in her hand, which took away the spontaneity. Cards have got to be a no-no because they stop you thinking.

'By the end I didn't rate *The Julie Goodyear Talk Show*. At the time I didn't think it stood a ghost of a chance of seeing the light of day.'

Julie did, though, and said confidently: 'My fans will get me this show; just wait till they see it. My public will decide my fate, not Granada.' And a battle to get the show further than one pilot began.

The fate of the series was in the hands of the ITV network, the central body responsible for giving regional programmes the national go-ahead. A network spokeswoman confirmed: 'We did see it, but it was on an informal basis.' In fact, Network Centre viewed it and binned it. An insider confessed: 'It really was not very impressive.' Granada merely said ITV could not find a spot for it in their schedules.

Granada added that, although the critics had panned it, the public had received it very well. 'We received a lot of positive calls,' said a press officer. A poll, conducted by viewing information service Teletext, showed a narrowly divided public, with 52.7 per cent saying the show was a hit and 47.3 per cent giving it the thumbs down.

Viewers are what counts when it comes to commissioning prime-time shows. Granada could still go ahead and make a series, which they could broadcast locally then offer to other ITV regions if they wished, or they could just decide to drop it.

On 16 November 1994, three months after the pilot went out, Granada claimed they still had not decided the future of *The Julie Goodyear Talk Show*.

Having boasted how the show was a dead cert, Julie must have been desperate for it to go ahead. It seemed as though she would do anything in her power to force Granada's hand. While the backstage wrangling continued, it appeared Julie was holding Granada to ransom. Annually, regardless of how long they have been in the show, *Coronation Street* actors sign a new contract. It was September and reports claimed Julie had refused to sign her £150,000 contract, telling friends: 'I love the *Street* but there has got to be more to life than playing Bet. I've still not signed the contract.'

A *Street* source said: 'She's keeping everyone guessing by not signing. The *Street* just wouldn't be the same without her. She knows it and Granada know it as well – it is just a matter of how it is going to be resolved.

'She's adamant on spreading her wings. She has been in the show for twenty-five years. If she's to do something else, now is the time.'

Then a story was leaked claiming Julie was pushing her luck by not signing. It said unless she toed the line she would be written out of the series. It also warned that bosses planned to tell her that the soap was bigger than she was.

Newspaper columnists warmed to the theme of the prima donna growing too big for her stilettos. In the *Sunday People* John Smith said:

I can't help thinking *Coronation Street* bosses should call time on Bet Lynch of the Rovers Return. Julie Goodyear's portrayal of the ageing Lancashire lass looking for love is becoming increasingly wearisome. Especially when, as I have pointed out before, her only way of portraying emotion is to adopt the look of a stunned horse.

Daily Mail columnist Lynda Lee Potter was just as scathing. She said:

Unfortunately, Ms Goodyear is showing very definite signs of suffering from staritis. Like Pat Phoenix before her, she seems to want to dress more like Mae

West than a hard-working, hard-up, albeit tarty publican. She's becoming more of a one-woman show than a team player. And she needs to be careful. She's only one member of a talented cast, not the leading lady.

The show has survived for thirty-four years, because it's bigger than anybody. It's more dependent on its writers than actors. And whenever any single member has got grand, haughty or believed that their popularity meant they had Granada over a barrel . . . they found, to their cost, that their days were numbered. And when they left or were booted out, their absence didn't make one iota of difference.

A week later Julie still had not signed and Lynda Lee Potter wrote:

One of the best bits of advice I've ever been given was: 'Never hand in your notice unless you are prepared for it to be accepted.' Over the years I've seen quite a few prima donnas storm into the boss threatening that if their demands weren't met they were tendering their resignation. To their amazement and horror, it was accepted. And if *Coronation Street*'s Julie Goodyear doesn't come to her senses very quickly, she could be in the same boat. She could well end up spending Christmas playing the fairy godmother in Wigan. And facing a bleak future touring the provinces in the kind of old potboilers in which Pat Phoenix, who wasn't actually a very good actress, spent her declining years.

Two days later, a story appeared saying Julie was prepared to sign a new improved contract. Her salary would stay at £150,000 but she would have fewer episodes and more time off.

No chapter in Julie's life would be complete without a tale of simmering passion. Hardly a year goes by without a story giving details of some affair or other and 1994 would be no different for bisexual grandmother Julie. The latest tale of Goodyear lust concerned her ex-screen lover, hunky trucker Charlie Whelan, played by California based British actor John St Ryan.

Viewers were already gripped by Bet and Charlie's erratic on-off screen affair, and watched open-mouthed as cheating Charlie did the dirty on Bet with beautiful but bitchy barmaid Tanya. The Rovers trollop had been scheming for weeks to get revenge after Bet sacked her for publicly humiliating failed model Raquel. Stabbing right at Bet's heart, Tanya stole Charlie, and the pair climbed into his lorry and drove off to Hamburg. As Charlie sped sheepishly away from Weatherfield with triumphant Tanya by his side, Bet was left alone in the Rovers snug, debased, degraded and dishonoured.

Off screen the situation between Julie and John – a regular stand-in for screen legend Sean Connery – seemed much the same as on. Julie appeared to fancy 6ft 4ins St Ryan as much as Bet fancied Charlie. Unfortunately, the craggy twice-married heartthrob was not attracted to her. 'She hadn't a chance,' said father of two John unkindly. 'Even if I hadn't been a happily married man, I didn't fancy her at all.' Ouch! what a knockback; Julie was obviously losing her grip. Used to men falling at her feet, it must have come as quite a shock when the forty-one-year-old actor told Julie he was not interested.

John was discreet about exact details of their relationship. 'There were certain signs from her,' he admitted. 'Certain things were done – but I could not make light of them without causing her distress. I don't see the point in bringing her down. I don't fancy her but I'm very fond of her.'

John would not take any chances, though; he even contacted his 4ft 10ins wife, Joyce, who was at the family home in California, and flew her in to act as minder. 'The only times I ever went out with Julie were when there was a member of my family there. I made damned sure of that,' he said.

Joyce was understanding and agreed there was a lot of John to fancy. 'He hasn't told me the full story of what went on,' she said. 'But I know that Julie fancied him like mad and everybody in the *Street* knows that he didn't take Julie up on it.' Like Julie, John could not boast an unblemished past. His first wife Pauline, from Bolton in Lancashire, told how he cheated on her and went off with his friend's wife. When they met on a blind date, John had not got his acting career off the ground.

John came from humble beginnings. His parents owned a chain of twenty newsagents in the Bolton area, but he seemed incapable of holding down a job. He became a policeman for a few months, then he delivered hire cars for Hertz, he went to work on a chicken farm – which he didn't like because the odd gas-filled carcase would explode – he also worked at a paper mill and a factory which Pauline nicknamed the 'fluff and dust factory' because he always came home covered in the stuff.

However, they married, had a child and were happy for a while until John started womanizing. 'He was working at Woolworth's and he struck up an affair with a pretty girl called Dorothy,' said Pauline. 'I only found out when she turned up with him on my doorstep late one night! There was a knock at the door. It was the pair of them. She said: "I've brought your husband home for you."'

Pauline later decided to pay a visit to her husband at his mistress's flat, which was close by. She said: 'I knocked on the door and Dorothy let me into the sitting room. There was John – lying naked on her sofa!'

The affair between John and Dorothy soon fizzled out, but John then fell for Joyce Hilton, the wife of a mate of his called Phil who used the same karate club. 'I thought Joyce was rather plain,' said Pauline. 'I couldn't see the attraction.' But John could, and he married Joyce as soon as he could. Now they have two teenage sons, Sam, sixteen and Shannon, fifteen.

With his chequered background John was perfect *Coronation Street* material. He would certainly be able to relate to the Walter Mitty character of Charlie, who at first pretended to be a macho cowboy.

By the time he started in the *Street* in January 1994, John had already appeared as Sean Connery's stunt double in films like *Medicine Man* and the *Last Days of Eden*.

Not surprisingly, John and Julie hit it off right from John's first audition. John, who is now back at his ranch near Los Angeles, remembers the occasion: 'I'd been flown over to Manchester for talks about the role of Charlie,' he said. 'I was in the producer's office when in walked Julie, looking her resplendent best as Bet. She was wearing a leopard-skin plastic mac and had a leopard-skin handbag. My first thought was "Jeez! It's Bet." Then she sat down, talked, and we clicked immediately. I found her open and very friendly, not a bit the big star. I thought she was terrific. She really impressed me. She offered to show me the set and took me around the Rovers Return. It was deserted, except for the props man who Julie persuaded to give us a couple of bottles of lager.

'Her parting shot was pure Bet. She told me, "Only do this show if you really want to – the money's crap."'

John took the job as Bet's lover and dumped his stetson in her parlour. They became good buddies and Julie soon started to show John round town. John, who wears a thick black moustache, discovered just what a laugh Julie could be when his son Shannon came to England for a holiday. Offering to show them the sights, Julie took father and son out for the night. 'Neither of us will ever forget it,' said John, talking to the *News of the World*. 'Julie took us to a gay bar without telling us. A guy at the bar asked Shannon, "Are you, then?" Shannon said no. Then the guy looked at me and said, "Is he, then?" I asked what was going on. Shannon said indignantly, "He's asking if we're gay!" The affronted homosexual huffed and said: "Well you're in a gay bar, lovies."' John was not upset by the incident. 'Julie was just having fun winding us up,' he said.

But he decided *Coronation Street* was not the place for him. 'I would never take a long-running part,' he insisted. 'A month is about as much as I'd want to go back for. But I'll never forget Julie.'

Not many people will, John, but there are precious few who stay around long enough to become permanent fixtures in her life, either on or off screen.

Epilogue

Julie Goodyear. Love her or hate her, they say, but you can't ignore her – either in the *Street* or in real life.

Former neighbours still delight in recalling her antics, while her pranks in the classroom are a legend at Queen Elizabeth's grammar school. Even fellow members of a youth club she belonged to more than forty years ago talk of the impromptu song-and-dance performances she put on for them.

It is impossible to have had Julie in your life, however briefly, without her leaving a lasting impression. Right from the start, the girl couldn't help it. At her first workplace, seventeen-year-old Julie was told to dress more demurely. She was causing havoc on the factory floor with her short skirts and tight sweaters. So she turned up in a modest white blouse gathered at the neckline, her sensational blonde hair tied in girlish bunches. Still the boys cat-called and wolf-whistled.

Julie Goodyear, both then and now, could not be

anything but a larger-than-life presence. She is a warm-hearted voluptuous lady with a huge appetite for life and everything it can offer. She's grabbed at all the good things she saw coming her way. Sometimes they've turned out to be not so good after all – but, what the hell, chuck. There's plenty more where that came from!

That's Julie's answer to life's many ups and downs. And it's Bet Lynch's answer, too.

On Thursday 25 May, 1995, Julie announced plans to quit the soap, saying: 'This isn't goodbye, it's au revoir. I could never leave the *Street* for good.' She added: 'I have given 25 years of my life to Bet, and I need some Julie time now.'

Julie said she wanted to spend more time with her three young grandchildren Emily Alice, Elliott Thomas and Jack William. She also wanted to tackle new roles. 'I need some new challenges', she said.

Bet has become a working-class icon and the public hate to lose a hero. I wonder if Julie is prepared for the struggle ahead?

Madge Hindle, who played Renee Roberts for four years and left *Coronation Street* in 1980, is still stopped by fans who address her as Renee. Even though Mark Eden, who played Alan Bradley – the despicable rat who beat up Rita – had his character annihilated by a Black-pool tram, he still finds it difficult to shake off the image. Recently, in a department store, he felt a whack on the back of his head. He turned around to discover a pen-sioner belting him with her umbrella. 'You're a bugger, you are', she said.

'It was only pretend', he protested.

Not to be fobbed off his assailant yelled: 'Oh yes, I know all about that! All that pretend business.'

Ditching the character is not the only issue. Workwise, ex-soap stars also face a problem. When Lynne Perrie, who played poison Ivy Brennan née Tilsley, left the *Street* she landed a top role in Stockport's lavish production of *Mother Goose*. When Jean Alexander, who played Rovers cleaner Hilda Ogden, finally hung up her flowery overall, offers flooded in from wealthy people in Cheshire offering her work as a live-in housekeeper. She went on to appear in several high-profile television series but, for years at press conferences, journalists still wanted to know about the *Street*.

Julie has made it clear that she does not wish to go from Weatherfield to a nursing home like her predecessor Doris Speed, who played the unforgettable Annie Walker, but can you see Julie playing one of the ugly sisters in *Cinderella* or jumping behind the bar at the Dog and Greatcoat to help out some hard-working landlord? No. Like Princess Diana, Julie has grown used to the spotlight. She might not like it 100 per cent of the time, but she knows where she stands when the TV cameras are switched on.

By the time Julie Goodyear appears on our screens again, if the BBC's schedules run according to plan, it will be a year since she slammed the door of the Rovers. So what has she been up to in those twelve months? Has she had to struggle to find work or did the offers come flooding in? First, we should recap on her exit from the Street, which was far from smooth.

For twenty-five years, scriptwriters wrote the juiciest storylines for their most flamboyant star. Once, Bet was nearly killed in a fire at the Rovers, and then there was the time she disappeared, to be tracked down later in a bar in Spain by her future husband Alec Gilroy. After being reunited with her son, whom she had had adopted as a baby, she coped with his sudden death. Bet has been married, divorced, wooed and dumped. Given her track record, viewers were expecting an explosive exit. In the end, Bet merely fizzled out and left with a whimper rather than a bang. On being presented with her final script, the Queen of the Street flipped. Julie was so disappointed at what she considered to be a "pathetic" plot that she stormed off the set. 'That's it, I'm finished. I'm, never coming back!' she announced.

So what exactly was it about Bet's departure that she objected to?

Newton and Ridley, owners of the Rovers, decided to sell off a number of their smaller establishments, including Weatherfield's finest pub. They gave Bet the option to buy. The storyline focused on her desperate attempts to raise £60,000 to purchase the pub. Bet approached her best and most solvent of friends, Rita Sullivan, to ask whether she wanted to invest in the Rovers. At first, Rita seemed keen to become Bet's partner but later she pulled out. They had a furious argument, and Rita told Bet exactly what she thought of her. Distraught, Bet then approached Vicky, her wealthy step-granddaughter. Vicky — under the influence of her money-grabbing husband Steve McDonald, who wanted Vicky's money to fund his own schemes — told Bet she did not consider the Rovers, or Bet, to be a viable proposition. This snub was the last straw. In a fit of what one TV critic described as 'any road rage,' Bet threw all of her regulars out of the pub. She then packed her bags, called a cab, put on her biggest earrings, winked at herself in the pub mirror, locked the door and left the Street without so much as a: 'See ya, cock.'

Having observed Julie reading the script, a Granada insider said, 'The air turned blue. Julie felt it was a pathetic way to get rid of Bet. She expected a really strong storyline, full of drama. Instead, she's going out with a whimper.'

Julie stormed off, but her professionalism won through and she decided that however weak she felt the story to be she owed it to her fans to film it.

Julie made her exit on 16 October 1995. To mark a new phase in her life, she had her long platinum blonde hair cropped into a chic, fringed bob. A significant move, as her backcombed, outrageously styled tresses had long been her trademark.

Since she waved goodbye to her dressing room at Granada studios, Julie has been sifting through mountains of offers, to the envy of other less fortunate ex-Street stars. One — from daytime programme-makers GMTV — particularly caught her attention. The ITV breakfast television producers wanted Julie 'on the sofa', interviewing both members of the public and the rich and famous, and offered her a weekly slot. The rate offered for the job was around £100,000 and not surprisingly, Julie was reportedly very interested. The money was tremendous, but it would also be suitable retribution for Granada Television who had shelved *The Julie Goodyear Talk Show*.

Julie also agreed that GMTV presenters Eamonn Holmes and Anthea Turner could interview her. This should have been a simple, uncomplicated business, but it turned into something of a nightmare for both parties.

The night before the interview, GMTV booked her into a £300-a-night room at the Savoy, the luxury hotel in the heart of London. A GMTV researcher asked Julie's agent if there was anything they could provide to make the star's stay more enjoyable. 'Pink champagne and flowers would be much appreciated,' they were told. The champers and roses were duly ordered, but never appeared. It was a minor hiccup and Julie did not seem particularly concerned.

The next day, Julie came to the GMTV studios, part of the London Weekend Television complex at the South Bank. She took one look at the set and realised that her outfit clashed with the sofa. 'Any chance of sitting on a different sofa?' Julie asked. 'No, sorry,' she was told.

Eamonn and Anthea were looking forward to chatting to the legendary soap star, but Julie decided that talking to Anthea — also presenter of the BBC's top-rated National Lottery Show — was not a good idea. She gave two reasons for this. 'Anthea makes no secret of the fact she knows nothing about *Coronation Street*,' reported a senior GMTV source, 'whereas Eamonn is a real fan. I also know, from a contact at Granada, that Julie never liked to be photographed with the younger members of the cast. For example, she wouldn't pose with Sarah Lancashire who played barmaid Racquel. Anthea is young, attractive and popular. So you can draw your own conclusions.' Demanding stars are not unusual in showbiz, but in this case the public became aware of the behind-the-scenes wrangles. A Sunday tabloid reported the whole episode as a huge row and claimed that Julie: 'Protested because her hotel had no pink champagne, demanded that the colour of the GMTV sofa be changed to match her outfit, and refused to be interviewed by Anthea.'

The next day, GMTV faxed a statement to all the national newspapers, apologising to Julie and explaining that the story had been wildly exaggerated. 'I felt quite sorry for Julie,' said the senior source. 'I had heard that she could be difficult, but she didn't make a fuss about the champagne. In fact, if it had been me who ordered it and it hadn't arrived I would have been furious on her behalf. When we told her we couldn't change the sofa she accepted it, but it is true that she didn't want to talk to Anthea or be photographed with her.'

Meanwhile, negotiations for Julie's GMTV sofa debut were superceded by a better offer from the BBC — her own daytime show. A contributor's slot, or your own show? There was no contest.

BBC1's *The Julie Goodyear Show* will be a one-woman road show rather than a studio-based chat show. In the twelve-part, weekly daytime programme, Julie will travel round the country chatting to members of the public who have extraordinary stories to tell. Julie, who prides herself on being a good listener with an ability to encourage people to open up, will tease out the details. BBC bosses, who reportedly offered Julie £150,000 to present the series, hope she will become their answer to ITV's popular and witty daytime hostess, Vanessa Feltz. Whatever happens, there should be an interesting ratings war.

The Julie Goodyear Show is not the only programme on the horizon for the star. *Coronation Street* executive producer Carolyn Reynolds surprised everyone by announcing that she wanted Julie to film an off-shoot series. Tentatively titled *Bet's Bar*, the series would follow on from Bet's exit. The plan is to unearth Bet in Spain where she has been managing a disco bar since leaving the Rovers. Julie says she is keen on the idea but has not yet signed a contract. A Granada spokeswoman said, 'Bet's Bar is on the back-burner at the moment. The idea is still floating around and Granada would like to do it, but no definite filming date has been set.'

The other project Julie's fans have been waiting patiently for is writer Kay Mellor's specially scripted film. Kay, who wrote the hit TV series Band of Gold, and whose younger daughter Gaynor Faye plays lairy Judy Mallet in the Street, has finished the script, provisionally called Girls' Night Out. 'I wanted to look at women in their mid to late forties to see what they did with their lives when the kids had left home,' said Kay. Girl's Night Out is about two women from a small town. One wins £50,000 on the bingo, explains Kay. 'At the same time, one of them falls ill, we don't know if she's terminally ill, but the film charts their lives really. It looks at their hopes aspirations, dreams, loves. I'd like to think that it's Thelma and Louise meets Beaches.'

Julie is first in line for the lead. 'I think Julie is keen to work with me,' said Kay. 'It would be nice if that worked out.' Again, no date has been set for filming. A spokeswoman for Granada Films said, 'The script is going through the usual round of rewrites; once we're happy with it we can discuss casting.'

So work for Julie has not dried up as it has for other, less fortunate soap stars. By the time she reappears on screen Bet Gilroy will have been given a decent mourning period which will make it easier for Julie Goodyear to shake off the inevitable comparisons.

On a personal note, Julie has had an extraordinary year. She was awarded an MBE by the Queen in the 1996 New Year's Honours list. When she found out she was so overcome with joy that she burst into tears. 'I'm a very happy Goodyear,' she said after the announcement was made. She toasted her 'gong', received for services to television drama, with pink champagne, of course, and added she was 'thrilled and delighted'. Julie was first introduced to the Queen on the set of *Coronation Street* in 1982. Julie — dressed as Bet — wore tarty clothes and gaudy Charles and Di earrings. This time, she swept into the Palace courtyard wearing a classy white suit and matching hat in a twenty-seven-foot-long chauffeur-driven white Fleetwood Cadillac. (She had planned to arrive in her Rolls Royce, but it broke down on the way from Manchester.) After Julie was presented with her MBE by the Queen, who took the award from a velvet cushion and pinned it on Julie's chest, she said: 'It was a very, very special day. I'm really pleased and I hope everyone's pleased for me.'

Meanwhile, her life ticks over. When Julie announced that she was leaving the Street, she said she wanted to spend more time with her grandchildren. True to her word she was pictured with Emily and Elliott, enjoying a day out, when she turned on the Christmas lights in Sheffield last year.

Julie has also surprised fans by swapping her plunging necklines for farmer's overalls and wellies. After years of living in the same unglamorous semi-detached house in Heywood, Lancashire, Julie has invested £200,000 in a twenty-seven-acre estate called Primrose Hill Farm, not far from Heywood. Taking her role in agriculture seriously, she has even joined the National Farmers' Union. She plans to rent some of her land to farmers for livestock and for planting. She also plans to invest around £500,000 to turn the run-down site into upmarket stables.

The property includes a farm, eighteen stables and a six-bedroom house which is also being refurbished. True to form she has instructed builders to add a bit of luxury by including a thirty-foot balcony, which will give her spectacular views across the grounds. She also plans to have a jacuzzi installed, so she can relax and ease her aching muscles after a hard day's work mucking out the stables.

At the moment, Julie's new life is far removed from her days as a teenager when she posed in a leopardskin bikini for the company magazine, and later, as a *Coronation Street* star who fought her way through armies of photographers scrambling to take her picture. But you can also lay odds on the likelihood that Julie will not stay dormant for long. Once she's back on screen, you can be pretty sure we will start to see some more colourful drama in the star's life. 'Ey up chuck! There's bound to be more trouble at t'mill.' And we'll all raise a glass of pink champagne and toast her comeback.

Bibliography

The following chapter notes detail interviewees and other sources used to gather information for *Queen of the Street: The Amazing Life of Julie Goodyear*. There are some who wished to remain anonymous and the author has respected their wishes.

Newspaper and magazine cuttings were sourced from the Press Association reference library, Mirror Group Newspapers reference library, Manchester Evening News reference library, Oldham Chronicle and Heywood Advertiser reference libraries. Additional local information was sourced from Oldham reference library and Heywood reference library.
Birth, death and marriage certificates were sourced from the Office of Population Censuses and Surveys, St Catherine's House, London.

PROLOGUE
Interviews with Elsie Bowden 6.4.94; Peter Birchall 26.1.94; Sue Skelton (now Sumner) 26.1.94, 24 & 30.10.94; Audrey Brogden 18.4.93 & 26.4.94.
Articles and reference books consulted: *Life and Times at the Rovers Return* by Daran Little; *Daily Mail* by Jack Tinker 13.8.94.

CHAPTER I
Interviews with Bob Paul 8.6.94; Edna Barlow 26.4.94; Edith Collinge 26.4.94; Joan Davis (née Deardon) 7.4.94; unnamed source, Ada Kemp 26.4.94; Elsie Bowden 6.4.94.
Articles consulted: *The Sun* by Ian Smith 26.9.83; *The Sun* by Ian Smith 28.9.83; *Sunday Mirror* 21.2.93; *Sunday Mirror* 26.6.94.

CHAPTER II
Interviews with Rod Simpson 2.2.94; Ida Boardman 6.4.94; Sandra Boardman (now Thornley) 6.4.94; Elsie Bowden 6.4.94; Alice Simpson (now Wellings) 7.2.94.

CHAPTER III
Interviews with Sue Skelton (now Sumner) 26.1.94, 24 & 30.10.94; Dot Huggins (now Stand) 2.2.94; Janet Howard (now Leech) 2.2.94; David Liddle 2.2.94; Pam Skelton (now Hughes) 9.2.94; Tony Whitehead 14.12.93; Annie Maskew 26.1.94; Sylvia Henderson (now McNally) 26.1.94; Anne Thomas (now Eatough) 6.3.94; Brenda Worrell (now Wilkinson) 16.12.93; Jack & Frieda Little 15.12.93; Peter Birchall 26.1.94; Sidney Yates 10.10.91; Kath Jepson 3.2.94; Peter Wild 27.1.94; Connie Parker 27.1.94.

CHAPTER IV
Interviews with Ray Sutcliffe 20.2.95; Sue Skelton (now Sumner) 26.1.94, 24 & 30.10.94; Jean Morris (now Barlow) 7.4.94; Jenny Morton (now White) 26.9.94; Peter Rushworth 27.9.94; Gordon Allen 26.9.94; Teresa Martini (now Wilkes) 7.4.94; John Bradley 14.4.94.
Articles consulted: *Heywood Advertiser* 1966; *Heywood Advertiser* 23.7.65; *Heywood Advertiser* 7.7.67; *The Sun* 26.9.83; *The Sun* 27.9.83; *Sunday Mirror* 13.5.79; *TV Weekend* 11.6.75.

CHAPTER V
Interviews with Pam Holt 8.4.94; Jimmy Rowbotham 8.4.94; Annie Coates 12.4.94; Carolyn Preston 4.10.94; Audrey Brogden 18.4.94 & 26.4.94; Geoff and Barbara Nuttall 28.4.94; Kenneth Alan Taylor 3.2.94; David Hamilton 16.5.94.

Reference books consulted: *Life In The Street* by Graeme Kay.

CHAPTER VI
Interviews with Jack Diamond 13.4.94; Audrey Brogden 18.4.94 & 26.4.94; Kenneth Alan Taylor 3.2.94; Geoff and Barbara Nuttall 28.4.94; unnamed source 15.4.94; Jimmy Rowbotham 8.4.94; Fred Feast 31.3.94; Graham Weston 25.3.94; Richard Shaw 12.7.94.
Articles Consulted: *The Sketch* 18.5.70; *Daily Express* 2.7.70; *Daily Mirror* 22.12.70; *Daily Express* 28.4.71; *News of the World* 16.1.72; *Sunday Mirror* 6.5.79; *TV Times* 17.4.82; *Daily Mirror* by Tony Warren 3.12.90; *The Sun* by Sandra White and Kevin Ludden 2.10.86.

CHAPTER VII
Interviews with Bobby Howarth 9.4.94; Cyril Smith 26.4.94; Fred Feast 31.3.94; Dr Robert Yule 25.10.91; Peter Birchall 26.1.94; Tony Whitehead 24.10.91 & 14.12.93; Sue Skelton (now Sumner) 26.1.94, 24 & 30.10.94, 30.1.94; Richard Shaw 12.7.94.
Articles consulted: *Sunday Mirror* by Tom Hendry 22.4.79; *Sunday Mirror* by Tom Hendry 29.4.79; *Daily Mail* 1.5.79; *Manchester Evening News* 10.9.80; *Daily Mail* by Geoffrey Mather 19.5.79; *Daily Mail* by Dennis Ellam 25.4.80; *Oldham Chronicle* 25.10.80; *Heywood Advertiser* 30.10.80; *Daily Express* by

Lynne Greenwood 20.7.77; *Sunday People* by Tony Purnell 2.3.80; *The Sun* by Bronwen Balmforth 14.3.80; *Daily Star* 30.5.80; *Daily Express* 12.9.80; *Sunday Mirror* by Tom Hendry 26.10.80; *Sunday Mirror* 9.11.80; *Sunday Mirror* 16.11.80; *Daily Mail* 12.11.81; *Daily Express* 4.2.82; *Manchester Evening News* 1.3.82; *Daily Telegraph* 2.3.82; *Oldham Chronicle* 2.3.82; *Daily Mirror* by Ian Ramsay 3.3.82; *Manchester Evening News* by Bernard Spilsbury 3.3.82; *Oldham Chronicle* 3.3.82; *The Times* 4.3.82; *Manchester Evening News* 4.3.82; *Daily Mirror* 5.3.82; *Oldham Chronicle* 5.3.82; *The Times* 6.3.82; *Manchester Evening News* by Peter Harris 29.9.83; *News of the World* 12.2.84; *Daily Star* by Neil Wallis and Frank Curran 1.10.86; *Sunday Mirror Magazine* by Paul Kerton 17.3.91.

CHAPTER VIII
Interviews with Edith Collinge 26.4.94; Alice Watkinson 29.4.94; Edna Barlow 25.4.94.
Articles consulted: *Manchester Evening News* 7.12.83; *The Sun* by Bronwen Balmforth 14.3.80; *News of the World* 12.2.84; *Manchester Evening News* 28.10.84; *Manchester Evening News* 28.10.84; *Manchester Evening News* 10.6.85; *Heywood Advertiser* 4.10.86; *Sunday Mirror* by Trevor Reynolds 5.10.86; *Woman's Own* by Nina Myskow 26.3.88; *The Sun* by Jim Oldfield 1.12.87

CHAPTER IX
Interviewes with Annie Coates 12.4.94; Judith Barker 30.3.94; Alan Olley 26.10.91; Kenneth Alan Taylor 3.2.94; Audrey Brogden 18.4.94 & 26.4.94; Geoff Nuttall 28.4.94.

Articles and reference books consulted: *Life and Times at the Rovers Return* by Daran Little; *The Sun* by Ian Smith 28.9.83; *Manchester Evening News* 5.12.83; *The Sun* by Ian Smith 5.12.83; *Daily Mirror* 5.12.83; *The Sun* by Ian Smith 6.12.83; *Daily Star* 6.12.83; *The Sun* by Ian Smith 7.12.83; *Manchester Evening News* 28.12.83; *Daily Star* by Harry Pugh 29.12.83; *The Sun* by Simon Hughes and Tim Oldfield 29.12.83; *Daily Mirror* by Ken Irwin 30.12.83; *Manchester Evening News* by Ian Marrow 30.12.83; *The Sun* 31.12.83; *Sunday People* 22.1.84; *Daily Mirror* by Ken Irwin 28.1.94; *Heywood Advertiser* 3.5.84; *Manchester Evening News* 16.5.84; *Daily Star* by Gordon Wilkinson 15.9.84; *Woman* 16.2.84; *Manchester Evening News* 11.1.85; *Heywood Advertiser* 18.1.85; *Daily Express* by David Stoakes 28.1.85; *News of the World* 12.1.86; *Daily Mirror* by Liz Hodgson 3.1.86; *The Sun* 9.6.86; *Daily Star* by Neil Wallis 14.6.86; *Daily Express* by Derek Hornby 17.6.86; *The Sun* by Jim Oldfield 29.9.86; *Daily Star* by Neil Wallis 29.9.86; *Manchester Evening News* 29.9.86; *Daily Express* by Roger Tavener 30.9.86; *The Sun* by Jim Oldfield 30.9.86; *Daily Star* by Neil Wallis 30.9.86; *Daily Star* by Neil Wallis and Frank Curran 1.10.86; *Daily Star* comment 1.10.86; *Daily Mirror* by Christina Appleyard 2.10.86; *The Sun* by Sandra White and Kevin Ludden 2.10.86; *Daily Express* by Roger Tavener 4.10.86; *Daily Star* by Richard Blake 4.10.86; *Sunday Mirror* by Brian Roberts 5.10.86; *Sunday Mirror* 18.1.87; *Sunday People* by Val McDermidm 18.1.87; *Daily Mirror* by Maurice Chesworth 19.1.87; *Daily Star* by Ian Trueman; *Daily Express* by John Coles 19.1.87; *Woman's Own* by Nina Myskow 26.3.88; *Sunday Mirror* by Mike Kerrigan, Peter William and Brian Roberts 13.5.90.

CHAPTER X
Interviews with Kenneth Alan Taylor 3.2.94; Sue Jenkins 24.4.94; Fanny Carby 18.3.94.
Articles and reference books consulted *Life and Times at the Rovers Return* by Daran Little; *Life in the Street* by Graeme Kay; *Sunday People* by Alex Stuttard; *London Daily News* 4.5.87; *News of the World* by Sandie Laming and Alan Hart 10.8.87; *Sunday People* by Val McDermid 17.5.87; *Woman's Own* by Nina Myskow 26.3.88; *Manchester Evening News* by Paul Taylor 21.7.87; *Daily Star* by Ian Trueman 9.7.87; *Manchester Evening News* by Don Frame 17.8.87; *Daily Mail* 18.8.87; *Today* 13.11.87; *The Sun* by Derek Shuff 14.1.88; *Daily Mirror* 5.2.88; *Daily Express* 3.3.88; *News of the World* by Alan Hart 23.10.88; *Sunday People* by Val McDermid 23.10.88; *Sunday Mirror* 30.10.88; *Heywood Advertiser* 2.1.89; *Sunday People* by Phil Hall 2.4.89; *Sunday People* 30.4.89; *Daily Express* by Jean Rook 26.9.89; *News of the World* by Tim Carroll 29.10.89; *The Sun* by Jamie Pyatt 6.11.89; *Daily Star* 1.9.90; *Sunday People* 9.9.90.

CHAPTER XI
Interviews with unnamed source, 30.10.94; Kenneth Alan Taylor 3.2.94; Ann Astley 25.10.91.
Articles consulted *Daily Mail* by Margaret Henfield 27.1.90; *The Sun* 9.2.90; *Daily Star* by Frank Curren 26.4.90; *The Sun* by Alistair Taylor 26.4.90; *The Sun* by Mike Ridley 2.5.90; *Woman* 16.7.90; *Daily Express* by Jean Rook 11.9.90; *News of the World* by James Weatherup and Keith Beabey 16.8.90; *Manchester Evening News* 1.9.90; *News of the World* by James Weatherup and Keith Beabey 16.9.90; *News of the World* by Alan Hart and Keith Beabey 7.10.90; *Manchester Evening News* by Carl Palmer 15.11.90; *Daily Star* by Frank Curren 16.11.90; *Daily Mirror* 16.11.90; *Daily Star* by Frank Curran 21.11.90; *Manchester Evening News* 21.11.90; *The Sun* by Sue Evison and Gordon Stott 10.2.92; *The Sun* by Sue Evison and Gordon Stott 11.2.92; *The Sun* by Sue Evison and Gordon Stott 12.2.92.

CHAPTER XII
Interviews with Ada Kemp 26.4.94, unnamed source 2.5.94.
Articles consulted *Sunday Mirror* by John Kelly and Brian Roberts 28.10.91; *Sunday Mirror* 26.6.94; *Sunday Mirror* by Brian Roberts 13.2.94.

CHAPTER XIII
Interviews with Vicky Ogden 30.3.94; Sue Jenkins 25.4.94; Kenneth Alan Taylor 3.2.94.
Articles consulted *The Face* by Steven D Wright November 1991; *Daily Mirror* 14.11.91; *Daily Star* by Tony Brooks 16.11.91; *The Sun* by Chris Hughes and Gordon Stott 2.1.92; *Daily Mirror* by John Kelly 5.1.92; *Daily Express* by

Stephen Thompson 9.1.92; *Daily Mail* 9.1.92; *Daily Telegraph* 10.1.92; *Sunday Mirror* by Gill Martin 12.1.92; *Daily Mirror* 21.1.92; *Daily Express* 21.1.92; *Sunday People* by Michael Burke 23.2.92; *Daily Mirror* by Patrick Mulchrone 29.2.92; *Sunday People* by Michael Burke 10.5.92; *Sunday Mirror* by David Rowe 10.5.92; *Today* 11.5.92; *Sunday Mirror* by Colin Wills 24.5.92; *Daily Mirror* by Tony Purnell 28.5.92; *News of the World* by Ken Irwin 7.7.92; *Daily Express* 5.9.92; *Sunday People* by Phil Taylor 15.11.92; *Sunday Mirror* by Brian Roberts 13.12.92; *The Sun* by Victor Chapple 15.12.92; *Daily Express* by Toby McDonald 15.12.92; *Daily Mirror* by Geoffrey Lakeman 21.12.92; *The Sun* by Andy Coulson and Dave Brown 21.12.92; *Daily Mirror* 24.12.92; *Sunday Mirror* by Brian Roberts 17.1.93; *Daily Mirror* by Matthew Hughes 29.1.93; *Sunday People* by Phil Taylor and Shaun Custis 7.2.93; *The Sun* by Kevin Ludden 8.2.93; *Daily Express* 8.2.93; *Sunday Mirror* 21.2.93; *Daily Mirror* 12.3.93; *The Sun* by Andy Coulson 12.3.93; *The Sunday Mirror* by Brian Roberts 4.4.93; *The Sun* by Pascoe Watson 17.6.93; *Daily Mail* by Patrick Mulchrone 17.6.93; *Daily Telegraph* by Jane Thynne 9.8.93; *Daily Mirror* by Tony Purnell 9.8.93; *Sunday Mirror* by Brian Roberts 10.10.93; *Sunday Mirror* by Brian Roberts 7.11.93; *News of the World* by Alan Hart 12.12.93; *Sunday Mirror* by Brian Roberts 27.2.94; *News of the World* by Dan Slater 30.10.94.

CHAPTER XIV

Interviews with Audrey Broghden 18.4.94 & 26.4.94; Carol Millward 16.11.94; Unnamed source 18.11.94.
Articles consulted: *Sunday People* by Dan Collins and Andy Byrne 23.1.94; *Daily Mail* by Andrew Riley 31.3.94; *Sunday People* by Louisa Hatfield and Andy Byrne 10.9.94; *Daily Mirror* by Justin Dunn 6.7.94; *Daily Mail* by Jack Tinker 13.8.94; *Daily Star* by Carole Malone 15.8.94; *Manchester Evening News* 22.8.94; *The Sun* by Charles Yates 26.8.94; *Sunday People* by John Smith 28.8.94; *Daily Mail* by Linda Lee Potter 31.8.94; *Daily Mail* 5.9.94; *Daily Mail* by Linda Lee Potter 7.9.94; *The Sun* by Charles Yates 9.9.94; *News of the World* by Dan Slater 30.10.94.

EPILOGUE

Interviews with Madge Hindle 29.3.94, Kay Mellor 22.2.96, Unnamed source, 4.6.96, Unnamed source 7.6.96, Lisbet Kesley, 7.6.96.

Articles consulted: *Sunday People* by Michael Burke, 3.7.94; The *Independent* by Jon Ronson, 18.10.94; *The Sun* by Peter Willis, 4.10.95; *The People* by Paul Byrne, 22.10.95;*The Sun* by Peter Willis and Alison Boshoff, 29.12.95; *Daily Mirror* by Nigel Pauley, 24.3.96; *Daily Mirror* by Justin Dunn, 30.5.96.

Knowledge is Power
Ken Morley

The compulsive autobiography of the man who breathed new life into *Coronation Street* with his brilliant portrayal of randy supermarket boss Reg Holdsworth. With its hysterical behind-the-scenes revelations, as well as a fascinating insight into Ken's rise from a poor childhood to become the star of Britain's number one soap, this immensely readable book is a must for all *Coronation Street* fans.

Secrets of the Street
Lynne Perrie

Lynne Perrie stalked *Coronation Street* for 23 years as the fearsome Poison Ivy Tilsey. Now, in the book the Granada TV bosses tried to ban, she lifts the lid on the real inside story of the *Street*.

Vera Duckworth: My Story
Liz Dawn

Vera is the uncrowned queen of *Coronation Street*. But her rise to fame has been far more sensational than anything the *Street*'s scriptwriters could dream up. Now she tells her true rags to riches story.

Oasis: What's The Story?
Ian Robertson

Brothers Noel and Liam Gallagher are the sensational and outspoken duo behind the most exciting rock band in the world today. With three major awards at the 1996 Brits, the fastest-selling debut album in British history, a second album that went gold in nine countries and sell-out concerts around the world, the band's continuing success seems assured.

Few people have seen Oasis the way ex-tour manager Ian Robertson has seen them and now, in a book that captures the anger, the energy and the music, he gives us a unique look into their amazing lifestyle.

Sting: The Secret Life Of Gorden Sumner
Wensley Clarkson

The only definitive biography published about Sting. For almost 20 years, he has been rock's most complex and intelligent star who has sold over 200 million records worldwide. Sting has fought his way to the top of his profession with a unique combination of cunning and genuine enthusiasm. Read about his sexual exploits, his experimentation with drugs, the early days with The Police and the full story of his attempt to save the Brazilian Rainforest.

The Nemesis File
Paul Bruce

At last ... the long-awaited paperback edition of the bestselling hardback. *The Nemesis File* spent the first four months of 1996 in the Sunday Times' Top Ten Book list. With a devastating new update, the paperback looks certain to repeat this.

Former SAS Sergeant Paul Bruce tells the extraordinary story of his top-secret assignment in Northern Ireland. This book will make history.

All prices include post and packing in the UK. Overseas
and Eire, add £1.00 to the price of each book.
To order by credit card, telephone 0171 381 0666.
Alternatively, fill in the coupon below and send it, with
your cheque or postal order made payable to
Blake Publishing Limited, to:

Blake Publishing Limited
Mail Order Department
3 Bramber Court, 2 Bramber Road
London W14 9PB

Please send me a copy of each of the titles ticked below:

❏ **KNOWLEDGE IS POWER** £14.99
❏ **SECRETS OF THE STREET** £4.99
❏ **VERA DUCKWORTH: MY STORY** £4.99
❏ **OASIS: WHAT'S THE STORY?** £9.99
❏ **STING: THE SECRET LIFE OF GORDON SUMNER** £15.99
❏ **THE NEMESIS FILE** £5.99

Name _____

Address _____

_____

_____

Postcode

PLEASE ALLOW 14 DAYS FOR DELIVERY.